THIS BUSINESS WITH ELIJAH

THIS BUSINESS WITH ELIJAH

Sheldon Oberman

Turnstone Press

Turnstone Press
607-100 Arthur Street
Winnipeg, Manitoba
Canada R3B 1H3

Cover: Elaine Halpert, hand-tinted photograph

Text design: Manuela Dias

This book was printed and bound in Canada by
Kromar Printing for Turnstone Press.

The characters in these stories are fictional, and any resemblance
to any person, living or dead, is purely coincidental.

Canadian Cataloguing in Publication Data
Oberman, Sheldon
This business with Elijah
ISBN 0-88801-174-1
I. Title
PS8579.B47T45 1993   C813'.54   C93-098162-6
PR9199.3.034T45 1993

To my parents, Al and Dorothy Oberman

Acknowledgements

My loving appreciation to my family for their support – Lisa Dveris, Adam and Mira Oberman and Baby Jesse – and my deep thanks to friends and advisors: Kate Bitney, Laurie Block, Lee Anne Block, Billy Brodovsky, Mic Burrs, Ruthie Dveris, Doug Glover, Rick Greene, Jack Hodgins, Walter and Diane Isaac, Bess Kaplan, Jake MacDonald, Dave Margoshes, Drew and Val Perry, Carol and Neil Rose, Andreas Shroeder, Myrna Summers, Frazer Sutherland, Anne Szumigalski, Turnstone editors Neil Besner and Pat Sanders, Jane Urquhart and Geoffrey Ursell. Also to the Manitoba Arts Council and the City of Winnipeg Arts Advisory Council.

Thanks to Kristen Andrews of Ragpicker's Antifashion Emporium and George LaFleche for assisting with the cover photo.

Song lyrics on page 92 are from "Tossing and Turning" by Bobby Lewis 1961 Harvard Music and Viva Music Molou Rene, Ritchie Adams Filmtrax Mogull Music Inc. Song lyrics on page 98 are from "The Lion Sleeps Tonight" 1951, 1952 and 1961 Folkways Music Publishers Inc., New York. Lyrics on page 116 are from Elvis Presley's "Jailhouse Rock" 1957 (renewed) Jerry Leiber Music and Mike Stoller Music. Song lyrics on pages 52 and 119 are from "Lady of Spain," written by Robert Hargraves, Tolchard Evans, Stanley Damerell and Henry Tilsley, 1931, Sam Fox Publishers, New York.

Turnstone Press gratefully acknowledges the assistance of the Canada Council and the Manitoba Arts Council.

The following stories were previously published: "The Sale" in *Border Crossings;* "This Business with Elijah" and "The Projectionist's Wife" in *Event;* "Hidden Wishes" in *Grain;* "The Lady of the Beanpoles" in *New Quarterly;* and "Spin Master" in *Prairie Fire.*

Table of Contents

THIS BUSINESS WITH ELIJAH

I ASKED HIM WHAT HE WANTED BEHIND MY PARENTS' STORE, AND he sang out he was the Prophet Elijah. He shook his sidelocks and he danced among the garbage cans. As I watched his hands coiling above his head, watched his fingers kissing his thumbs, I wanted to dance as well, to close my eyes and sway and let my voice bleed with his into the endless sky.

Instead, I ran.

I skittered over gravel and crashed up the back stairs to our apartment over the store. My mind was burning with his eyes and burning with his hair sparking blue and green and with his thin body spinning on a fence post faster, faster, and his crooked back splitting wider, wider, billowing out fiery wings.

I slammed the door shut. I crouched against it. A long moment passed and I began to breathe. The hall was hot and airless. Heavy winter coats hung on either side as if to muffle any outer noise.

"It just gets worse and worse." My father's voice was rising from the kitchen. "We'll never get out of this damn hole."

"That's not true, Murray." My mother was straining to keep

calm. "We just need to catch up on our payments. Then we'll get back our line of credit and we can get the new spring stock."

"And what'll we tell my ma? That we have to borrow from her – to pay our bills – so we can go even deeper into debt?"

"If we don't get new merchandise, who'll come to the store? Who'll want to shop?"

On and on.

I looked up at the painting on the wall: it was a dime-store reproduction of Millet's *Angelus*. A peasant farmer and his wife stood in their field, heads bowed in prayer as the Lord's land turned golden with the setting sun. I often imagined how they were digging side by side, the wet earth sticking to their boots, their hands as rough as their crude tools, labouring without word or thought until the distant church bell rang the evening's Annunciation of the Angel, how they paused, glanced at one another and began the shy singing of their prayer.

My father's voice seemed to groan from behind the painting. I followed his distress along a crack in the wall that ran from the picture frame, back along the hallway into the living-room. There the crack disappeared under the wallpaper, a pattern of flowers and grains swirling out of cornucopias. I saw my father standing beyond the border of that land where the wallpaper met the white glaze of the kitchenette. He was bent over the table spread with bills and receipts, frowning at the ledger on his plate.

"Ma always says that we should sell the store, otherwise we'll end up even worse."

"And then what'll we do?" my mother snapped. "Go back to the factory? Is that what you want? Or maybe you want to move back home to her? Did your ma say that, too?"

My father sat with a sigh and brooded into the book, underlining figures on the page, row after row.

I said nothing. My parents were working. Their clothing store was with them from the moment they woke up to the moment they lay down. They were especially busy, for it was the Eve of Bank Day, their day of reckonings. Also, it was Passover. They had closed the store early, hurried upstairs, and had me put on my good clothes and go outside while they completed their end-of-March accounts. I, being only ten years old at the time, was expected to wait outside the store, to watch the people on the buses heading home, to talk only to people I knew; but most of all to stay clean, to stay quiet and to be ready to go to Baba's.

But not to see Elijah. And not to interrupt with any news of miracles.

So I slouched out the door and past the other apartments toward the window at the end of the corridor. It had a view of nowhere – only the brick wall of the next building little more than an arm's length away – but my yearning for a miracle led me on.

I removed the screen and hunkered onto the window-sill where I hesitated with clenched teeth until I found my courage. Then I leaned out and I caught a rung of the fire escape.

I was looking for Elijah in the clouds. That was where I thought he'd gone, rising above the garbage cans and through the net of telephone wires to shape and reshape himself high above the sun. I climbed up the rusty ladder onto our second-storey roof only to find the sky was empty.

But below me, our block of Main Street in Winnipeg's North End was full. Shoppers were everywhere searching for the latest marvel, and hoping it would be reduced in price. Across the street inside The Fantasy Salon, Liz was circling round a customer, charming up a Jackie Kennedy hairdo for the weekend. Next door to her was Saint Joseph's Bingo Hall and Legion, where the city workers were hustling in, always the first ones there and the most devoted, calling for draughts of Black Label beer, kolbasa and pickled eggs. Then City Butchers, with its crowd of customers in the front, flies buzzing in the back. The crumbling Babylon Apartments was at the south end of the block. Its cracked windows blared a half-dozen different songs, all with the same heavy-hearted throb.

Across the intersection at Borkow's Funeral Chapel the shoppers kept a respectful distance. But even there, the limping man with the chauffeur's cap was hurrying in, delivering somebody's funeral clothes in a cardboard box, a loose pair of shoes shuffling on the top.

On my side of the street I could only see the store signs: CHAPLIN'S PHARMACY, Gustaf's barber pole and, directly under me, my parents' sign, STEIN'S STYLE SHOPPE. Next, a hanging shingle – Instant Alterations. Invisible Repairs – belonging to the tailor with emphysema whose wife had fled back to Hungary leaving him to rave and wheeze and sew. It obscured the sign at the north end of the block, so I could read only the POP of POPULARITY GRILL. Past that was THE SPECTACLE, already switched on and trying to dazzle in the fading light though everyone had seen its feature, *Ben Hur,* with Charleton Heston, when it was first released a year ago at The Gaiety downtown.

"They shouldn't call it a business section," Mr. Werner, our caretaker, once said. "They should call it a busyness section."

I knew I'd never find Elijah on this street.

I crossed the flat top of our building to the back porch roof, slid halfway down and lodged myself against an air vent. Grey nubble from the shingles tumbled to the eavestrough but I gripped my legs around the vent and scanned the lane and side streets.

What I discovered was quietude. Not silence: the air was alive with screen doors and clothes-lines, dogs and hammers, a service truck rattling down the lane. Yet they seemed separate and harmonious sounds quilted into a patchwork of yards and houses. They spread upon a stillness.

Still no Elijah though I felt him close at hand as if his voice were spiralling in the song of a knife-and-scissors man hawking down a side street or in the break of pigeons rising from their coop.

Something hovered behind the movie house.

I raced for it, scaled the slant of the porch roof, crossed the flat top, down the metal rungs, through the window, the flights of stairs, the spread of gravel, concrete, broken glass. But it was only the shadow of a back lane scavenger, a bloated woman who'd bagged her life into a shopping cart. She was as dusty and layered as the bundles she was pushing like a punishment. Even her eyes were layered. She could never be Elijah. She'd have to moult for a hundred springs even to see Elijah.

Behind the cafe, a delivery man was snickering to the cook. "You should have seen that crazy bugger. He was in back of the bakery juggling three hard loaves of pumpernickel, singing out some nutty immigrant song. Kids were jumping up and down like there was no tomorrow. I tell you, if I'd had a camera, I could have sold that picture to a magazine!"

I hurried past.

ONLY LATER, AS I CLIMBED BACK up the stairs, did the delivery man's words echo back to me and I realized he had seen Elijah. Elijah was moving through other lanes, trailed by other children, ones who did not run away. I curled against the topmost stair, and my chest ached with emptiness.

It ached long and deep before I heard the whispering sing-song, "Danny, Danny," and the slippered steps of Old Mr. Werner. It was he who'd first told me about the wonder-working Elijah, the glories of King Solomon and the Ba'al Shem Tov's magical adventures. "Danny, I'm all dressed up," he said. "This is something new for me." He was climbing up from his basement workshop where he kept his bed and hot plate, climbing up to the Passover, God's Days of Redemption. "I'm telling you, I am doing this just for you." Standing two stairs below me, he reached out to my shoulder and I uncurled to his touch. "Danny, you got to tell me the truth because I don't know. Am I looking good enough for your family?" He wore a loose and faded suit. His tie showed three blue swallows flying above a sunset. His skullcap was balding velvet.

"You look terrific, Mr. Werner. You're like a model or an actor in the movies."

"Yah, yah. I can guess which one. *Curse of the Mummy*. I know the movies you like to see."

"No, Mr. Werner. You're great. You're like that wise old guy, Charlie Chan."

"Okay, so now we're both wise guys. So help me button my collar." He smelled of shaving soap and talcum powder, though his face still bristled with patches of racoon grey. I found myself bending to him, not only from the knees but from the heart, wanting to kiss his cheek. And wanting to tell him about Elijah, but I hesitated, because I was ashamed that I had run away. Then I heard my parents behind the door, rattling keys and rushing on their coats. They'd be looking for us.

I patted down his collar. "Mr. Werner," I said, "I'm really glad you're coming." For we were all going to Baba's: my parents and I and Mr. Werner, whom I had begged to come and then had begged my parents to invite and, finally, had begged Baba to accept by making the old man out to be a lonely widower whose children left the faith and who would feel most alone on these holy nights. Somehow I had managed it. My first miracle of Passover.

I'D NEVER THOUGHT, BACK THEN when I was still a child and ruled by whatever ruled my parents, that Passover seders had anything to do with God. I thought of them as ceremonies of submission to The Family. My parents rehearsed me for days beforehand – not in the meaning of the ritual meal or the blessings or the four questions that I, as the youngest male, was supposed to ask, but, rather, they prepared me for the snares of my uncles and aunts, the taunts of my cousins, and how to please my baba.

Baba above all. Baba above everything. The very entrance to her MacGregor Street apartment block proved her power – stand in the lobby with its broken mailboxes, its tattered rug, and smell her herring, her bubbling corned beef, her boiling chicken. These were Baba smells. Climb her stairs. Knock on her greasy brown door. Listen for her Baba sounds.

"Rena!" Baba's voice was a high, strained gargle from the kitchen. A clatter of pots. "Rena, somebody's at the door! You deaf?"

"I'm going, right away. I'm going." Thin and gloomy, Rena

opened the door. She was always the first at the Passover meal: setting plates and taking coats, catching what she could of others' words and looks, being extra hands, extra ears and eyes for Baba – Baba who was so large, especially when I could not see her. Baba who was enormous on the telephone, her voice hoarse and shouting. And who grew larger still in my parents' telling and retelling of her demands, her judgements, her displeasures, until she became a giant.

Baba stomped down her hallway. She swallowed me in a fatty hug, laughing that she had me. My parents searched the floor to find their smiles, and all the while Mr. Werner watched and watched. "This here's my Danny!" Baba bragged to us all. "He's my favourite grandson." She turned to Mr. Werner. "And you? You are Murray's landlord?"

"I am Yossel Werner. A good holy day to you."

"Where you from?" Baba was suspicious. "You come from Poland? Or maybe Hungary? You got some kind of different accent."

"I came from Otvotsk, not so far from Warsaw."

"Warsaw? One of Hitler's ovens, pah!" Baba made her ritual gesture of spitting out the evil word.

"But now we're all Canadians," Mr. Werner said. "And we are all here alive and well."

"It's good you brought two books for the seder," Baba said. "We only got a couple. Next year, somebody better bring more."

"Mr. Werner knows how to read all the blessings for the meal," I announced. "He can make sure we'll have a real good service."

"Good – you show my boys what to do," she laughed. "You get them praying and I'll get them eating. But first, Danny, you come with me." I was pulled away, into her "bubbling pot" kitchen with its paint and linoleum curling in the steam of her thirty-year soup. She pinched my flesh and sat me on a stool where I watched her chop and stir. Baba's skin was loose, bleached as a boiled chicken's, soft as gefilte fish. I wondered if it had ever been firm like mine. They said she used to lift weights, real weights. The family ran a steam bath where the sons lifted barbells as if to prove that nothing could keep them down. The steam bath was their sanctuary where they would heat and strike themselves with swatches of oak leaves and groan under a pummelling massage. Three of her sons became weightlifting champions and she would at times work out beside them, mastering both iron and steam to keep her boys her allies.

Zaida, my grandfather, could take neither weight nor heat, at least not directly. The Depression which kept him poor also offered him escape. He travelled to far-off cities where he worked for years, sending back everything he could, like a man trying to buy his time.

Baba ran the family. She faced all problems with a hard eye, a closed hand and a dirt floor peasant's crudeness which further dismayed her gentle husband. In Russia, she'd been a victim of hunger and hate; here, discreet abandonment. She used the only powers she understood to keep her children close. She set each child against the rest with petty jealousies, resentments, hidden fears, and this kept them all clinging to her for support. It was never clear to me, then or now, these many years later, how well she understood her methods or whether the others realized their roles, but such things work even without understanding.

Eventually Zaida returned, to sit and sigh by the radiator, trying to rescue the family from the tangles of their plots and counterplots. He offered reason, compassion, humility and a painful display of self-blame. What they wanted was power. At last, exhausted, Zaida found his final, quiet way out. From then on, he was referred to as a saint, which simply meant that he was dead and had never been a threat.

Saul, the first son, preferred distraction. Family folklore had it that he had just missed being crushed by a piano dropped by movers. He came to interpret this event as some sort of revelation on the dangerous nature of burdens. He chose God instead. A mothering God. A worrying God. A God so anxious about Saul's frailty that He sent him criss-crossing the world in a quest for perfect health.

Whenever Saul ran out of money, he worked as a collector for religious charities. Wise in the manufacturing of miracles, he'd make his rounds on two trembling canes, and within a week or two he'd be springing, full of his God's blessings, into an overseas travel office. I never met Saul in the flesh; he moved away before I was old enough for memories and his returns were always unexpected, brief, almost apocryphal. The only proof I had of his existence were exotically stamped letters crammed into Baba's sewing drawer. They offered cures for depression, heart disease and cancer. They decoded ancient prophecies and begged immediate support.

Rena poked into the kitchen. "Ma, they're all here now. You coming out, or what?"

"How can I come? Look at everything I got to do!"

"Okay, okay, I'll help. But get Danny out of here, there ain't no room."

Rena never had words for me; only glares. While I may have acted afraid of her, I was mainly going through the motions. She simply could not raise Baba's forceful smells. Rena had only a mustiness and a trace of something burnt.

The wives, armoured in backcombed hairdos and black lace, chatted empty-handed in the hallway. The three brothers – my father, Steve and Leo – grunted and gripped one another with iron handshakes. They laughed hard and shoved each other until chairs scraped and their wives cried out.

"Stop it! It's enough already."

"Murray! The lamp!"

"For God sake, Steve, that's your good suit!"

It was Passover, a time to recall our history.

THE FAMILY SETTLED AT THE EXTENDED TABLE; Baba's chair empty at one end, then Rena and her children, the three brothers and their wives. At the far end on a stool was Mr. Werner. My other cousins and I got the added card-tables. My aunts and uncles flipped through the Passover prayers in grudging recognition of Mr. Werner as a stranger and a guest.

Mr. Werner lifted his cup for the blessing of the wine, his eyes dark with memory. He chanted in the way of his father and his father's father. All dead. All dead.

Other eyes glazed with boredom, wandered over the frill of a blouse, the fabric of a shirt, the jewel in a ring. They darkened only with suspicion. This table also had a history.

Sammy, Rena's son, rose to stammer the first ritual question, the question that should have been mine to ask since I was the youngest male. But I did not know the Hebrew.

"Ma nishtanah ha lailah hazeh, mee kol ha laylot? Why is this night different from all other nights?"

"Because," sang Mr. Werner in the ritual response, "we were slaves of Pharaoh in Egypt, and the Eternal One, our God, brought us out with a strong hand and an outstretched arm."

He uncovered the matzoh, our bread of hasty departure. But Baba was already pushing it to the side, along with the ceremonial herbs and salt water, making room for supper. So Mr. Werner had to rush through the Questions and the Commentaries, to skip over the tale of the Four Sons and the story of Jacob. Still, Steve yawned as his mind shuffled playing cards. Leo slipped away to the bedroom phone to make some 'connections', and before Mr. Werner could sing of the writhing rod of Moses and the Pharaoh's broken will, Baba burst through with a flood of soup and roast, sweet chicken and stewed fruit, cutting off the Exodus entirely.

We grabbed at the dishes. We heaped one serving onto another. At first we tore and chewed without tasting, as if the food might soon be snatched away. We were not hungry as much as aroused. It didn't matter that we were decades from the poverty which shaped these habits, or that there was far too much food; we grunted for the loads of meats and fish. We called for more.

Only Baba did not eat. How could she? This was our communion with her, proof of our needy love. We ate of her. Later, in her own time, she would eat the eaters.

We tired. Ached with heaviness. I could only suck and savour. I lifted my fragment of the matzoh which Mr. Werner had ritually broken, then passed to each of us, brittle as old parchment. I chewed it into sweetness as I watched him mourn into his seder book while the radiators hissed murder, pogrom, persecution. I mused about ghosts, wondering if my zaida could be a ghost trapped behind the wallpaper. I pretended my Aunt Rena's dead husband was a tiny ghost hovering over a wine stain on the tablecloth. Another plate boomed down and the spirit fled like a frightened insect.

Steve studied the braised beef drowned in gravy. He rubbed his lips with a napkin. "So, Murray. How's the store? You pulling in the big bucks?"

My father flinched from behind his mound of salad and Jello. He tried to remember Deborah's advice, how he should answer when Steve went for the cuts of heart and liver.

"Well, you know how it is in the clothing business, Steve. Lots of sales but lots of overhead."

"Aw, come on, Murray! You're making a pile. Your Deborah's got you working day and night. You don't even get time off to spend it. Hey, Ma, how about some more cream soda?" Steve looked pleased at drawing first blood on his brother. He liked scoring high and fast, which made him Big Steve at the poker club, the big winner rolling in the dough, the dough he peeled off in fives and tens to toss at flattering kibbitzers or to slip to his high-styled wife from Montreal who laughed it all away. But at the family table, he gave nothing away to anyone except to Baba because here Big Steve was still Little Stevie scraping and scrambling for his mother's soup pot love.

Baba set down a half-dozen bottles of soft drinks. "What kind of money can Murray make? Whenever I'm in their store, nobody's buying. Who's going to buy at those prices? I ask you, Deborah, what makes you think my Murray is a fancy businessman? He had a good job as a packer. Now, you'll make him lose everything."

My father lowered his eyes. He pushed bits of salad around his plate. Either way, business success or business failure, he'd be condemned.

Baba poured the drinks into heavy tumblers. "Murray," she

said, "that blouse you gave me, it's no good. It tore under my arm. Maybe you'll bring me a better blouse?"

Rena burst out at her daughter, Shaini – "Stop spitting food. Stop it or I'll get mad!" – becoming even angrier that she was missing Baba's and Murray's words, words she could keep to cook in her own oven, words she could serve at their next dinner. She poked Shaini's lips with a spoon of baked carrots. "Now eat! . . . Look at you. Three years old and you don't listen to nobody!"

"Ma, never mind the blouse. How about some stockings?" It was Leo smiling over his palm-sized address book thick with pencilled notes. "I'm meeting with a guy tomorrow night. I can get you all you want." Clever Leo who claimed he never needed any sucker job, not as long as he had contacts. "Hey, Murray. I'll get some for you, too, cheaper than the wholesale. How many do you want, two gross, three gross?"

But what if they were hot? My father didn't deal in heisted goods. "That's okay, Leo. I got plenty of women's hosiery. A big order came in just last week. Where am I going to put any more?"

Leo stiffened. He would sulk for Ma. "Fine! Go try to help a brother. I don't even get a 'thank you'."

"What's the matter, Murray?" Baba leaned over the clutter of plates. "You can't return the other stockings? Jacky Winestock won't take back his merchandise? I used to feed him right here at this table!"

My father lowered his head. His hands groped for words. Until my mother spoke. "It's a business situation, Ma. But it's great that Leo wants to help us out. We appreciate it, don't we, Murray?"

Baba drew in her resentment. Leo tapped his out upon a plate. Steve was grinning, pleased with this new rift. He knew that now my parents could not ask Baba for a loan. "Hey, let's forget it, already!" He cracked a laugh. "Murray must be sick of women's stockings, brassières and girdles. Jeez, peddling that stuff would drive me nuts. Look, tonight's a holiday. I want to toast my ma!" Steve lifted the silver goblet, full to the brim. "Ma, you made one hell of a meal! Here's to good times!"

12

"No! You don't drink!" It was Mr. Werner, his glimmering eyes fixed on Steve. "That's the Prophet's cup. Don't you know anything?" The goblet was set in a special place to await Elijah's invisible visit to the seder, the prophet who had risen to Heaven on a whirlwind and who descends to honour every home's Passover meal.

"I saw him," I said without thinking. "I saw Elijah." Mr. Werner, Steve, the whole table turned to look at me. "He was behind the store. He was dancing and singing and getting ready to fly. He was going to fly!"

Even my cousins were still. Then, as if balancing something delicate between us, Mr. Werner asked, "Danny, what did your Elijah look like?"

"He had long curls and a long beard and a black coat. And his back was all hunched at the top. I wasn't the only one who saw. Max, the guy who drives the bakery truck, he saw him, too." What if Elijah would really visit our seder? What if he would sit right next to me?

Steve's laughter broke overhead. "I'll bet he saw that crazy Doukhobor! The one with the dirty beard that the guys call Castro. He sleeps on the river bank wrapped in newspapers. You're lucky he didn't grab you."

More voices clattered overhead.

"Naw, it's the rag collector, Yonkle. You know the one – he's always sneaking into weddings for the booze."

"A shame! Jewish welfare should do something."

"Some prophet. He collects bottles in back alleys. What you got there is a nickel and dime profit! Ha! Ha! You get it, Ma? It's a joke."

Their laughter turned my hurt to anger and I broke away from the table. "Let me go! Let me get by!" I had to edge along the wall, pushing past their chairs and their swollen backs that grumbled and twisted with tufts of hair and creasing necks, past smells of cigar and sweat, bites of perfume and hair spray. "Damn! Hell! Crap!" I was coughing out the worst words I knew even as I tangled in the straps of my mother's purse. It spilled out Kleenex smeared with lips, compacts of powder, a gaping mirror. She reached towards me but I slapped her hands away. "Leave me alone!" as I entered the no man's land pursued by shouts and warnings.

Until I was held by Mr. Werner's mild voice threading through it all. "Who knows what the boy saw? Do you know? You don't know." All other voices dropped into broken mutters. Mr. Werner's voice was deep and strong. "My father, Avram Werner, may his name be blessed, he saw an angel. It was the day the peasants came with axes to make a pogrom against the Jews. An angel appeared and showed my father where to hide his family in the bushes. All the time that we were hiding he saw the angel shining down, protecting us inside a great fire. And what did the peasants see? Maybe bushes. Maybe a pile of dirt. But my father, he saw an angel."

The tablecloth rustled. A chair creaked and straightened into silence. A knife was laid quietly upon a plate. Mr. Werner raised his finger. "So Steve, you want to drink wine? That's good. We are supposed to drink wine on this night. And with our wine we make our prayers. Danny, you open the door for Elijah."

It was the prayer of Shfoch Chamatcha spoken as the door was opened. It welcomed the spirit of Elijah, prophet of reconciliation, herald of the Messiah and the End of Time. I felt the cool rush; Elijah's spirit was tinkling and laughing, flying over stains and bones, dancing on the silver rim of the wine cup, sweeping out the hot, stale air. It pushed me, too, back into the room, to Mr. Werner who rocked over his leather book, one finger crooked above the page, motioning, "Come, Danny. Come."

His hands slipped around my shoulder, scratchy against my shirt, and when the prayer was ended, I sat down next to him, pressing against his bony knee. Everyone else left the table. Some clattered in the kitchen or shook open newspapers around the coffee table, others whispered in the hall, and glanced at us and glanced again. But Mr. Werner was close beside me.

"Danny, this is Hebrew. Can you read it?" Black twisted letters. His book was not like the other ones. It had no woodcut illustrations of long-haired Egyptians with their whips or bent slaves wrapped in ragged sheets.

"I don't know how to, Mr. Werner."

"That's okay," he said. "Do you know what Egypt is, eh? What's Egypt?"

"It's a country in Africa."

"Is that right? That's very good! And what else? What else do you know about Egypt?"

"We all lived there once, like thousands of years ago."

"Yah, Danny, so was it a good place or a bad place?"

"The Egyptians were mean. They made us work way too hard. We had to build the pyramids."

"You know a lot about Egypt. But did we stay there? Did we stay in that bad place forever?"

"No," I answered. "There was Moses, the one in the movie, *The Ten Commandments*."

"In Yiddish, he's called Moishe. God loved us so he sent Moishe."

"Yeah, and Moses made the Egyptians let us go."

"It took a miracle. It took ten miracles!" Mr. Werner began a weaving love prayer, a circling song without beginning or end as he rocked and I rocked along beside him, humming into his breath, warm and sweet from Manishevitz wine. And when we stopped, or, rather, when we let it go to sing somewhere else without us, he opened his eyes and asked, "Danny, you know what 'Ma nishtanah' means? It means 'What's different'."

"Ma nishtanah," I repeated.

"And 'ha lailah hazeh' means 'this night'."

"Ma nishtanah ha lailah hazeh."

"Yah, Danny, you said it just right. You're a smart boy. Mee kol ha laylot. That means 'from all the other nights'. Put it all together and it means 'What's different about this night from all the other nights?' "

"Because we're not in Egypt?"

"That's right. And because tonight we learn how we can get out of all the bad places."

I pressed closer into his book and into him, my shoulder under his arm, my ear rubbing against his dry whiskery chin as if he could carry me, light as smoke, light as words up to the clouds. We gazed into his book of stains and tears and twisting letters, singing, "Ma nishtanah ha lailah hazeh, mee kol ha laylot?" Our voices entwining, we swirled above the table and out the window in a shy thin song, a strong brave song as we creased and folded, sighed and swayed into one another.

"Ma nishtanah ha lailah hazeh, mee kol ha laylot."

THE SALE

MURRAY HEARD HIS SON'S FOOTSTEPS ON THE APARTMENT FLOOR above the shop. He thought, he's woken up but he won't see they're gone. Not right away.

The footsteps overhead made Murray restless, wanting to be busy with a heavy job, like packing the winter stock and carrying it to the basement, then hauling up the spring clothing from last year. But he knew he had to wait until after the sale. He thought of asking Deborah if he should sweep the front steps and sidewalk once again. The spring melt had left a crust of dirt and sand all down the street and the wind kept blowing in all sorts of trash.

Murray swept often to make the store look clean and modern and popular, a place where smart shoppers kept coming and going, finding bargains, finding exactly what they need. This was part of his personal sales strategy. Deborah, who had been an assistant manager at Eaton's, told him often, "A merchant's not like some kind of a muscleman pulling people off the street. A merchant works out sales strategy, he finds the way to make people want to buy." So Murray swept the front and washed the floors and windows. He made sure he was always neat and clean. He smiled and stayed smiling whenever there were customers in the store.

Murray had been a weightlifter, almost the western champ; everyone said he was crazy to have quit. People still stopped him at times to tell him the title had practically been his. Murray never knew what to answer. He'd wink and sometimes say, "You're darn right!"

Murray had loved the weights: groaning against cold metal, raising it high and clear, especially during competitions with his pals cheering and the screaming ache of his muscles as if he were pulling the world off its foundation and holding it above him in a roar. And afterwards, the men all slapped, prodded, cheered him along, calling him their boy, their champ, saying he could take on anything. But it had taken him nowhere. Only into Joe-jobs in warehouses while those same pals were showing up in suits and silk ties, boasting about their fancy cars. More and more Murray had felt exposed and foolish.

When he had met Deborah, she understood it right away even though she was ten years younger. "What good is holding up a weight? A pillar can do that. A machine can do that. Meanwhile some boss is pushing you around day in, day out. Who's going to take you seriously outside the gym?" As soon as he had heard this, he was sold. He quit his job and the two of them opened up the clothing store on the Monday after their wedding.

Murray made the decision about the sidewalk on his own. He would sweep it later. First, he'd tackle the packages of women's hose, rearranging them by sizes instead of brands. He wasn't going to check with Deborah, either. He'd just do it and let her decide if she liked it after it was done. Besides, he saw that she was at the back, caught up in her own decision-making, marking down the prices on a rack of winter skirts. Her face was tight with concentration. Murray knew what she was thinking: how much to let go? 25%? 35%? 50%? It wasn't easy. Ever since Christmas things had been tough; everyone was broke and even with the sale, they were having what she called "another bad season."

Deborah always said, "A clothing store has its times just like everything else." Murray understood this well. Everything's got seasons – football, baseball, the farmers, even a marriage. And March was slow. And it was chilly, so nobody was shopping. He had to be patient. Keep busy. Stick to his sales strategy.

Sweaters were piled on the discount table near the front. When a customer came in and messed them up, Murray folded them again. If this happened often enough, he reasoned, somebody might buy something and the pile wouldn't be so big. No matter what, when the sale was over he would lay them all in cardboard boxes marked Winter 1960/61 and hope they'd stay in style for next year.

"You can't show them if they're out of style," Deborah always said. "You want the place looking fashionable, not like just another North End bargain bin. It's got to be unique." That was why they named it Stein's Style Shoppe. Deborah said the words had a sophisticated ring.

Murray began sorting the hose into sizes but he couldn't concentrate; the footsteps overhead were becoming frantic. There was a thud like a box being dropped. Then a series of scrapings and the scattered roll of marbles. A moment of stillness. Murray decided to separate the hose into colours, too. But not yet. He'd wait for what was bound to happen next. By the count of eight there was a scramble down the apartment's back stairs descending into the shop. Each step felt like a rap on Murray's chest.

"Mom! My comic books!" The boy swung through the back door, surprising Deborah as she was untangling a clutch of hangers. "Mom!"

"Ssssh! Be quiet!" She rattled the hangers in her hand. "You know you're not supposed to yell in here!"

"But I got robbed!" he hissed. "All my comics are gone for sure and I don't know what else!"

"Daniel, please! Remember last night? Dad and I talked about how you're getting older . . . how you don't need certain things any more."

"They were under my bed . . . all together in the box. At least forty, maybe more."

"Look at me, Daniel. We talked about how you spend your time. And we all agreed that by ten years old, some things should change."

"You took them? Did you take my comics?"

Deborah turned to the rack, straightening the skirts. "You'll find new things to do, more mature things . . ."

"That's my stuff! You can't take my stuff!"

". . . like being with other boys and girls."

"Like who?" he asked and kicked the rack. "There's no other kids living on Main Street. There's no kids even close."

Murray watched Deborah rub her brow, watched her close her eyes and begin to knead the nape of her neck. He felt he shouldn't stare but he was remembering other times when the two of them would work far into the night. Deborah, tired and stiff, would look over and call in her familiar way, wanting him, only him. So Murray decided it was really all right to stare and he let himself admire her raven hair and her body, still as shapely as when they'd first met. He thought of how she looked so much like Jane Russell who'd starred as a rancher's high-spirited daughter and again as a saloon singer in those western movies at The Spectacle. Her lips were moving, silently mouthing something to herself. Murray had to concentrate to read them; she was repeating the same word, "Damn. Damn."

Deborah's getting her headache, he realized. It was only eleven o'clock but she was already getting it. Those headaches, he thought, they spoil everything.

"Daniel," she said quietly, trying to offer some calmness to the boy. "It's Saturday and you know how busy we are on Saturdays. We've discussed this before and we can discuss it again . . ."

"We didn't disgust anything."

"Discuss."

"It's not fair," he said. "You're not fair."

"That's enough! Go talk to your father!"

Murray saw her shoulders tightening. "Deborah, it's okay!" he called out. "Just take it easy!"

"Murray, talk to Daniel!" Click went a hanger, click, another. She was straight-backed, deliberate. The skirts needed prices. The rack needed skirts. Customers would be coming. Everything had to be in order.

He knew how she could lose herself like this. Being constantly busy. Working till ten, up again at seven, going day after day until she'd finally wear out. Then that awful mood would come with hard words about selling the store or getting a bigger store, or having another child – changing anything, changing everything. Finally tears or clouded silence while Murray stood nearby but not too close, feeling helpless in a maze of racks and counters. And without even the beginning of a strategy.

In the meantime, there was Daniel to deal with, slumping towards him, demanding sympathy. Murray gathered the packs of hosiery, trying to look busy. He hunkered over the display shelves, his large hands frustrated by the slippery packages that would not stay put.

"Dad?" Daniel glanced up warily as if Murray were some untrustworthy giant who would only respond to pleas or bargaining.

"What is it, Danny?"

"It's about my comics." The boy's head tilted back. "Mom says I have to talk to you." He seemed so pale and thin to Murray, almost elfin, a confusing knot of needs and wants, carried along by moods and fantasies. Deborah had said it best. "That boy's in his own little world. Something's got to be done."

The front door swung open and a cold, dusty wind swept along the floor. A slim young woman entered, her eyes scanning the counters in search of sale tags. Just behind her was a man in a khaki parka. Murray tried to signal Deborah but she didn't seem to notice.

"Dad, I have to talk to you," said Daniel.

"Not now, Danny. There's customers." Murray would have to take them. His hands pressed the sides of his slacks. He grinned, trying to catch their attention. The woman was already rummaging through cardboard packets of men's underwear. Finally, the man looked up. Murray went for him.

"My name's Murray," he said. "So what are you looking for today?"

"Naw, nothing . . . you know . . . just waiting for the old lady." The man hunched, burying himself deeper in his parka. He was young, about nineteen, and new to the neighbourhood. Murray had seen him on the street. He had been impressed by how the young man moved with a balance and intensity as if primed for sudden action. Murray had thought, the guy's not solid enough for weights, but he could be a goalie or a boxer – light middleweight. Now Murray was surprised. Here, close up, inside the shop, the young man seemed so sullen and awkward.

"Maybe you'd like a good shirt," Murray said, grinning again. "We've got a sale on real tough ones, from Scotland. One hundred percent wool!"

"Well, the winter's over, eh?" The young man's eyes brushed to the window. Across the street a crew of workers jostled into the Legion.

'But these shirts, you can wear them all year round. They're practically like jackets."

The man continued gazing and Murray was drawn to look across the street as well, recalling the taste of beer, the laughter of men around a table. Until something rattled in the back. It was Deborah, pulling more hangers out of a box.

"It was a tough one," Murray said, trying to concentrate on the young man. "I mean, the winter. The winter was a real tough one this year, huh?"

"I don't know," he replied.

"You had to be dressed for it. Not that we sell construction clothes. We just carry the men's regular line. I guess you work construction, huh?"

"Sometimes." His voice dragged. His eyes narrowed on Murray.

Murray droppd his gaze and noticed the man's work boots, worn and cracked. "I mean, I've seen you some mornings . . . heading for the bus stop. So I wondered if maybe . . ."

The man glared at the woman as if she were to blame for

Murray's questions. She perked up at once. "Dean doesn't take the bus no more. That was when he worked at Temporary Help, but now he's on permanent with the butcher. He's like an apprentice, aren't you, honey? Deanie, you want the briefs or the boxer shorts? The briefs are a better price."

"I don't care. Hey, what do I care?" He shuffled in the narrow aisle, testing the zipper of his parka. He glanced to the street, then lowered his gaze past Murray to the woman. "Just get something, okay? I'm taking off."

"Dean?" She called to him but he didn't slow down. "When you coming home? What about supper?"

"Yeah, supper." He was out the door, scowling into the wind, his parka open, hands deep in his jeans pockets. Murray watched him trudge past the front window. He waited for him to enter his view again at the street corner, watching as he dodged the traffic, crossing Main Street to the Legion.

"What about these shorts, are they going on sale?" The woman's voice was cold with blame.

"What? Those are Harvey Woods shorts. They never get reduced. But how about these Stanfield briefs, they're great!" Murray grinned, trying to crack through her frown with fierce sincerity. "They're strong and they don't stretch. They're guaranteed! Just look." He knew he was too aware of his own enormous hands, of the woman's glare, of Danny behind him, looking puzzled. He tore off the cardboard flap. "Here, feel them. They're terrific. I mean, I wear them myself!" He knew he was getting too close. He was supposed to step back, let the customer decide. Deborah's words were repeating in his head, "Murray, you've got to give the customer more room." And this woman was so small, he thought, really just a tiny young thing. And nervous, too.

Murray tried to explain. "I like to . . . well, a lot of men like to wear them . . . because they last so long." He smoothed the underwear on the counter, not looking up. Her hands seemed frail even as they tightened around her purse.

"That's okay," she said. "I was just looking. I saw you had a sale."

"We got lots on sale . . . even some boxer shorts, but not the Harvey Woods."

"Yeah, well, maybe another time." She headed to the door, buttoning her coat.

"Janet!" Deborah called out, coming down the aisle, full of welcome. "It's Janet, isn't it?" She touched Murray's shoulder, meaning, *Go. I'll take her.* "Janet, didn't I see you at Bingo Thursday night? I sit at the front so I can flirt with the caller. It doesn't help – I still can't win. Were you there last night? Did the jackpot really go in just sixty numbers? I should have gone but I was marking down all those skirts. Have you seen them yet?" The woman smiled, her hands relaxing. She followed Deborah up the aisle towards the skirt rack. "You'd better get your man back in here. A handsome guy like that, we've got to dress him up!"

Murray felt his face blushing hot and red. Head bowed, he hurried past the lingerie, the women's sweaters, coats, past the cabal of the two women laughing by the skirts and through the children's section to the basement door. He stormed down the basement steps into the murky darkness at the bottom.

The air was cool and moist and everything was still.

"Dad? Daddy?" Daniel was calling from the top step.

Murray stayed silent, resenting the high pleading tone, the sharp light.

"Daddy?"

"What now?" Murray's words had a creature's voice, a troll's voice. Did the boy flinch?

"I've got to talk to you."

"Then come down."

"What about the dark?"

Murray pulled the chain but the light merely thinned the dark, a dim bulb dying on the end of its cord. It was only enough to outline the shovel leaning against a mildewed wall.

"I'm going to the furnace," Murray said. "I'm going to feed it coal." The building was the only one that Murray knew of that still used coal for heat. He was always telling Old Man Werner, the landlord, to switch to gas. Coal was expensive and too much trouble. Yet somehow, from somewhere, the black load arrived, thundering down the chute to the floor beside the furnace.

Privately, Murray was always glad to see the coal.

He concentrated on the pile. He grasped the shovel with balanced hands. He lowered it to the floor six inches from the perimeter, then paused, aiming for some perfect point. He held his breath for the precise moment and then lunged the shovel under and up for a solid heavy scoop. He held the shovel in mid-air, testing its weight, raising and lowering it as if it were something to be judged. Then, into the furnace.

The flames sank and sighed. Murray allowed himself a grunt of satisfaction and bent forward, staring into the fire.

Daniel shuffled into the wavering light. "It's like a monster."

"What is?" Murray felt the flames dancing across his face. He prodded a lump of coal back to the pile and edged the border to shape a circle.

"The furnace. It's like a monster with fire coming from its mouth. There was this witch doctor and he got all the natives bowing to a monster. Only it wasn't a monster. It was a giant statue. But nobody knew. They thought it was real because the mouth made scary sounds and gave them orders. Meanwhile it was just the witch doctor doing it all." The boy was becoming increasingly excited, his voice rising, his arms animated. "And then Tarzan busted in with elephants! He's trying to stop the witch doctor from burning a big game hunter. The witch doctor was ready to slide the hunter right down into the statue's mouth. The hunter's tied up and all he can see is this big burning mouth and . . ."

"That's enough!" The furnace door clattered shut. The fire behind the grate striped Murray into bars of shadow and flame.

"Huh?" The boy bolted back.

"No more stories. A bunch of goofy day-dreams – that's what you're getting out of those comic books."

"But lots of kids read comics."

"Yeah? Well, they're not living in them, not sitting all day with their faces pasted between the pages. You've got to get outside, do something, make some friends. Forget those comic books."

Daniel's lip trembled. "Did you . . . did you burn them?"

Murray sighed, weary of being so hard. "Come on, Danny. I wouldn't do something like that. What do you think I am?"

"Are you down there, Murray?" Deborah's voice descended from the top of the steps. "Murray?"

He lowered his head to the coal. "I had to feed the furnace."

"The furnace! It's already roasting up here. You're always running down there to feed the furnace."

"Okay, I'm coming."

"Well, there's customers."

"I said I'm coming!" Murray checked his hands for dirt. He rolled down the sleeves of his dress shirt and set the cufflinks. He tightened the knot of his tie, then tightened it again until he felt it rubbing at his throat. But he did not leave. He picked up the iron rod and unhooked the furnace grate. One more shovelful.

Daniel turned, mourning into shadows. Suddenly he brightened. He saw something in the storage room, the light of the furnace reflecting off a glossy cover. "My comic books!" He rushed into the small room and knelt beside the box, checking that they were safe and all together: Batman, Superman, Spider-man.

"Leave them where they are." Murray's voice was low, regretful as he shut the grate. "Just forget them, okay?"

Daniel looked torn, hesitating on one knee.

"Look, we've got to go," Murray said. "I'm turning off the light."

Daniel stumbled to his feet. He rushed up the steps two at a time.

"Danny, just start playing outside. How about it?"

The boy was gone. As Murray reached for the light cord, he noticed a streak of coal dust on his hand. And on his white sleeve, a black rub that would be hard to wash away. Deborah would have him take the shirt off right away. She'd scrub it in the sink, murmuring in her familiar, weary tone, "Oh, Murray."

How could it have happened? he asked himself. He had been so careful; he always tried to be so careful.

MONEY

THE SIDEWALK BETWEEN SCHOOL AND MY PARENTS' STORE WAS A maze of cracks I used to leap and skip for my innocent mother's sake: "Step on a crack and break your mother's back."

But, by ten years old, I was too aware of others on the street and I no longer jumped the cracks. Instead, I spanned them with a practised grace, shifting subtly, avoiding almost every one.

When I did misstep, I no longer turned in a circle to unwind the deed and try again. I simply scored a point against myself like in the games of balls and teams and teachers' piercing whistles. Still, I remember how uneasy I would feel, the old taboo of breaking my mother's back whispering through my thoughts, as if I hadn't changed the game at all.

It was simple once I turned off Inkster onto Main Street. I aligned my feet on either side of a lengthwise crack, lush with green camomile, and I followed it past the pharmacy to where my mother would be waiting.

There the game became darker and more disturbing.

The building was divided into two stores with adjacent

doors sharing the same alcoved entrance – the door to our store was on the left and Gustaf the barber's door was on the right. I had to climb four steps.

I tucked in my shirt and tightened my shoelaces. I pushed my right hand in my pocket, clutching a hard Christmas candy, a gift from Beatrice McKay, an old wizened neighbour. I kept it as a lucky charm to help me pass the display windows that were on either side of the steps.

I advanced with my left foot.

I did not look through Gustaf's window. It was enough to imagine him frowning at me, stiff and white beside his porcelain chair, his comb and scissors held on guard, as if he knew some dreadful thing that I had done, something I couldn't remember, and because of that forgotten act, he would someday march right through that window and grab me.

I believed that I could avoid this only by concentrating on my mother's window. On its three plaster mannequins. The middle one was what my mother called "The Torso." Its pearly white brassière looked so much like armour that I imagined The Torso had once been a complete woman, powerful and brave like a comic book superhero. She yearned to grow back the rest of her body so she could grab a weapon, shout battle cries and take revenge. Beside her were two lady mannequins; peaceful, sublime, as if they were watching something wondrous in the clouds. Their plaster was chipped in places, their wigs were brittle and faded, but their hands were raised to console The Torso, wanting her to know about that thing that she could not see or hear or touch. They were also sending me a message of perpetual protection as I climbed the steps.

Forget Gustaf. Think only of us.
Forget Gustaf. Think only of us.
Forget Gustaf. Think only of us.

On the fourth step, I seized the brass knob with my left hand, rushed in, and with my shoulder slammed the door behind me. Home free.

The store seemed empty at least of my mother; the shelves were packed with clothes almost to the ceiling. In front of me the old nickel-plated cash register seemed to float upon the glass counter-top. I played my finger along the intricate design until my mother came.

She presented her worn smile and a faded, "Hello, dear." We didn't look at one another. She checked her receipt book. I studied the furrows on her forehead, the lines she made when reading her receipts. Her face had different lines for customers, though just as deep. She turned a page and asked, "What did you do at school this morning?"

Neither of us ever noticed what I answered. Only a mumble was needed. The next move was hers. She settled behind the cash register so it became a part of her with her head and arms emerging. The till rang out. Its NO SALE sign flapped up beneath her neck. Her hand swung down and my hand swung up. Coins dropped into my open palm.

"This is for lunch," she said. "Now dear, don't forget – stop by when you're heading back to school."

THE POPULARITY GRILL WAS ALMOST FULL when I arrived. The two U-shaped counters were heavy with street workers bent over their hot gravy sandwiches. Mr. Nojuk worked the grill but seldom looked up, even when handing Rita another dish. Mr. Barry, the music teacher whom the workers called a "beatnik," was dropping coins into the jukebox to play "Michael Row the Boat Ashore."

I avoided his smile, for it was always hard to greet a teacher out of school, even Mr. Barry who lived just down the lane. I took my special seat at the end of the counter. It was really Rita's but she never sat down during lunch.

"Hiya, Danny!" Rita called. "I already got your bacon frying. How's that for service to my favourite customer?"

"I thought I was your favourite, Rita!" It was Roberto, the butcher, cleaning his fingernails with the tooth of his comb.

"You, Roberto? All your favourites are at the track."

The street workers chuckled harshly. The butcher waved them down. "Well, at least my Dizzie Lizzie loves me, don't you?" He slipped his hands around the waist of Liz, the student hairdresser from The Fantasy Salon.

"Come on. Don't!" She slapped at him with a menu.

"Lady Elizabeth," Rita mocked in High English, "is this strange man bothering you? Do you wish me to place some saltpetre in his coffee?" More laughter from the workers.

"You should have been with me at the track last night, Lizzie," said Roberto. "You would have been a lot friendlier. And richer."

"Oh sure!" Liz tittered, opening the purse she always kept on her lap. Her compact blinked open and shut again.

I watched Liz, trying to understand what made her laugh, for I'd noticed that she laughed at strange moments, but when others laughed, no matter why, she'd lower her eyes as if she were being blamed. Liz pretended to study the menu, then nodded to Rita. "I'd like the grilled cheese with a Seven Up."

"You could've had steak, Liz," Roberto said.

"Just wise up, Roberto," Rita snapped. "If Liz wants to see horse meat, she'll tour your butcher shop."

The counter roared. The butcher's eyes narrowed and he shifted in his stool, leaning close to Liz. "The long shot, number eight, came in first just like I said it would. And it paid twenty to one." He stood up to shove his hand into his front pants pocket. "Guess who bet ten bucks on the nose?" He held up a roll of tens, as the line of workers fell silent. Rita frowned with her arms full of dirty plates. Mr. Barry looked up from his book and even Mr. Nojuk lowered the bacon back onto the grill, staring with his head cocked to one side. "Liz could have been in on the bet," Roberto taunted. "You see this? Two hundred smackers in hard cash. This ain't cheese and Seven Up, this is steak and champagne!" Only I kept laughing, delighted by Liz, who seemed as stunned as some cartoon character.

I finished lunch right after Roberto and followed him outside so I could watch the way he swaggered down the street. I knew I shouldn't act like him. Liz, Rita and the rest all called him stupid and a show-off. But Roberto always won. And not just at the race track. He won at the trickier games of jokes and teases, brags and warnings. He made everyone look and listen. No matter what they said about Roberto, they paid more attention to him than to anybody else.

Liz came out of the cafe soon after me, and passed by acting casual but trying not to look at me. At the corner, she began to rush, teetering on her high heels so that her blonde tower of hair shook with every step. I veered into a vacant lot where I spied as she caught up to Roberto behind his butcher shop. I watched them get into his shiny Eldorado, Liz speaking quickly, bowing her head as if Roberto were right and she were wrong, until he turned the key and drove away with her, leaving behind a cloud of oily smoke.

I practised how Roberto bellowed, "You see this?" I raised my fist to the empty lot just as Roberto did to the cafe filled with doubters.

I hesitated. Something about the lot seemed out of place or at wrong angles. I backed up, looked around. The weeds, broken glass, the yellowed shreds of paper all looked as ordinary as ever. Then it struck me – the old telephone booth had disappeared.

I felt as if I'd been tricked. Impossible. The booth had always been there, just like the stores, the sidewalk, the street lights at the corner. It belonged there. I'd checked it every day for change, pushing open the folding doors, fingering the shiny metal return, backing out before the doors snapped shut. It didn't matter that I'd never found anything, the booth was a part of what I did each day, nothing that seemed so special until it was lost.

I moped over what was left, drawing my foot across an empty square of dirt. The grey crust opened along the edge of my shoe. There . . . silver – yes, the sly grin of a coin . . . and just as quickly, gone.

I fell to my knees and got it – a dime, just as easy as that. As I rubbed it clean, I kicked at the ground and found another one and then two nickels all where the telephone booth had been.

31

I remembered a man in the booth cursing and poking through the slatted floor. He'd fumbled his coin and it had dropped through the wooden slats where he couldn't reach it. Plenty of people must have lost coins that way, I reasoned, and all those coins would have dropped through the slats to settle in the dirt. The slats were gone. The coins were left behind.

I focussed on the square of dirt as if it were a map: graphic hills and valleys, every pebble and splinter of wood, distinct, vivid with possibility. I didn't dig as much as sift, pinching at weight or shape, finding nickels, dimes, even quarters.

I raked my fingers through a deeper layer, section by section. The soil was rich with coins and each one swelled my excitement. I began dredging up moist red crusts, the rot of the wooden base.

Something else emerged: sowbugs, fleshy scaled things with a hundred arms. I'd torn them from their secret passages. They scrambled over my hands, over the coins, over each other and tumbled back into the earth. I jumped to my feet. I wanted to kick dirt over them and get away.

But the coins were there, too, singing in a hard, high pitch. I felt paralysed, wanting to break free but fearing if I left the coins they'd call to someone else. Then someone else would be rich and I'd be poor.

So I stooped. I pushed my fingers into the earth. Coins, dirt, sowbugs mixed together.

I didn't feel my hands, I witnessed them, pushing into the dirt, shaking off the bugs, picking at the coins and thrusting them into my pockets. Everything became a blur except the mechanics of collecting. Still, I felt the tightness of my jaw, heard a moaning through my teeth.

When I broke from there, I ran to hide in a gap between two stores. I thought, what if someone saw me hunched in the dirt with all those bugs? A worker or Rita, or even Mr. Barry? That wasn't sand in a playground box and anyway, I was too old to play with sand. What would they say about it in the cafe?

But the coins weighed heavily in my front pockets, as if they were still singing to me, "It doesn't matter. We're all that matters!"

I rushed to the shop, feeling their pull as I bounded up the stairs and slammed inside to show them off. No one was there. My mother would be in the back room. That gave me time to pull out the coins in fistfuls and heap them on her counter. Still no one came. I scraped the grit and slapped off the dust on the back of my pants. I stacked them and I lined the stacks in a row. Finally, I added them up, nine dollars and forty-eight cents.

My mother entered, pressing down her blouse, her face already set in her customary smile for business. "Oh, it's you, Danny. You're so late. You should be headed back to . . ." She saw the coins and halted.

I felt I only had that moment to explain. "I found them," I said. "The old telephone booth's gone. And they got left there. I was coming from lunch and and no one saw but I got them . . . and . . . and . . ."

My mother took over, slowing me down with questions, corrections, revisions. Until I was trying to tell the story her way, guessing what I should say, how I should speak, should stand, but especially what I should be skipping over: the bugs, the dust, the rotting wood, the "dirty parts" of what had happened that might upset her. I lost my way and could not speak at all, could only push over the piles and spread the coins beneath her gaze. "Look," I said. "Just look."

We both fell silent. My breath was hot on my hands as I scraped two quarters against each other to study the grit flaking off the coins. This wasn't what I'd expected. There was no celebration, no yelling and laughing, no dancing around; only this hush and the grit sifting onto the counter.

My mother finally spoke as if asking me a riddle.

"Danny, you're a lucky boy. That's such a lot to find. Do you know how hard it is to earn? Now what should you do with all this money?"

I thought, show it off, throw it in the air, yelling, "Steak and champagne!" like Roberto. But I knew that wasn't what she wanted.

I thought of how many comic books the coins could buy.

Or tickets to the movies. I'd even buy her something, too. Like a greeting card. But that wasn't it at all. Her words, her silence, even the raising of her brow were clues I had to trace to the one true and perfect answer.

"I guess, uh . . . what I should do is . . ."

"Yes, Daniel?"

I noticed my lucky candy on the counter, pulled from my pocket with the coins. I remembered how Beatrice McKay had rattled her tin of candies over me as I'd looked up to see myself reflected in its bottom, all gawking and dwarfish. As the candies shook, the old woman chanted, "I take one and only one hard candy every day. And why only one, why not as many as I want?"

"I don't know," I had replied.

"So my candies last till Christmas when a new tin comes my way." She'd pulled off the lid and placed the candy in my hand as if it were a precious stone.

I didn't dare to eat it so I kept it as a lucky charm. The wrapper had become grimy with lint and dirt but I knew the candy would still be sweet.

"Come on, Danny." My mother's brow was furrowing. "What should you do with the money?"

"I'll stick it in a tin," I answered. "I'll spend just a little at a time. Like for treats. That way I'll keep it until . . ."

My mother smiled, nodded, her eyes halfway closed. Almost. Almost right. "Danny," she said, her words sweet and brightening. "You can do even better than that. You can save it the way your father and I save money."

"Like in the bank?"

Her mouth broadened into a full smile. She settled behind the cash register. It rang out and CASH flapped up beneath her neck.

"You deserve a lot of credit, Danny. For being sensible. You can go with your father after school and put this money in the bank. You'll get to meet Mr. Crowley, the manager. He'll be impressed. He'll give you a bank book with your name on it just like ours. And he'll write in it exactly what you're worth."

Her hand swung down. It collected coins and placed them in the special compartment of the till. The hand swung down one last time and my hand lifted to meet it. A fresh clean coin dropped into my opened palm. "That's for a treat," she said. "Now hurry up, you're late for school."

I gripped the coin but felt uneasy as if something had been left out or worse, betrayed. But I had my mother's approval. I should feel happy. She'd tell my father about my money. At night when I was in bed and they were in the kitchen doing their accounts, they would talk about me.

I walked outside as if a crowd had gathered to applaud. Something gleamed beside me in the barber's window. But I no longer cared if it was Gustaf or anyone at all. The forms behind the other window – torso and mannequins – all seemed to waver and dissolve. I saw only my own reflection.

After all, my mother had assured me that I had something more than piles of coins for spending. I had real money, like the numbers that flapped up from her cash register. I'd get those same numbers in my own bank book. I could already imagine them waving and calling to me, figures I could hold inside my head.

$9.48

THE LADY OF THE BEANPOLES

A LBERT BARRY WAS DIGGING A CLUMSY TRENCH OF A GARDEN IN HIS small back yard off Main Street, his garden fork thrusting through mouldy leaves, probing deeply into earth, almost to the bed of Red River clay. Separating. Turning. Mixing.

Yet he knew he wouldn't get the vine-splendid beans and stout carrots of his next-door neighbour, Mrs. Slawik. Her prosperous tomatoes weighed so heavily in the hand, they were like something he could swear by.

Last fall she had let him have the pick of all her seeds. He had started them growing in milk cartons on his window-sill, the same way she did, with the same water, soil and sun but they hadn't favoured him as they did her. He'd caught her disappointment as he'd brought the seedlings out to transplant by her fence. She'd sniffed the way she did at Danny Stein as he was ruining his sneakers in the spring runoff. "That back-lane boy," she'd said. "He's growing every which way but he's not growing up."

Composting wasn't helping Albert Barry, either. His mouldy V8 juice had better enzymes than her spoiled pickles.

His eggshells and grapefruit rinds mulched just as well as her Old Country borscht and cabbage rolls which were, according to his books, a violation of all rules on proper rot. Yet Mrs. Slawik's garden smacked dark lips for more while Albert Barry's turned a cold, clay shoulder.

"Mrs. Slawik!" He called to her, not awkward or shy as long as he could speak from behind his fence. "Say, Mrs. Slawik, I've been gardening next to you for two lean years. How about telling me your secrets?"

She was patting her seeds into short tight rows, never bothering with markers. "No more than I needed tags for my five kids," she always said. Broad hips and sturdy legs. Grey eyes and silver hair. A smile, thin and pale as the newest moon. "Secrets? When I'm young like you, Mr. Barry, then I got secrets. Now I'm too old. All I got is habits."

"Then how do your habits grow such big tomatoes?"

She waved him off with a laugh and a promise that she'd fill his grocery bags if his crop was poor again, and she shuffled off into her house. He knew that she was flattered, for her garden meant more to her than her well-scrubbed rooming house, her mothballed Easter bonnets and all her faded photographs. Mrs. Slawik's garden was as close as she could get to the peasant farm in Ukraine where she'd been born – a world of fifty generations framed here by sixty feet of fence.

Albert Barry came from a straight and narrow line of bankers and ministers who never saw a piece of land as anything but a site for mortgages or burials.

He carried on their dedication to clean hands by teaching school recorder and conducting Boys and Girls Mixed Choir at Luxton Elementary, a few blocks away. He continued that dedication even when his wife found what he described as "another tune to beat her drum to" and left him for a jazz musician heading east. Barry, conscientious to a fault, missed neither a beat of music nor a day of teaching. However, he did shorten after-school band practices and gave away his collection of Gilbert and Sullivan operettas. He also began attending a church basement coffee house, where college boys in tab collars were singing the newly fashioned folk songs. It was then that Albert Barry accepted, on faith alone, their testaments to the dignity of sweat and the sanctity of dirt. He bought himself a garden fork, a pair of denim overalls and a stack of books on backyard farming.

Yet he hardly raised anything beside his own expectations and the eyebrows of his neighbours. It wasn't as if he'd even eat the vegetables he tried to grow; he took most meals at The Popularity Grill, where canned peas and parsley were strictly for colour on the plate and the special of the day was always hamburger.

The more Barry dug, the deeper he reconsidered. His fingernails were filthy. His underarms were soaked. His father's aversion to mould and pollen was burning in his nostrils, swelling up his eyes. He could hear his father preaching in his head. "There's no percentage in a garden, Albert. Cut your losses, son. You should not try to turn a profit with a garden fork." It was one of his father's many 'should nots' that kept the muscles knotted in Albert Barry's neck.

He rubbed at his stiffness and felt a blister on his forefinger just where it would play the F on the recorder. Old Dad was right as always, Barry thought, but kept on digging. I was meant to hold a tuning fork, not a garden fork. If I had a penny's worth of practicality, I'd convert this misery of a garden into parking stalls for Ray Horobec. Ray worked out of his garage down the lane. He was always looking for more space to botch another customer's transmission or to patch some rusted Chevrolet so it would shine like virtue till it was sold.

Just as Barry began to plot the cost of asphalt in his mind, he was jarred by his garden fork scraping something hard below. It shivered up his spine and grated on the edge of his front teeth.

What's down there? he wondered, testing with the fork. A brick? A stone? Maybe one of those ruptured pipes the city workers love to hunt all summer with their backhoes.

He pried at it, muttering at himself, "You damn fool, you're harvesting a crop of rocks just to break your father's heart." He worked at it with the fork until he felt it loosen. He knelt, probing, and reached something smooth and firm though too slippery to grip. Wiping away the muck, he spotted the gleam of gold.

And he thought of Lydia's wedding ring as he had spun it again and again for hours at the kitchen table, watching it glitter like a hollow golden seed. The ring he'd found stuck in the soap dish after Lydia had left him.

He wondered, why am I digging this damn thing up? It's probably some pipe. I could break a line if I disturbed it. Still his fingers played on the shining metal in the earth until the muck caved over it, burying his hand, clotting his flannel shirt sleeve, to leave only the stump of an arm.

He removed his muddy shirt, folded it carefully, kneeled and scooped away the earth until he saw a streak of gold.

ALBERT BARRY HAD BEEN A BOY who once went wild for gold, who'd charged through the tangle and decay of vines in the gap between two garages. Flinching at rough leaves. Crashing over a huge Scotch thistle. Just so he could grab what three girls in party dresses shrieked that he should never touch, though they had lured him on, after games of Spin-the-bottle and Pin-the-tail, and had gotten him even dizzier with a Maypole romp around a laundry pole as they teased him, saying, "If you touch it, you'll be sorry." "Don't you even dare to look."

Don't dare to look inside a steamer trunk that they'd said was rich with bounty, goblets and golden crowns seeded with pearls and diamonds. Because a horrible fate would get him if he tried to open it. A witch had guarded the treasure with bloodsucking things that would pull him in with a thousand suction cups and ripping teeth, first tearing off his clothes, and then –

"Lies! Lies! You girls are all such liars!" he'd yelled, trying to shout them down.

"And then your skin's ripped off and –"

"Nuts!" he'd shouted. "You're just nuts and crazy!"

"And then the witch will make a zombie to look like you, so your parents won't ever know you're locked inside the trunk and screaming through her poison slime."

"There's no such thing," he'd sneered, "because nobody can live without a skin."

"Albert Barry, puff and blow," they'd chanted at him. "Albert Barry, you don't know!"

"You're just stupid girls trying to scare me from your hiding place!"

"Smarty pants! Full of ants! You just go and see." They'd flounced their skirts as he rushed for the trunk.

His heart had drummed a wild charge as he swept past a burst of nettles and thistles slashing at his face, while his ears were ringing with the wail of girls – "She'll get you! She'll get you!"

Until he swept away the rot of leaves, broke the trunk lid off its hinges and tore through ragged clothes cloudy with dust, only to scrape the slivery boards beneath.

"Dirty! Dirty!" they sang as he gaped at them empty-handed. "Dirty! Dirty!" spreading their tongues, tossing their hips for insult.

Dirty Bert in a dirty shirt
All he wants to do is flirt
Poke and stare, he don't care
Makes a mess in his underwear!

ALBERT BARRY WINCED. "Now look at me," he muttered. After twenty years of trying to grow up, I'm on my knees, playing in the mud.

Searching the earth with blind hands, he finally grasped the smooth, firm thing. He laboured with it and the ground began to swell. He tightened his grip, drawing it out as earth heaved and split, releasing a foot-long human form: head, waist, legs, all

41

clotted with muck. Not yet free. It was attached to something on a pole. He brought it all out steadily until it stuck again. Two more gentle tugs and the last part, the base, came out like a plug.

When he hosed it off he found it wasn't gold at all, just some brassy electroplated thing and rusty at that, though it seemed fairly well preserved.

Fool's gold, he told himself. I suppose that proves it was meant for me.

It had no wiring for a bulb so he reasoned that it couldn't be a lamp. Still, it seemed to be domestic; some sort of 1930s misbegotten Greek and Roman styled household thingamajig.

The statue on top intrigued him: a young woman with flowing hair holding a rainbow above her head. She was nearly naked except for folds of robe draping from her hips. Her face might once have gleamed, but now was blank and pitted. He rubbed her flat belly and nipple-sized breasts, scraped the grit from a long lean leg. She stood upon a sphere that he imagined must represent the world, a very worn and tarnished world conveniently fastened to a stand.

An ashtray stand, he thought. That's what it is and the statue is its decorative handle. Amazing. Absurd. And somehow awfully wrong.

The tin ashtray crumbled from the pole. He broke off the base where the decay had eaten through and the statue was left standing on a simple iron pole. Holding it at arm's length, he wondered how it came to be buried in his back yard. There were too many previous owners of his house to guess who might have put it there. It hadn't been merely dumped, he was certain of that. The garbage cans were only steps away and it would have been snatched up in those back lanes where the garbage crews could never stay ahead of Winnipeg's North End foragers and gatherers.

Perhaps whoever owned it didn't want to let it go, he thought. Too out of fashion to keep but with too much residue of value to toss away, it may have been stored near the back porch and forgotten as the dirt piled up – a prize for future archaeologists. Or was there a deeper intention to its being buried here? Was it meant to protect the place from evil spirits? Those Old Country immigrants, they've got superstitions that haunt their every move.

Mrs. Slawik returned with a pruning knife. Barry watched her ease into her willow bush and cut curved branches of pussy willow. The blade flashed as she paused, noticing the statue in his hand.

"What you got there, Mr. Barry? Something your students made for you?"

He broke into a grin and held it high. "I teach music, Mrs. Slawik, not metal work. This is a lawn ornament that I bought downtown, in Eaton's basement. I was looking for a plaster elf like Mrs. McKay has on her lawn but they were all sold out. So I picked this up instead. How do you like her?"

She snorted, not taken in for a moment. "It's time you find a girlfriend, Mr. Barry. That one won't keep you warm."

"I've got no luck with real girls, Mrs. Slawik. Besides, I think she's kind of pretty."

"Too skinny, not enough meat."

"Not even for a poor vegetable gardener?"

Mrs. Slawik studied the maiden with a sideways stare. For a moment, she was thoughtful among her branches, her fingers rubbing at the glowing bark, the moist wind whispering through her hair. "Mister Barry," she said, "you stick her by the gate where you plant your beans. Don't wait until tomorrow. You put her there tonight. Then later, some beanplants, they'll climb up. She might be a good thing for your garden."

He nodded respectfully and they both turned away.

THERE WAS SOMETHING ABOUT that first warm night in May with the air so moist and yeasty. It would not let Albert Barry fall asleep. He'd wanted to sleep so he could dream but he couldn't keep his eyes shut. He'd felt whispers up his back and such a hunger in his arms that he spoke his thought aloud. "I've been alone too long." And the four years he had shared with Lydia suddenly felt like the loneliest time of all.

There was something else he was missing, something in the garden. So Albert Barry came out of doors again. He heard night noises all around: a siren wailing down Inkster Boulevard, that wild red-haired Riley boy playing tin can soccer down the lane, the hollow roar of Main Street's traffic and some TV somewhere chattering out the late-night news.

Yet his garden seemed separate from all that and he listened for its slow cooking of a thousand seeds underneath the ground. Still, that wasn't why he'd brought his dusty bottle of red Italian wine.

It's for the lady, he told himself and mused on how he'd been so out of touch and out of tune and had never really known it until now.

The statue stood in front of its grove of broomsticks and galvanized pipes, all of them stuck in the ground and tied with string to hold a future crop of beans. Her arms were held high as if to draw down rain and call up seeds and greet anyone who called to her, even those who didn't know her name. The statue was not nearly high enough to be a beanpole but Albert Barry was keeping that a secret between Mrs. Slawik and himself.

"Our gardening secret," he murmured.

He took a full deep drink and gave one to the statue, the red stream splashing on its feet and rusty globe, running down the pole into the upturned earth. The garden got the next one in a circle poured around them both. Then, assuring himself that he wasn't yet a total fool, he finished off the rest.

When he felt the magic growing in his guts, he looked to Mrs. Slawik's window. He had an impulse to invite her to a polka around the pole, yearning to see her years fall off with every circle round until she turned into a maiden once again. But he knew that the old woman was probably snoring in her bed with enough dreams of her own.

Looking past her window, he imagined a row of windows, Lydia's first and then those of the few other women whom he had known before her, every window blank, reflecting a barren sky.

"Don't look," Barry told himself, half remembering some

fear, childish or primitive, of losing one's self to an empty mirror. Yet he fell into mulling over everything he had meant to feel and meant to say to Lydia but never had, until Lydia finally could not wait any longer and shut the door behind her as she left. He thought of the years that followed and the stubborn silence in him that all his choirs and orchestras could never break.

He kicked dirt into the muddy hole where he'd pulled the statue out, wishing he could find a way, a clue, another chance. "Or at the very least, a decent crop of beans," he said aloud with a regretful laugh that turned into an odd little hum. It led into an ancient tune whose name he didn't know. First he was singing it and after a time it seemed the tune was singing him, then swaying and drawing him into a shuffling two-step. Its rhythm took him around the pole in a dance as out of fashion and peculiar as any Art Deco pseudo-Roman-Greco female ashtray ornament. It set him spinning, slipped him out of his slippers and lifted up his head. It waved his arms and pumped his blood faster and fuller with his chest heaving, bellowing the night air in and out as if to inflate him larger than his life had ever been. It even managed to squeeze out a couple of hurrahs before his knees finally bowed him out and Albert Barry collapsed in front of the statue. Where he sat to find his breath and gradually to find himself graced by a full white moon that floated free of laundry lines, telephone wires, TV antennae to hang above the statue's upraised arms.

It was then he felt the moonlight soak the earth and heard seeds breaking open under him as if they were sprouting in a maze. As if they were moving under the fence and across the lane with roots stretching east to the Red River and north past Stein's Style Shoppe, City Butchers, past the movie house and on till Main Street turned to highway freed of curbs and shops. Roots running west past Salter, MacGregor, McPhillips, King Edward avenues to tie friendship knots with prairie grasses. Roots that would rumble south to break the walls of City Hall, to crack the Royal, the Imperial Bank of Commerce, and then the bars of City Zoo and on to the swimming pools and patios of Tuxedo.

His ears were ready to hear the crack and split. His moist eyes were ready to see the sun wind up the world for one more turn. Albert Barry was ready for the most golden light to flow through the maiden's arms, opening every crusted heart, beginning with his own.

For Old Man Werner's fence posts to come alive again, sprouting young green leaves; for Mrs. Grenier's sickly pigeons to rise bright as flames and weave laurels above the street lamps; and for pale Mrs. Nojuk's withered apple tree to bear children, who would dangle from every branch, their mouths singing out golden clouds of pollen.

But most of all, Albert Barry was ready for the young bean plants to climb up to the maiden whose pole had taken root so firmly in the earth.

HIDDEN WISHES

I FEEL THE HURT AGAIN CORRODING IN MY CHEST JUST FROM
remembering Rita. It doesn't matter that it's been so many years
or that I was a boy of ten and she was a woman of thirty-two. I
loved Rita and she betrayed me.

I suppose the hurt is the one thing that I could keep of her.

And now – a photograph. My mother's dealt it out from a
pack of cast-off photos that had never found a place inside the
family albums. It shows Rita in a woven hammock, all in a
blur. She must have moved as the camera tried to catch her. It
wasn't ever easy to catch Rita. I hold it up to the light. Yes, it's
her – that luminosity waving in a bathing suit. My father and
mother, young and pale, are grinning behind her. They're
about to push her off the hammock or to swing her up or
maybe they're trying to trap her in its netting.

"Those were the good times when we were all so young,"
my mother says with an edge of jealousy. "Younger than you
are now."

And I am older than Rita was then, I tell myself, though I
can't quite believe it.

My mother slides the picture behind the others. "Rita's dead, you know. Yes, she died a couple years after moving down to New Orleans. Oh, you were writing your grade eight exams – I didn't want to upset you with bad news. She starved to death, poor dear. Some sort of trouble with her stomach."

I nod noncommittally and watch her deal out other ghosts, arrange them on her table, read out their varied fates – all in honour of my visit. Of course, I won't believe her. How can Rita be dead and I still feel this way? Even if she had died, it wouldn't have been from a failing stomach. Her death would have come from her heart: a broken heart or a lost one. A starving heart, I suppose, though it never starved for me.

Rita McKay was my mother's friend, who waitressed at The Popularity Grill, down the street from our clothing store. Rita was also my special pal, tall and slim with hair that seemed to change with her every mood from black to fiery red to shimmering blonde, but always with a plume of smoky grey rising from her cigarette. Rita would give me a big hello when I'd arrive each day at the cafe to have my lunch. She sometimes served me with a treat: potato chips beside my corned beef on rye; Pez candies arranged in my initials, D.S. for Daniel Stein; sometimes a note hidden in the sandwich like in a fortune cookie. I'd decode the words printed backwards. One said, "!neppah reven yam tI !muhc pu reehC." Another read, "!pu sdnats eh nehw kooL .stnap sih no dratsum dellips yelworC sgabyenoM dlO." Once she stuck a plastic swizzle stick in my glass of Orange Crush. It was shaped like a woman with the words CLUB COPACABANA ablaze across the dress. As I stirred the ice-cubes I watched the figure twirl inside my glass. Rita swished her skirt and trilled, "Caramba!"

She'd signal me whenever huge Mrs. Sweeney waddled to the till to pay her check. She claimed the woman kept fifty-dollar bills in her brassière. "Just watch her, Danny," Rita whispered. "One of these days she'll run out of change!"

I ONCE STOLE FOR RITA: a foot-high brass statue of a woman with naked breasts. It was in the back garden of Mr. Barry, my grade five music teacher. I sneaked outside before anyone was on the street, climbed the fence, and broke the statue off its metal pole. I dodged through a maze of yards and lanes and doubled back to my hideout, a derelict van rusting in the lot behind our store. That's where I hid it, thrusting it deep into the burst padding of the driver's seat.

I wanted it for Rita. I didn't know why. I never found the nerve to tell her, much less offer her the thing. Instead, I'd curl up with it in the dark cave of the van, with the sunlight piercing through in dusty shafts, and I'd rub it like Aladdin rubbed his lamp, making wishes. I wished Rita and I were trapped together by an earthquake. I wished us lost in some prehistoric jungle, our clothing half torn off, swimming rivers and climbing trees for food. I wished a scientific experiment went wrong, turning her into a mermaid who needed me to keep her safe and hidden. My fantasies grew so wild, so confusing that they gripped me in a fever. Finally I was afraid to touch, to even see the statue.

So I went to Old Man Werner, who was from the Old Country where they knew about strange things. I straddled the stool as he was sawing beside his bench and I puttered with the nuts and bolts, trying to sound casual when I asked my question. "Mr. Werner, can anyone get in trouble making wishes?"

"Anyone?" he asked.

"Yeah."

"Anyone such as me or you?"

"Yeah, anyone."

He grunted. "Anyone, even you, can wish for what you wish. What's wrong with that? Even trees and grass can wish. They wish for the sun and rain to make them grow."

"But if you make wishes on something. It's more than just regular wishing. Like if you ask the thing for stuff."

He put down his saw and brushed his canvas apron clean of sawdust. "You mean like praying to a thing?"

"I don't know, people pray to lots of things. I've seen it."

He frowned. "You've seen superstition. A thing is just a thing. What can a thing do?"

"Then you can't get hurt just from making wishes on it?"

Mr. Werner hung his apron on a hook. He shoved his tools onto shelves until there was nothing more to shove. He fumbled drill bits into their slots while grumbling about "making the whole mess straight." I knew enough to wait in silence. It wasn't until he finished twisting shut his jars of nails and screws that he would even look at me.

"In the old times," he said, lifting a block of wood, "they made idols, things that looked like what you call . . . a . . . a superhero or an animal – a pig, a cow, a snake – and they'd pray to these things." He tossed the block onto the scrap pile. "Foolishness! A prayer has power. You don't pray to a thing. It makes the prayer go bad and who knows what could happen then? My father, may he rest in peace, he called that kind of praying a sin."

I had my own ideas of sin. I thought of how I'd pulled the wings off flies, or made prank calls by dialing random numbers, then holding the receiver at arm's length, listening to the voices plead, "Who's there? Who are you? What do you want?" I thought of my last wish – let the world be destroyed, everyone be blasted away by fire and wind, with only me and Rita left to Adam and Eve the earth together.

I felt ashamed.

I DIDN'T DARE TO RETURN the statue and it seemed like sacrilege to dump it in the trash. So I buried it beside one of Mr. Werner's fence posts.

Still, it drew me back. I would glance at the mound whenever I passed as if the statue were growing ready to spring up and call me, "Thief! Kidnapper!" Even worse, perhaps by telling it my hidden wishes I had given it some kind of power over me.

I could not ask Mr. Werner for any help. He might say there was something wrong with my wanting Rita. He didn't know her. Or know that I loved her. Or that I'd always love her.

I understand now that Rita was a starry beauty who laughed and joked before my eyes but mooned in private over what my mother called "bad luck in love."

All I knew back then was that Rita loved a party. The nightclubs she'd first known had all closed in their time and were replaced by others and then by others again. I heard her say she calculated her age by the number of clubs and dancehalls she'd seen come and go. "Better than counting your mistakes," she'd laugh with a rasp, "or the wrinkles around your eyes!" Her throat was seared by an endless chain of cigarettes, an American brand called Lucky Strike. She must have laughed that way even as each of her friends slipped away into engagements and marriages. And she'd have kept on laughing through house warmings and christenings, her laughter becoming harsher and harder as she became the "single woman" at the parties, singled out by other women with a shifting glance or an arm held closer to a partner. As time went on, there were fewer and still fewer parties. Maybe this was why she learned to drink alone.

Rita's laugh was quite carefree and mischievous one September night coming through the phone; she was calling us to rush right over so she could "uncover" her "mystery object." She claimed she had it delivered three months early "to avoid the rush." We were intrigued as always. Only Rita could wake my parents from their tired talk of business and keep them up past bedtime.

We hurried to the gabled house of her aunt and uncle. They'd taken Rita in as a girl and even with all her wild ways, they would never let her go. We congregated at the dining-room table with drinks for all as she unveiled her "1961 space-age model of the True Tree Everlasting." She removed, one by one, the seven scarves that served as seven veils to reveal a three-foot shock of white aluminum. It was an artificial Christmas tree. She said, "This little guy won't fade or pine away. Not like all those nothing-is-forever evergreens that Uncle Alec keeps on dragging in." She had us raise our glasses as she intoned, "I christen thee my Tinsel Tom. I'll stand on guard for thee as long as you stay up firm for me. Okay, everybody, bottoms up!"

That glittering mock-up of a tree ruffled both her aunt and uncle. "I don't mind it as a joke," said Beatrice. "But we'll have a real Scotch pine in the corner like every other Christmas, all strung with popcorn and my gingerbread angels."

Alec scoffed. "That girl and her crazy gimmicks! Some day, they're going to haul her off!"

All this was posturing; the three of them were always upstaging in front of visitors. As long as we could serve as audience they hardly faced or spoke directly to one another, yet, always kept each other in their sights.

Rita put on "Volare," then "The Girl from Ipaneema." She taught my father how to rumba and had my mother spinning in a souvenir sombrero that she'd brought back from Mexico. I clapped and stomped and stared as if they were suddenly appearing on a movie screen.

Rita was the star, like those women of the evening movies whom she'd always rave about: Ava Gardner, Elizabeth Taylor, Gina Lollobrigida. I'd seen them all in secret. I'd hidden in a toilet stall at The Spectacle theatre after the children's matinee until the adults had crowded in the lobby. I'd slipped into a seat by the back wall where the usher wouldn't see me and I watched those women on the screen quite unobserved, women who had the power to make men miserable or joyful with a single word, a single gesture. My Rita was one of them, singing and snapping her fingers, splashing Captain Morgan Rum into a highboy glass with bangles ringing to her every move. She knew how to drive men crazy. Drive them to drink. Drive them over cliffs.

But never me. "You're my favourite. You're my Darlin' Danny," she told me in front of everyone as she dropped ice-cubes in my mug of Hires Root Beer. I knew then that Rita was my star light, star bright lady, even as her record player crooned, "Lady of Spain I adore you / Right from the night I first saw you / My heart has been yearning for you," while she danced in the centre of the room all by herself.

I begged her, "Rita, don't get old. You won't get old, will you?"

She blessed my words with laughter. "Me get old? Why would I want to get old?"

I decided I had no more need for wishes; I could speak straight from my heart and I proposed that very moment. "Rita, will you wait for me? I'll grow up and we'll get married." The whole room howled, but I didn't care.

"What a great idea!" she called out. "Who wouldn't want to wait for a dreamboat like you?"

I shone with pleasure. Rita and I had made the wish together. Together, boy and woman, we'd make our wish come true. I only had to break free of my childhood and she'd be waiting.

Alec turned off the record player and shut the lid. He declared, "Enough of those phoney gigolo songs. It's time we had a good old sing-along!" He played a flourish on his accordion that led into "When the Saints Come Marching In." Beatrice joined him with her hands tightly clasped together, her voice ringing firm and loud. I asked Rita to show me how to dance, but she wouldn't even raise her eyes and pretended to crush something into Beatrice's Oriental rug. She was instantly and dramatically bored, knowing, as we all did, that she wouldn't get to play another of her songs.

She packed away her records, complaining to my mother, "Now he's got Beatrice all heated up! Soon she'll be blasting out her spirituals like an old church organ, practising for eternity. Glory hallelujah, you'd think God was deaf!" We had to cajole her to stay in the parlour and then to sit at the piano, all the while sympathizing as she protested, delayed, insisted on conditions. But she could never resist a crowd and soon she was banging out "Roll Out the Barrel," first in parody, then in earnest, trying to outsing and outmug Alec and Beatrice both.

My parents and I danced what Alec called our "sofa polkas," sitting side by side, holding hands and stomping feet while he swung about the room with his accordion threatening Beatrice's shelves of bric-a-brac and all her commemorative Royal Family plates that hung above the wainscotting. Alec played "Casey Jones" with extra choruses he'd learned as a conductor on the trains. Beatrice's voice gained power while his puffed like a steaming locomotive.

Eventually both Alec and his accordion collapsed into the corner where he fired and stoked his pipe. "Wheezing and squeezing," he hacked, "that's what I do best," and he made a grab for Beatrice's hips as she wheeled in the tea caddy.

"Get that smelly old man away from me!" She rapped his hand with a serving spoon. "He could at least mind his ashes!" she said, arching her brow for our benefit. "We'd all better escape to the verandah. Between that old man's pipe and Rita's cigarettes, they've smoked us out."

We didn't need any excuse to sit on their screened front porch. We always took our places there for Beatrice's tea and pie and Alec's dark tales of world disasters. We settled into the evening, guessing at each shadow on the boulevard.

On the hour, the cuckoo clock called from the hallway, and Alec, as always, raised a forefinger as if to signal a train about to leave. After forty years on the C.P.R., he had a conductor's reverence for time. Yet, with a few beer and some nods to the darkening elms, he'd talk about time running out, predicting the collapse of civilization, warning that the signs were everywhere for anyone with half a mind to read them.

"We're going from bad to worse. Everyone in cars and no one walking. Damned automobiles have ruined the neighbourhoods, turned everybody into strangers. No wonder crime's so bad and all this immorality – no one has to care what anybody thinks. And nobody cares to think. We may as well tear down the verandah like all the rest and either drive to Hell or lock ourselves inside with a damned TV." He struck his pipe against his heel, letting the sparks fly where they may.

I was shocked. I often felt appalled at how adults could so totally condemn the future which was mine, not theirs. I wanted someone to silence Alec before his curses got any worse, but my parents were nodding passively and Rita wasn't listening at all. She was on the edge of a hard-backed chair contending with her aunt, "No, I don't want a nice cup of tea. I want to finish my drink. Oh, yes I do!"

Alec grumbled on, "Here's Diefenbaker pulling this country into depression and there's Kennedy looking for civil war with all his civil rights. And what about that Bay of Pigs business down in Cuba? Rita raves about her 'sexy Mexico' but she won't say how they chased her out of Havana – and that was only two years ago, last New Year's Day. You ask her. That place had more damned revolutionaries than it had fleas, and all of them crazy on tequila!"

A heavy silence dropped between Alec and Rita, and the other conversations stalled as if caught between two breaths. Alec rose to poke at the Black Forest cuckoo clock in the hallway. "There you go," he announced. "It's twenty minutes after." We all knew Alec's theory about specific moments of the hour. He believed that the human intellect ran in one-hour cycles with three twenty-minute phases. The top of the hour coincided with the top of our intellectual concentration while twenty minutes before and twenty minutes after the hour were the two mental low points, equally distant from the top. Alec claimed that this was caused by the pull of the moon and the rhythms of breathing which affected the pressure on our brains. So, at twenty minutes before and twenty minutes after every hour, the mind wearied, conversation lapsed, and all thoughts slipped into a dull reverie.

Rita sulked, clinking ice in her frosted glass. "Just look at Uncle Alec fiddling with his clock. God, I'd like to rip that thing right off the wall." We shifted in our seats. Beatrice tapped her foot with a slow firm beat. There was an unstated boundary to their constant teasing and Rita had just stepped across it. She must have known it, too, because she immediately switched back into her pose of gay impudence. "Besides, time only counts if it's a good time. Isn't that right, Murray?"

My father smiled, but the mood had changed. We'd witnessed these dark currents in her before and in Alec. We'd trained ourselves to overlook certain emotional highs and lows, considering them theatrical or eccentric or simply something accidental spilling from the bottle. So, after some ritual discomfort, our thoughts drifted off, lulled by the evening breeze as Rita gazed heavy-eyed through the verandah screen.

A car's horn blared out of the night. Rita sprang up, fluttered on her coat and chirped "Adios amigos!" as if she were going to have herself a time more wonderful than Alec or Beatrice could ever imagine.

Alec checked his clock. "It's far too late," he hissed to Beatrice as she bent to serve dessert. "It's no time to be calling on a respectable girl."

The screen was so veiled with ivy that I could barely see Rita crossing the yard. She seemed to be breaking through a labyrinth of vines towards a darkness streaked in chrome. She half turned as if to wave, but I lowered my eyes. I didn't want to see her reach that car. Rita had broken her promise to me.

I felt a swelling in my throat, a corroding in my chest. I spooned a dollop of neapolitan ice-cream onto Beatrice's hot pie crust, watching it melt into the bitterness of rhubarb. I stirred and wished. I wished that I could stop her, that I could shoot a ray gun that would shrink her with a green pulsating beam until she was transformed into a small figurine lost in the jungle of the grass. I would find her and lift her in my hand. I would take her to the cuckoo clock and shut her up inside there for myself.

The car horn blared again. Rita sang out something to the shifting clutch, the grinding gears. A door clicked open and slammed shut. Then a muffled roar. It's no use, I thought. I've lost her now. She's forgotten me and let some stranger have her – someone I imagined to be dark and fierce behind the wheel, who steered with one hand as she lay upon his lap.

Sparrows were fluttering in the ivy. Alec fetched a broom from the hallway closet. "Damn all your squawking and making whoopee! Shut up!" He struck the screen. Wings burst into the night. He struck twice more. My mother touched my father's arm; we wouldn't be staying for second helpings.

Alec tossed the broom into the corner and sank heavily into his wicker chair; I dragged myself out of mine, too tired to even sigh or to nod to Alec my silent alliance. He scraped the ashes in his pipe. "Between those birds and the bloody cats in the alley," he said, turning to me, "we can forget about a decent night's sleep altogether."

THE PROJECTIONIST'S WIFE

GRETE KLATT LEANED AGAINST THE INNER WALL OF HER TICKET booth as her son's postcard slipped from her fingers. She tried to focus on a detail of Art Deco moulding running past her cheek but it remained a blur. She fumbled open the latch of the metal door.

Stupid. I was so stupid, Karl. I closed the door too soon.

The conical booth was cramped and airless but her husband, Anshelm, always insisted that the door be fully closed before anyone came to buy tickets for the show. Anshelm was fiercely proud of their old movie house, The Spectacle, and especially of this ornate ticket booth. He called it "the grand prow of my theater, like the ancient Rhineships." Then, smiling thinly, he'd call Grete "the silent wooden figurehead."

The postcards had been Grete's only relief inside the booth – their scenes of castle towers, canals, French boulevards and Alpine villages taped on the encircling wall were peepholes into a grand world that their son, Karl, had been exploring for so many months and describing to her with such passion.

Until January, over a month ago, when all mail from Karl stopped. Then these views became unbearable, each of them a vacuum drawing Grete into the vast emptiness that had taken him.

You're out there somewhere, Karl. But what if you've gone too far? What if you're lost and never coming back?

Grete had been tearing Karl's cards off the wall, not knowing what to do with them, where to put them, only needing to get them away. They'd resisted. The rolled bits of tape stuck to her fingers and to her dress. She stacked postcards on the counter but they formed a crazy house of cards that would not pack together nor fall apart. As she pulled Michaelangelo's *Pietà* from the wall, it stripped off a patch of grey enamel paint. Grete's vision began to alter and the card slipped from her fingers.

She leaned forward, pressing her wrists on the cool steel counter, her forehead against the wicket window, gazing through the tinted glass at the lobby's entrance doors. The six glass doors divided Main Street into a triptych, or rather, three framed pairs of nearly identical panels each showing a connected segment of the street: a strip of sidewalk, four lanes of traffic, a dividing boulevard, more lanes, more sidewalk, a strip of stores and a spread of signs above them. The sky was cut off entirely.

This was her daily view for fourteen years, ever since they'd emigrated from Germany; add a bit of white in winter, a bit of green in summer. She'd never considered it anything other than her ordinary lot until this moment.

It turned so strange, Karl. The glass doors looked like a set of frames and the things moving outside – the cars and people on the street seemed to pass from frame to frame in such a jittery way like an old silent movie – even people I've seen for years – Mr. Borkow from the chapel and Mrs. Slawik with two of her big grownup sons –

all of them were walking and gesturing like everything was coming loose. And all I could do was watch.

Grete dumped all but the last cards, as they were, into a paper bag. She decided she would take the bag home and place it under Karl's desk. Her hands were trembling as she set the roll of admission tickets on the spool. It was 4:20 on Friday. The letter carrier would soon come but if there was still nothing from Karl she would have to wait till Monday. Grete, so accustomed to living within her private sphere of thoughts and feelings, felt battered by her fear for him. All her defenses were wearing down.

Why don't you write? What's stopping you?

Her chant to Karl was silent, as if by speaking to him in her mind, she could hold on to him.

What if I went insane? Ran into traffic, yelling out your name? Drivers would honk their horns, people on the street would pull me back as if I were drowning. They'd carry me to your papa who would frown and turn away because I'd shamed him. I would never dare go out again, imagining the neighbours following, whispering circles all around me.
How could they understand the way I need you? The way I cannot be without you anymore? Not because we were so close. But because we weren't.

Karl's postcards had been a kind of advent promising Grete the closeness that they'd never had. His descriptions were impassioned, enthused: English architecture, French politics, a painting in a gallery, an odd Dutch custom, and such detailed insights about those he met on the road, in the hostels and cafes, as if each carried a message just for him, some pausing in the midst of their adventures, others stirring from the trance of uneventful lives, revealing themselves to Karl alone.
And Karl in turn revealed himself to Grete.

Why me, Karl? And why now? After all the years we had together, all the hours in the house, or working in the theatre. You hardly spoke more than a few words at a time, and not one word that felt like these. Did you learn these thoughts from books? Or from some friend? Do you talk to others in this way? Or is it only when you write?

Grete never wrote any of this to her son. Her actual letters were a well-worn patter of motherly advice and the petty who and what of family gossip. These other thoughts, called up by Karl's cards and letters, remained echoing in her mind where before there had only been a cool stillness. Once, she tried to write them out but the words alarmed her on the page as if they'd come from someone desperate, almost crazy for attention. Not from Grete Klatt, the projectionist's wife. So she kept them to herself. But the words were growing forceful and lately there had been moments when she could hardly hear people's chattering, the clatter of her work or the traffic's growl beyond the doors, all those wilful, emphatic sounds outside herself that had always kept her knowing who and where she was.

We should have been close, Karl. We were both such quiet people. I wanted to believe our quietness was something that we shared — like some membrane left over from your birth — one they couldn't take away. Did you ever think that, too? Maybe I thought this as an excuse for never talking. Now I think that I was frightened to speak, afraid the wrong words would make things worse.

With your younger sister and brother, it is all Me! Me! Me! So I cook and clean and sew. I set things before them and set myself back. That's what they seem to want. Maybe that's what I want, too. They'll grow up, marry others like themselves and come back only to ask for more of what they've always had.

But you were my first child, born in those awful ruins during the war. The broken stones must have released something into you - something sad and wise. I saw it in your eyes — like a troubled sky. Always watching, especially me. Were you waiting to tell me something? Did I make myself too busy for you to speak?

*When you got older you'd stay inside your room, growing tall
and thin in the dark, watching your aquarium like it was a
television. Dr. Barsky said the stage would pass. Everything passed.
But you left and still we never really spoke.*

*Then you sent your postcards, so full of words in such a little
space like you were telling me everything you could – only there was
no room to say any more, but you expected me to understand, to
know just what to answer.*

Karl's postcards were also addressed to his father, though
Anshelm seldom read them. He'd been against Karl travelling
in Europe.

"You'll go to university," he'd told Karl. "That way you'll be
a somebody, not a nobody tramping down the road." Anshelm
had butted his freshly lit cigarette and turned back to his table
of beer and politics at the German Club.

Karl never argued with his father, but for the first time he
did not obey. He bought a knapsack and slipped away,
mumbling an awkward goodbye to Grete.

At first, Anshelm refused to notice. Later, he refused to
believe. When the first card came, he studied the postmark as if
it were a trick. He skimmed the lines until he could point out a
single phrase. "There!" he said. " 'Got soaked by the steady
rain.' Now Karl has learned about England! Nothing but muck
and dirty fog! He'll be back soon enough!"

He wasn't. Karl went on to Holland, Belgium, France. His
last postcards were from Germany.

Dec 16, 1961

Dear Mama and Papa,

Frankfurt street crews work good and hard! Jawohl! Dirt
must never show. They'd scrub our movie house like new
again and even clear the gum from under the seats. Papa
couldn't train me that well. Maybe that's why Frankfurt has
the cleanest movie houses and dirtiest movies!

The hostel keepers wake us at 7 a.m. with a
loudspeaker. 'Achtung! Achtung!' They think we need cold

showers and mountain hikes in lederhosen. I heard
Wagner's Gotterdammerung. What a manic-depressive!
Write me, Poste Restante, Hamburg. I'll be there Xmas.
– Love, Karl

Dec 18, 1961

Dear Mama / Papa,

Berlin dissected, schizophrenic. Old seniles/young
crazies. Marble statues/barbed wire. Grand houses full of
squatters. Met a young German Jew (Last of the Mohicans)
near 'The Wall' – a street musician singing in Hebrew. Some
give him money, others make threats – showing their guilt
either way – he calls his songs prayers for the dead. 'Who's
dead?' I asked. He answered, 'Me. You. All of us.' and threw
some coins at a Mercedes Benz. Museums fantastic – modern
German art – tortured passion/cold forms. Tell Papa – great
beer & wienerschnitzel. Next week, Hamburg – your home
town! – Love, Karl

Dec 22, 1961

Guten Morgen!

Just got into Hamburg by night train. No sleep just
rumbling dreams. Couldn't find the youth hostel – got a
gasthaus near the station. Nothing to see so far – it's all
rebuilt – grey sky, grey buildings, even the food is grey. Met
an old fellow, Helmut Kraus, in a cafe on what used to be
your street. Says he knew Papa in the war. Does Papa
remember him? Helmut's giving me a tour tomorrow. After
all I'm the son of a son of the Fatherland. Why not the
Mamaland? Or the Brother and Sisterland? I'll send a letter
soon. – Love, Karl

It was Karl's last message.

Grete turned over the card, rubbing the soft surface. It was a hand-tinted photograph of a mediaeval church.

An old postcard, Karl. Older than you. They shouldn't still sell such cards. You might think the building is still standing. That is like selling you a lie.

I was so afraid of that church. Every day I had to go there for Mass. I was already seventeen years old but I stepped so carefully into the square, imagining that even the cobblestones were holy and could bleed or groan. I'd bow my head as I approached the entrance with its row of stone saints frowning down from the roof. I felt them telling me, 'We are judging you for God. You must clean yourself of sin. You must love God. You must love us. You must want us to be angry and to punish you when you are bad.'

When the first bombs fell, the nuns told everyone, 'Stay inside the church. Bow your heads and pray.' But I ran out, choking in the smoke with the ground exploding everywhere. I looked back and saw the stone saints shaking and I thought, they're angry at me. They're shaking the walls and falling down, smashing down to punish me because I disobeyed.

The nuns died for their faith and the others who stayed there died, as well. They all became angels without me. I ran and hid in the bomb shelter, covering my face. I'd brought God's anger pounding down on everyone because I did not truly love him. I had sinned and I would never be redeemed.

The letter carrier startled Grete at her glass wicket. He grinned through the opening. "Hey, Mrs. Klatt, where's Anshelm? You didn't finally dump him, did you?"

She broke into her nervous smile. "Oh, no . . . I mean, we are now opening for an early feature. So I come out sooner to sell tickets and Anshelm is not here. He goes upstairs to prepare the film projector."

"Well, here's another letter from the Old Country."

"Oh, I was so worried! Thank you!"

He looked puzzled as he slipped it through. "I guess it's a

mother's job to worry. I just brought the last letter Tuesday."

"On Tuesday?"

"Jeez, if I could get my girl, Charlotte, even to phone me once a month! And she's just out in Portage la Prairie. You got a good son there, Mrs. Klatt."

"A letter came on Tuesday?"

"Your husband's been giving me the stamps. Those German commemoratives were real top quality. These ones from Morocco look pretty good, too."

"Of course, yes." Grete carefully cut the stamps from the envelope. "The letter and the cards that came last week – they had good stamps as well?" she asked.

"Oh yeah, Karl always sends them with different stamps. He's a very thoughtful kid."

If I ask your papa for your letters he might only lie. If I make demands, he could destroy them out of spite. He must always be right, must always be a giant in everybody's eyes. Even his family's. I touched your handwriting on the envelope and imagined him holding all your cards and letters, looking huge and powerful like some close up picture that fills the screen. Then the picture twisted like when the film gets caught in the projector and melts in the heat of the lamp. He was turning black with that hard white light breaking through.

She pressed the envelope onto the metal counter, ironing out the creases with her hands; it was not the time to open it. An old couple was helping each other through the doors. The lobby was soon alive with faces: a bus driver on a split shift; Mr. Barry, the school teacher, with Elizabeth, from The Fantasy Salon, both of them smiling awkwardly; the man who brought food in his coat pockets and complained about the prices; three teenaged boys sharing some coarse joke; a half-dozen others. She nodded to each one, selling each a ticket.

Grete heard Anshelm opening the door to the inner lobby. She slipped the letter into the deep pocket of her smock. Anshelm took his place by the door, tearing tickets, joking with the bus driver, smiling to the rest. The teenagers got a sharp schoolmaster's nod. The Stein boy loitered in the lobby studying the Coming Attractions. He smudged the glass unwittingly and Anshelm shooed him out.

"Did you see that 'audience'?" Anshelm muttered, entering the booth to search for his Players cigarettes. "What a bunch of flies these damned films draw!" His greying yellow hair fell stiffly over his eyes as he poked into the drawers.

"People don't dress up for an early movie," Grete said, sliding the envelope into her purse and clasping it shut beside her.

"They wouldn't know how to dress for their own funerals. My cigarettes were in this drawer. Who's been snooping in the booth? Was it Doris? I've told that girl to stay behind the snack counter."

"You might have left your cigarettes in your office," Grete said.

"Ignorant mob, that's all they are. I can't show any film of culture; all they want is something loud and fast to keep them swallowing popcorn. I've no more time to waste, I have to run the projector. Send Oliver to buy me another pack."

"Oliver doesn't come to usher until the second show. I'm sure I saw the cigarettes on your desk."

She waited a full ten minutes into the movie before she drew out the letter. Weighing it in her hand, she could almost see Karl looking at her as he sometimes used to do from the doorway of his bedroom. Anshelm would be at the kitchen table, slapping his newspaper, railing about some fool's disaster or a devilish conspiracy. Karl's eyes would drift to Grete working at the stove or fussing about the table, as if he expected her to challenge Anshelm, or speak her thoughts, or to say anything at all.

You must try to understand your papa, to make allowances. He had such plans. When I first met him during the war, he looked glorious in his uniform and sounded so brilliant with his poetry and philosophy. He was leaving for the front to film news documentaries for the German army, though he told me that he was nobody's soldier. He said he didn't care which side won. He called them all 'blind fools led on by lunatics and scoundrels.'

We married after just three weeks but we hardly saw each other until the war was over. Then everything was different. You were almost two years old and our house was no more than a pile of bricks. His family's factory was destroyed. Their estate was behind the new Russian border. The only work we could find was clearing rubble onto horse-drawn wagons.

Yet your papa was undefeated. He'd thrown away his uniform for worker's clothing but under his shabby pants he still wore the high black boots of an officer. One evening, he climbed a hill of rubble onto a broken marble balcony. He looked across the ruins that used to be the glory of Hamburg and he shouted, 'Good riddance to this trash. We will be superior to the past. We will rise above it.'

What did I know? I was a frightened girl with a hungry child. I clasped my hands together in a prayer of thanks – again and again just like applause.

Doris tapped her nails against the window of the booth. Grete froze, then, with a show of calm, she slipped the letter into her pocket of her smock.

"Sorry, Mrs. Klatt, but a lady complained. There's some guys near the front who're making noise."

Grete said, "I will tell them to be quiet. Go back to the snack bar. If someone comes, you collect admission." She touched the letter through the fabric of her dress.

If I could only rush out through the fire door, escape to my little patch of flowers in the back. I would kneel on the earth, pull at weeds, water the marigolds, violas, pansies, while all this trouble drained into the earth. Do you understand me, Karl? Let my feet turn into roots, my skin to bark and each fingertip grow leaves to hold the light. Mr. Grenier's pigeons would fly around me, cooing for seeds. Then seeds could be my words and I would never have to think of what to say or how to act or ever have to go back in that airless booth. But Doris is watching me. And the ground outside is covered in snow. And I would never dare.

Grete passed through the swinging doors. At first, she saw only the movie on the screen and the dim outline of heads, all uniformly turned to the picture – a Viking battle scene, men with torches scaling a castle in a thunderstorm, axes and spears waving from the battlements, screaming rain-swept faces. It cut to a dungeon scene – a young man tied on a wooden bed. Another man in a leather mask approached with a fiery sword. A third man in a hooded robe stood at a distance, nodding.

"Get the bugger! Kill him!" A silhouette rose against the screen. Beside it were two others, huddled in laughter.

Grete pointed her flashlight. She'd seen these boys many times before, passing in front of the theatre, jostling one another, spitting on the sidewalk.

"You must be quiet," Grete whispered. "Others are trying to watch."

"Yeah, sure." The tall one scoffed, sliding back into his seat. "Old Sauerkraut!"

"What did you say?"

The boy raised his arm in a Nazi salute. The screen's glare cast his face into caricature. "Ve vill be qviet or be exterminated. Ja!"

"You must stop that," she pleaded. They jeered back. One tossed a spray of popcorn at her feet. She looked up to the projection window, desperate for Anshelm's authority. She knew that he'd be standing there, aloof behind his projector, scanning the screen from his observation port. He never bothered with the audience while a film was playing. "Let them huddle in their dark cave going 'ooh!' and 'aah!' as if they're watching something real. It's just Plato's latest shadow show – another kind of fantasy for a new batch of fools. Not me. My place is up on top, running things with my projector."

"Jawohl, mein Fuhrer!" The two others joined the mock salute as Grete hurried away. Glancing back, she saw them standing on the seats looking like shadows of the warriors on the screen.

Grete rushed up to the projection room to tell Anshelm. He gruffed, "I'm taking over. You stay up here." As he left she slumped into the chair, yielding to the beating of her heart.

When she felt the letter stiff inside the pocket of her dress, she drew it out, tore away the envelope and tried to bring the words into focus. Even without reading it, she saw the change; Karl's small willowy script had grown into feverish twists and scratches. The last lines slanted down into a scrawl.

Jan/62

Papa and Mama

Marrakech, Morocco – a hot maze packed with dark humanity. Black men, brown men with heavy eyes and thick lips. The men stare out from hooded robes and women laugh behind their veils. The souk – the marketplace – festers with every sort of appetite. Sellers squawk and jabber and pull at us to buy anything. Would you like to see them all eliminated, Papa? Or forced to work for someone else's greatness?

I'm not disgusted by them. I'm fascinated. And they're fascinated by me. Especially by my blond hair. One sweaty fellow at a stand grabbed me by my hair. He lifted a long sharp knife that he uses to slice watermelon and pressed it to my throat. When I could think of nothing but my own blood spilling on the ground, he muttered something foul and bit my ear. The other street sellers laughed. Then I laughed, too. Now we're all friends.

I'm writing again, two days later. Sunrise. Reuven and I are on the flat roof of the Hotel de France moaning for a breeze. Trying to sleep up here on cushions. Heat doesn't end. Or maybe it's the fever. Now some muezzin is singing prayers from a minaret. I see people on the lower roofs and in the street, their faces in the dirt, bowing east. Yet they won't bow to a statue or even draw a picture. They believe that all images are profane, idolatrous. So what do they imagine in their minds? Could their dreams be anything like the pictures on your movie screen?

Reuven is sleeping on a mat near the edge of the roof. It frightens me, the way he tosses and turns so close to the edge. That's how he is. He won't change. Not even after that scare in Munich. The police tried to blame him. And his poor guitar – it was all he had to live by.

He's in a bad way now. He can't fight off all the hate in his life. He says it's not just because he's a Jew raised in Germany. It's also because he's a German raised inside a Jew. It's like all the past keeps getting played inside him. I wrote you about what happened to his family and about the death camps but I couldn't write everything. It would have been too awful. It was too awful to even hear.

Why don't you write me back? Are you both angry? Or ashamed? I need to tell you these things. I almost stopped writing. But it would have been as bad as not listening to Reuven. Yet without you writing back, I feel trapped between his words and your silence. The pressure gets worse and he keeps telling me more and more.

Yesterday, I couldn't stand it. I said to him, 'Shut up, damn you!' and left the room but he kept talking as if I were still there. Later I came back to apologize but he said, 'It doesn't matter. Even if you ran away, even if I died - I will keep talking and you will keep hearing me.'

Earlier tonight, he wandered out into the streets like he was in a trance. I followed from a distance. He went out the town gate into a stony emptiness. The sky was cloudless and the ground was glowing like the moon. He tossed something behind him. I saw it was his passport. Suddenly, I got so angry that I caught him and pulled him around, wanting to swear or hit him. I saw tears rolling down his face though he wasn't even blinking or making any sound.

I started to cry. I don't even know why. I haven't cried since I was five. I know what Papa would say. But I will cry anyway, even now.

Papa. I keep trying to understand what Old Helmut Kraus told me about you. I know how you would justify yourself. You'd say that you did nothing. That you were better than the Nazis – untouched by their stupidity. You only filmed it. But didn't you have to look at what you were filming? Did you think the camera's lens would keep you clean? Is that how you could act like nothing real had happened?

You have no compassion left. Your feelings must have suffocated behind your camera lenses. You can look out at the world . . .

The script became too scrawled to read. Grete's hands grew heavy and she rested the pages on her lap, pressing them flat and warm. She watched the graduated turning of the reel, the film threading through the gears; sprockets, spindles, gates. She reached out, letting the celluloid run between her fingers.

The machine keeps pulling and film keeps moving, thin as a strip of skin that could break at any moment. But the machinery won't let it.

As she turned away, she noticed the dull glint of iron, an ornate padlock at the back of a deep shelf behind a stack of films. It was clamped to a large metal storage box, a box she hadn't seen since they'd emigrated. She'd almost never been inside Anshelm's projection booth. No one was allowed in, not even to clean. "Only I touch my equipment," he'd say. "It's too precise, too valuable. It won't tolerate clumsiness."

But why this padlock? The room has its lock already. Nothing, Karl, is as wilful as a lock. Iron biting into iron. It makes me think of Papa in bed at night, grinding his teeth, his back to me like a wall that sweats. Never any words for me, not even groans or snores. Only that grinding.

Grete put away the letter and searched Anshelm's leather coat for his keys; she found an intricate iron one that released the lock. Inside the metal box beside some battered film cans were a half-dozen postcards and three letters, all recently from Karl, two unopened. She clutched them, trying to decide whether to risk taking them all or to rescue one at a time.

As she put back the first two cards, she noticed the markings on the film cans – German army issue – all identification scratched out except in one place where she discerned Anshelm's name as captain in official type: Hauptmann Anshelm Klatt.

She had no desire to look inside. Yet it seemed that Karl's hands, not her own, were opening the closest can, lifting out the reel. And Karl's eyes, not her own, were examining the strip, holding it to the bright bar of light that leaked through the side of the projector.

Footage from the war, Karl – something your papa might have filmed, that must be why he kept it – is this what he watches late at night when he says he is 'reviewing'? This film is a negative – it reverses everything – giving these men white uniforms, white guns – turning these naked people black. Some are crouched as if to hide themselves. Others stand covering their private parts. In the next frames, they go down on their knees. Here is a close up of a face in uniform laughing or yelling, teeth all black. And in these later frames a woman stretches out her arms while the others are lying in rows upon the ground. Now more white guns.

I can't keep looking, Karl. What if I see myself? Or even you? These people could be anyone, everyone. Except for Papa; he would not be there. He would be behind the camera.

Grete returned the film to the film can, the film can to the box, then placed the cards and letters exactly as they'd been. She didn't want to read them, fearing what they would say, grimly aware that despite the greetings of "Mama, Papa," Karl's letters were no longer written to her. He had forgotten her, in his anger.

Now you are only thinking about Papa, imagining how he feels, how he acts so you can fight him. But that's how you will become like him. You would answer no, that's not true. You would say his anger is cold but yours is hot. Still, I recognize Papa's voice in yours – so bitter and condemning. Just tell me one thing, Karl. When all your angry words are out, what will you have left for me?

She sat numbly for a long while until the reel began to clatter, as the film was running to its last few minutes. She hurried to the lobby to fetch Anshelm.

Doris was fussing with the popcorn machine. "Mr. Klatt wouldn't even let me go outside to look," she sulked. "Honestly, it's not like someone's going to steal the soft drinks."

"Look at what?" Grete asked. "What has happened?"

"I know those guys – they hang out at Pop's cafe, sitting on the window ledge, whistling. They always say the stupidest things."

"Doris, please tell me."

"They're such delinquents, it makes me sick. Mr. Klatt went in to shut them up, and right away they came charging out the other doors on the far aisle."

"Where is Mr. Klatt now?"

"Oh, he marched right outside after them. He didn't even have his coat on and they were dodging around and throwing snow and calling him names. They wouldn't go away till he said he'd called the police."

"The police?"

"He was just giving them a scare, but as soon as he came back in they painted that German sign outside, right on the big poster window. You know, that sign that's from the war."

GRETE FOUND ANSHELM on the street unlocking the shallow window that displayed a full-size movie poster. A large swastika was spray-painted on the glass.

Anshelm grinned fiercely, hunching over his tool box. "Ha! Those young devils! They don't know who they're dealing with! I can get their names."

"Anshelm, the reel is running out."

"Let it go. It's the end of the movie, anyway. This damn spray paint won't wash off. Everybody is going to see what they've painted on it. At first I decided to take the window off its hinges and hide it downstairs. But now I have a better idea." He swung open the window so it hung between them. Grete looked at Anshelm through the large pane of glass. The lines of the swastika cut across his neck, arms, waist.

His mouth kept speaking, its breath frosting in the air. "I

thought to myself, if I take away the window, those boys could come back and steal the movie poster. But then I found their can of spray paint and I thought of something clever – something those fools could never think of. Watch this!"

Anshelm sprayed along the outer lines of the swastika, joining the gaps to turn the swastika into a completed square. The four inside lines that radiated from the centre then appeared to divide the completed square into four smaller squares. "Now nobody can see that it's a swastika," Anshelm boasted. "I've disguised it. I've made it look like a block of four square windows. Do you see? That's my intelligence. Isn't that my intelligence, Grete?"

The sounds all seem so swollen – traffic, wind, creaking hinges, or is he grinding his teeth, the way he does when he is sleeping? Everything's so loud with choking.

Such a crash! A conductor's arms – that's how my arms move, Karl – as I crash them through the window. Just like I am bringing an orchestra to an end, all with breaking glass. The cars roaring, the pigeons beating at the sky, Anshelm yelling words, these are all instruments in my orchestra. Even Papa's sputtering as he stumbles back.

And the bits of glass are so beautiful. Everything's in pieces with the wind blowing through the broken window, and over me, singing all over me. And over Papa. Over you, too, Karl, wherever you are. If you can hear me, then you must hear this wind singing.

But Papa doesn't hear the singing, yet. That's why he's grabbing me by my wrists. But when he sees that I am cut, sees the blood coming down my arm like a ribbon that's unravelling, he gets so very pale and stares. I start laughing. I lift my cut to his face, touch my blood to his cheek. 'Red tears, Anshelm,' I say to him. And to all the people coming out the doors. 'Look, everybody, these are my tears.' I will tell you, too, when you return. I'll speak it out so clearly there won't be any mistake. I will say, 'Don't be afraid, Karl. I have red tears for everyone.'

SECRET TONGUES

ALEC'S DEATH IN APRIL JUST A MONTH AFTER HIS WIFE BEATRICE'S secretly thrilled my mother. "It's just as if they'd planned it," she told my father, adjusting her funeral hat to a rakish angle in the mirror. "That's the power of true love." She turned to offer him her tragic gaze but my father was on his knees beside the bed hunting for the match to his Argyle sock. "Alec's departure," she announced, undaunted, "was a blessing in disguise."

The only death I'd ever seen was a sparrow's. My mother hadn't called that "a blessing in disguise." The bird had dropped on our door step like a small dry turd and I was lifting one of its wings when my mother spotted me. She dragged me to the bathroom and scoured my fingers with laundry soap, yelling to my father, "Murray, there's a dead bird on the steps! Throw it into somebody's yard. God, it's such bad luck, I'd better light a candle."

My father, still searching for his Argyle, grumbled something about Alec getting "a bad deal." He rose with quite a different sock covered in dust, but with a wink and a finger to his lips he sat beside me on their bed and pulled it on. As he lowered the cuffs of his pants, he described how "Alec, that poor palooka, took a real tough fall." Alec had been walking home from the Legion late at night and, not seeing the construction on the street, had dropped right through an open manhole. My father nodded confidentially, "I could see it coming, what with the shape of his liver and him retired with nothing to do and only Rita left for company in the house."

According to my father, Beatrice's death in March had also been "a pretty solid bet." She'd gotten "awfully religious" and caught something nasty singing in a Pentecostal choir. Whatever it was, it became even worse when she insisted on planting daffodils far too late in a very chilly autumn. It grew into what he called "a woman's ailment" that went from "bad to worse to terrible" all through the winter until she finally died in March. "And we had to bury her," he said, "before her bulbs had even sprouted."

The more I tried to understand certain things my parents told me, the more their words bewildered me. I vaguely understood that I wasn't supposed to understand, only to store the information in my brain until I became adult. Then, all the odd bits and awkward ends would sort themselves out and fit together into some marvellous body of knowledge that made perfect sense. In the meantime, I was to nod solemnly and keep my mind a blank, the way I did whenever crazy Mrs. Kupakis stopped me on the street to confide to me in Latvian. My father rubbed my head with his knuckles, "There's a good boy, Danny."

"Murray, let's not be late for the service," my mother warned, "or we'll end up at the front and I won't see a thing." She hunted up some last-minute gear: bobby pins, a handful of cafe mints, and extra Kleenex so she could have "a real good cry." She turned back to her vanity and, without taking off her gloves, she applied mascara with a small plastic wand, grinning fiercely. She batted her eyes, spit into her Kleenex and cleared the black stuff off to start again. "Oh, by the by," she said. "I bumped into Walter Borkow from the chapel. He promised me he's giving Alec a first-class service."

"Damn rights," my father mumbled, lining up his shirt sleeves as a cufflink squirmed between his fingers.

I asked, "Is Mr. Borkow going to bury Alec or burn him?"

"Danny!" The cufflink flipped and skittered across the floor into the closet. "Look, Daniel," my father said, poking for it in a pile of laundry. "It's just a dead body. It doesn't feel a thing."

"That's right," my mother added. "Alec doesn't care about his body anymore because his soul is going to heaven." She lowered the veil over her face so only her red lips were visible. They seemed to float by themselves inside a stormy cloud. "There's nothing to worry about. There's nothing to be afraid of," the lips assured me, parting and joining with each syllable. "A funeral is just a way to say a last goodbye to someone who we loved. It's really very beautiful." The lips sealed into a smile.

"I loved Alec, too," I said. "So why can't I come?"

The lips pursed, then split apart. "You're too young to know about that kind of thing!"

MY PARENTS COULD BE just as cryptic about finances, family politics, neighbourhood scandals and half the evening news. The closer they got to saying anything important, the more mysterious they became, using signals: whispers, glances, even special coughs and grunts. Sometimes they shifted into Yiddish, their parents' mother tongue, for affairs that children and other strangers could not, should not understand.

And, of course, there were the secrets of the bedroom. I'd hear my parents late at night – my mother moaning, my father choking out some strange word – their tortured prayers rising through the heating vent beneath my bed. "Oh Gott! Mein Gott!" as the other groaned. Afterwards came the crying, the laughing in relief, the hushing into silence. I understood only one thing – their deepest secrets were dangerous and compelling.

Not like Rita, Alec's niece, who seemed to have no secrets, who spoke whatever came into her mind, bantering outrageous, forbidden things no matter how much my parents tried to distract her. It was all a joke to Rita.

She told me everything. And I understood nothing. I didn't dare ask her to explain. How could I admit to her that I didn't understand? Not while I felt so close to finding out what my parents kept from me – the knowledge that I was not supposed to have, could not be trusted with, could only get when I became a man. I reasoned that if I could discover it, then I'd become that man.

"Oh, Danny darlin', you're my little man," Rita would say and pat the couch. "Come on, keep me comfy." I'd lounge beside her, watching for the slight tightening of her jaw, the rising of her chest, preparing to laugh at every joke, determined to show that I could "get it." I'd listen for her voice to lower and grind on something confidential, the cue for me to smirk, wink and say something, anything that might sound as if I, too, were "in on it." This delighted Rita who'd sometimes repeat what I had said, laughing uproariously while my parents frowned to one another.

I kept up my pretence, hoping I might chance upon some clues that would lead me to whatever it was they knew – the "it" that seemed so menacing to my parents and so hilarious to Rita.

"RITA MUST THINK A FUNERAL is some kind of holiday," my father said, wrestling with his tie. "I knocked on her door to give her the flowers; I even had a little speech for condolences. And what does she do? She pulls me in for a rum and Coke. She didn't even have the mirrors covered."

My mother was busy rubbing her worn high heels, searching the leather for a shine. "Murray, you got it all wrong," she said. "The English don't cover up their mirrors when someone in the family dies. That's only a Jewish custom."

"And I suppose it's an English custom to wear a bright yellow sundress to an uncle's funeral, the guy who took her in when she had nowhere else to go? Because that's what she had on."

"You don't know what she's going to wear," my mother said. "She'll surprise us all, she always does. Now, did you buy the good bouquet with the pink carnations like we agreed?"

"Sure, and she stuck it in a mason jar behind a vase – a vase of long stem roses from you know who. She even put his card in front for everyone to read. 'Thinking of you every day,' it said. Can you believe it?" My father tossed the knotted tie onto the bed. "He's thinking of her every *night* – that's more like it. I'm telling you, Deborah, now that both Beatrice and Alec are gone, she's heading out of control."

"Dad?" I asked. "Who's 'you know who'?"

He turned on me, as if I'd sworn aloud. "Daniel, get right outside. And you'd better stay out there till we come back!"

I WENT STRAIGHT TO MR. WERNER. The old caretaker was the only one who always answered my questions and who was always where I could find him – in his basement workshop bent over something never quite completed. This time he was assembling a fishing rod that I was going to present to my father on his birthday.

My father, generally lax and easygoing, had been campaigning on and off for the last year against what he called my "goofy day-dreams." He'd confiscated my comic books and banished me out of doors to find some gang of pals, start playing sports and become the boy he used to be.

I got it in my head that a gift might appease him. At first I thought to resurrect an old statue that I'd stolen and then buried by Mr. Werner's fence. I thought of painting it up like some flashy girlie thing that might amuse my dad but something stopped me and shifted all my thoughts toward a rod instead. A Bradley Spin Master fishing rod. I emptied my bank account of its $9.48, took the bus down Main Street to The Man With The Axe – The Store That Chops Down Prices – and I bought the kit, hooks, line and sinker all included.

"Yah, yah," Mr. Werner said. "The whole fishing caboodle. I got those other parts somewhere here. I was getting right to it." He searched among stray copper pipes and rolls of wire, summoning a fine cloud of dust that rose to a ray of sunlight streaking through the cellar window. The dust turned to gold and swirled around him.

"Mr. Werner," I said. "You know all kinds of stories and how things work. My teachers know lots of other stuff. And my parents know things, too. But the more I keep trying to figure out what everybody's telling me, the more I get mixed up. Like, do you think maybe I'm dumb?"

His laughter rose in musical notes, then settled in a sigh as he stroked the dust from his loose flannel shirt, his white bushy eyebrows. "Ah, Danny, you and your mind! Your mind is so hungry, it's got to have all the answers on one big plate so it can eat them all together and all at once." He lifted the sections of the rod. "Look, you tell me what you think. If I throw these pieces into the air, are they going to fall together to make your fishing rod?"

"No."

"Good. So you understand – some things don't happen in one big shout." He nodded for me to watch as he began with gnarled hands and squinting eyes his slow and careful assembly: he joined the sections of the rod, fitted the rod into the handle, attached the empty reel. "When I first came to this country, I knew from nothing. I couldn't even put ten words together. I could say 'Hello,' 'Goodbye,' 'Thank you' and 'Excuse me, I do not speak any English.' " He laughed again as he tied an end of the fishing line to the cylinder of the reel. He signalled me with a crooked finger, "Danny, hold this spool of fishing line and back up really slow. Then your present will be ready for your father."

"How come?" I asked, as we backed away from one another.

"How come what?" he questioned back. "What do you mean, 'how come'?"

My back bumped against the mortar of the wall. "How come I have to back up all the way here?"

"Watch a little more, ask a little less," he answered. "Then maybe you'll understand better by yourself." He sat on a wooden crate at the opposite wall, obscured by shadow except for the silver shimmer of his hair. We were at the furthest ends of the workshop, joined by the sea-blue nylon line that he began reeling in. I held the spool by both ends of a screwdriver stuck through its centre so as he turned the reel, the line pulled on the spool and it began to turn.

I watched and understood. He was reeling in the line and my job was to keep the spool at my end feeding it out.

Mr. Werner saw me smile. "There, Danny. You see? You didn't have to ask. And I didn't have to tell you." Mr. Werner rubbed his fingers across his mouth and shaped a smile of his own.

"I still don't know much," I said.

"When I first came to this country, I'd never even seen a banana. They gave me one and I tried to eat it, peel and all. What did I know? I was like a baby."

"Yeah, but I'm born here. I've been here all my life. I hear grownups talking all the time. And I still can't figure out half of it."

The old man's nod was like a bow. "You're right. It's hard to not understand. It don't matter if you're young or old." He reeled the line more slowly, to the thin rhythm of his breathing. "They used to say that in the beginning when the Two Worlds were side by side, that everything was understood by everybody. You spoke with angels just like with the neighbours. You even talked with animals and trees. The Sparks of Creation were everywhere giving off such clear light and there wasn't even shadows. But that's over now. Now hardly anything is clear. Even between me and my son. I say to him, 'Hello Arthur, I'm so glad you came to see me.' Suddenly, he looks worried. He takes off his glasses. He asks, 'Why? Is something wrong?' "

"So how come things changed?" I asked.

"Maybe too many bad thoughts, bad feelings. Things broke apart. The Sparks got covered over. This world got so heavy that it sunk down – like that board in the playground."

"The teeter totter?"

"Yah, just like like that," he said. "And the Other World lost its weight and got pushed up. Maybe something went wrong there, too. I don't know. But now everything in this world is out of kilter – people running around all their lives wanting everything from everyone and none of it does them any good."

The reel was winding on with slow click clocks. "Maybe that other world's not even up there any more," I said. "Maybe it's like the Planet Krypton. Right after Superman left it for Earth, the whole place exploded."

Mr. Werner shook his head. "No, no. It's still there. Sometimes, for a moment there's a thread, a word, a breath of wind – we make a connection."

"Like by accident?" I asked.

"Who knows what's an accident? To the Ba'al Shem Tov, nothing was an accident." Mr. Werner stopped reeling in the line. He'd always stop whatever he was doing when he spoke about the eighteenth-century wonder-worker from Carpathia. "The last person to read the Book of Mysteries and live. The one chosen by the thirty-six Lamad Vavniks, the Hidden Holy Ones who keep the world from falling even further." Mr. Werner's finger pointed upwards beyond the heavy beams above our heads. "Rabbi Israel ben Eliezer, the Ba'al Shem Tov, Master of the Holy Word, Blessed be his Name – he was a lightning rod between the Worlds, that's what he was."

I settled against the coolness of the wall. Mr. Werner was beginning another story.

"The Ba'al Shem always knew when he was being called. A dream, a bird, maybe someone said a simple thing – it meant something altogether different to the Master. He'd raise his walking stick and speak the holy word for 'carriage'. Aha! A carriage with four horses would appear right out of air and carry him to where he was needed. One time, the carriage took him to the funeral of a bride. She was being lowered into her grave while the bridegroom, the family, the friends all circled round and cried; everyone had given up all hope. The Ba'al Shem pushed through and stood above her. His spirit sank past her body and in the deepness of the earth, he found her soul imprisoned by a ghost.

"The bride's soul cried out, 'Rabbi, help me. Years ago, as my jealous sister lay on her deathbed, she made me promise that I would never marry her husband. Now I've accepted him as my bridegroom. I was young and thoughtless when she made me swear; I didn't understand what it would mean. Must I be condemned to this?'

"The ghost came forward to defend itself. 'She gave her sacred word as I lay dying and then she broke it. The bride belongs to me!'

"Decide. Who had the greater claim to this struggling soul – the bride herself or the ghost who was betrayed? The Ba'al Shem Tov read the signs of Heaven's judgement, then he announced, 'The rights of the living are greater than anything owed to the dead.' He called out in holy words, 'Come back to life,' and the bride's soul broke free. Just like water fills a jug, her life returned!"

Mr. Werner rose from his crate as if witnessing the joy that must have flooded through the crowd, turning funeral into wedding. Finally, he looked to the fishing line, limp and forgotten on the cement floor. He began to reel again, pulling the line taut between us.

I thought about what I would do if I had knowledge like the Ba'al Shem Tov. I'd call down a silver bolt of light. A flash. A burst of smoke – I'd summon genies, discover the future, amaze the world with my superhuman understanding.

"Magic," I said. "You can get anything if you know magic."

"You get nothing with magic," Mr. Werner snorted. "Tricks that don't work when you need them. Curses that blow up in your face. No, the Ba'al Shem Tov called down miracles. One time, the Paritz, a black magician, attacked him with an evil spell. The Ba'al Shem turned it back on him just like a hungry wolf."

"Was it like a real wolf?" I asked. "Did it kill the guy?"

The old man shook his head. "Nothing like that. The Ba'al Shem didn't want to hurt nobody. You can't become better from making someone worse. He only wanted wisdom – and it came to him like birds come when you show them love. One day the greatest Book of Mysteries arrived, The Book of Adam.

It was written in the language spoken before the Tower of Babel fell apart, every letter shining with its own light. Only six others had ever read that book to its end: Adam, who was taught to speak by God, Abraham, Joseph, Joshua ben Nun, King Solomon and the tzaddik, the holy man, Reb Adam. Others tried, but each made some mistake and died.

"The Ba'al Shem Tov took the Great Fast – no food, no water from Sabbath to Sabbath, and he purified himself in every way, so he could enter the greatest Book of Mysteries without getting lost inside. He opened his mind to every thought, in every tongue, and he followed all their meanings to the very end where all languages, all thoughts, all mysteries join together into the first words of the world – so he could read the Forgotten Tongue and learn what even the Hidden Holy Ones did not understand." Werner stopped and leaned forward, frowning, as if he'd run out of breath, though he seemed to be hardly breathing at all.

"Is that how you learn to make miracles?" I asked.

He stared at me for a moment, then shook his head. "I shouldn't be filling your head with all those Old Country tales. Ghosts and curses, those stories are no better than your comic books."

"But what about all the miracles?"

He scowled, rubbing at his brow. "I never saw any miracles. All I know is that my parents, neighbours, all of them back then, they believed those kinds of things. But what good did it do them? They all died, even their village was destroyed, and not one brick was left standing on another." He turned back to the reel, frowning into the troubled water of some rising memory.

"You can't stop now," I begged. "That's what my parents always do – they always keep back the important stuff."

He raised his hand as if to hold me off but wavered and sat down. "All right, I'll tell you more but I don't make no guarantees it's true."

"That's okay, I just want to hear it. What did he do once he learned the secrets from The Book of Adam?"

Mr. Werner settled in. "My father, may he rest in peace, he told me that the Ba'al Shem Tov learned how to call the Governor of Dreams who could teach him even more. The Governor became his guide and showed him every secret place on earth and in the dark clouds between the Worlds – he even brought him to the Prophet Elijah who agreed to guide him further. They travelled in a flaming chariot that was carried on a whirlwind to the highest point of heaven, what the Kabbala calls The Bird's Nest. No one can even guess what he learned there. But it was not enough; he could not learn how to get what he wanted with his whole life."

"What was he after?" I asked.

"For the Two Worlds to join once again. So we could be together with everyone we've ever lost."

"I'd get to see Alec and Beatrice?"

"Yah," said Mr. Werner, "and I'd be with my wife, Miriam. Sometimes I feel her so close, it's like she's right here about to touch me."

I looked in the shadows where he stood but saw only the wooden crate and some linoleum coiling off its roll. "It wouldn't happen, would it, Mr. Werner?"

"It didn't happen, that's for sure," he answered. "But the Ba'al Shem Tov kept calling with sacred words, not eating, not sleeping, not looking left or right." Mr. Werner's voice began to rise. "Not even stopping when the angels begged, 'No more. The Time's not right. The Worlds aren't ready yet!' The Ba'al Shem wouldn't listen. He sang out, 'Come now! We've suffered for too long. We can't wait any longer!' shaking the Gates of the Other World . . . until finally, the Messiah had to call to him and the soul of our holiest rabbi, the Ba'al Shem Tov, was taken away from us."

Mr. Werner sat back down, lowering his gaze to the fishing line. The only sound was the slow spinning of the reel. He seemed so shrunken, huddled on that empty crate. And the beam of light had moved away.

Finally, the fishing line ran out, with only the end of it tied to the spool that I was holding. Mr. Werner reeled it in, reeling me in with it. I stumbled towards him, drawn not so much by the pull of the line as by the glistening in his pale grey eyes.

"Look who I caught!" he smiled. "I caught a boy! I bait my hook with just one story – I catch a boy with a thousand questions!"

"It's too bad about the Ba'al Shem," I said.

Werner nodded. "Good? Bad? Who knows? You can believe something's so good and then it crumbles in your hands. Other times you get such awful news but it turns out to be for the best. The people were inspired by his struggle. They came to him as he lay dying, they asked him, 'Tell us, what have the powers taught you?' 'Joy,' he answered. 'It is joy that carries us to the Other World.' Many still follow his last words. They live by joy, though it's not as easy as you might think. So who can know even if the fall of the Ba'al Shem Tov was good or bad?" Mr. Werner strung the fishing line through the metal loops of the rod and tied a lead sinker to the end. "Here," he said, handing me the rod. "The job is done."

I balanced the fishing rod in my hands. It was almost weightless yet so long it could scrape the cobwebs on the basement window. "Are there still guys who can do stuff like the Ba'al Shem Tov?"

"That's over two hundred years ago," he answered. "Nobody's getting miracles anymore, not like his." He saw my disappointment and gave me a wink. "But way before him, they were catching even bigger miracles – you'd call them whoppers!"

Then we had our fun. "What'll it be?" Mr. Werner shouted. "Samson? David? Noah on the boat. What'll it be?" He was Joshua outside Jericho swaying side to side, trumpeting the ram's horn in the air. He struck the work light overhead so it swung to his tune and his shadow danced across the cracks of the basement wall.

I yelled, "Me, too. I want a part!" He had me act out Solomon, the King, holding my sceptre between two quarrelling women. I commanded, "Give the baby to both of them. Cut the child in two!" and Mr. Werner played all the other parts – the wailing mother, the stony mother, the brainless soldier with a hacksaw for a sword. He even played the baby who googooed through it all.

Next I stood on the work bench and my fishing rod was the staff of Moses. Mr. Werner became the Red Sea roaring at my feet as he shook thunder from a sheet of tin. I raised my rod. I crashed it down. I split the sea in half. Mr. Werner transformed into the Pharaoh swept away into the depths of the scrap pile. I cheered in the only Hebrew I remembered, "Shalom! Mazel Tov! Ma neesh tanah!" as I paraded my people through the mud to the sunlit stairs of the Promised Land.

"Now I want to be the Ba'al Shem," I said. "Let's make the fishing rod his magic walking stick. I'll read from that book of Adam's and go exploring for the Bird's Nest."

Mr. Werner, breathless, leaned against the workbench. "No more. I'm back to being an old man again. Believe me, it's the hardest part to play."

I dashed outside without him, thrusting the rod into the hot glare of the sun.

FOUR LANES OF RUSH HOUR TRAFFIC roared on either side of me, but I knew where I was going and what I had to do. I lifted my rod from the concrete island. I called out, "Let me through. Everything stops on the count of three!" As I reached the final number, the green light turned to red and all the wheels and gears groaned to a halt. I raced across the street to the funeral chapel's high black door.

I couldn't get the brass-bound door to open. I pushed with my shoulder until the studs bruised my arm. Not even a rattle. As I leaned on the fishing rod, trying to catch my breath, I wondered how I could get inside.

I tried to puzzle out the wormy Gothic letters on a small sign hanging overhead, as cryptic and challenging as my parents' warning, "You're too young to know about that kind of thing." Or the Book of Adam that so many tried to read and failed. But I wasn't afraid. I kept the letters clear before my eyes, concentrating all my thoughts to figure out the words.

𝕱𝖚𝖓𝖊𝖗𝖆𝖑 𝕾𝖊𝖗𝖛𝖎𝖈𝖊 𝖎𝖓 𝕻𝖗𝖔𝖌𝖗𝖊𝖘𝖘

It happened as I thought – the distant yawn of a back door opening up for me. I rushed behind the building in time to see the riding boots of the chauffeur stepping over a metal threshold, the aluminum service door clattering shut behind him. The chauffeur had a stiff artificial leg that made him seem half human, half machine, as he worked himself across the parking lot. He stopped beside the Borkow hearse – a long sheet of blackness stretched with chrome that glinted in the sun. He wrapped a pair of mirrored sunglasses across his face. He opened the driver's door, folded himself up and disappeared inside.

The chapel's service door was loose and gaping – no one there to stop me. I entered the building as casually as if I knew the way by sight.

But there was no oak-panelled lobby with fine columns as I'd imagined, only a sloping ramp and grey enamelled walls scored with long scratches as if some sort of trolley had been scraping past. The ramp led me into a dimly lit basement, a wide room filled with coffins, some gaping open, others closed, all of them raised on sawhorses draped with canvas. As I crossed the room, the coffins seemed to float past me on either side, not up the ramp towards the light but downstream, sinking into darkness.

There was no music, either. I had imagined I'd hear an organ and the glorious singing of a congregation – all the adults I knew – my parents, teachers, the storekeepers, even the city workers who lunched at the corner cafe – all of them singing as I moved along the brilliant passage to the front of the chapel where I'd find Rita, pale as ivory, head lowered, looking down on Alec's body. As I'd approach, I'd see a shimmering through cathedral glass – Alec's ghost. I'd whisper, "Alec. I can see you. It's me. It's Danny!" and he'd reveal – I don't know what – but as he'd speak I'd understand everything just like the man I'd been waiting to become.

I'd join Rita; I'd know exactly what to say so she'd rise up to hold my hand, and then we'd join my parents and all the others, singing out strange words that I would instantly know.

But there was no music at all in the funeral parlour's basement. Only the scrape of my fishing rod dragging on the concrete and far ahead, faint, droning words from some microphone, crackling with static. I made out Alec's name three or four times along with "beloved" and "honoured by his companions," and some bigger words I'd never heard before. The voice resonated as I entered a low-ceilinged room with stacks of chairs. No sign of anyone – only a filthy sink and some dog-eared playing cards scattered across a table. The voice coughed, flattened back into a nasal hum, and droned on, filling the stairwell beyond the room.

I shouldn't be here. I know I shouldn't, I told myself.

A short flight of stairs led me into a dark hallway. At the far end I saw a doorway blocked by a tall attendant with his back towards me. He seemed little more than a hunched silhouette, partially obscuring the coloured sunlight in the room beyond him. It was the chapel. I rushed forward, thinking only that I had to reach that light. I was more than halfway there, stepping into the furthest stretch of the attendant's shadow, when he swung around at me.

"Hey you!" his words gurgled in his throat. "How'd you get in here? Huh?" He was stooped so low he seemed to have no head at all.

I tried to stop and lost my footing. I was slipping on my heels as he grabbed at me.

"Gimme that!" he said. Suddenly he had weight and force. He seized my arm and pulled away my rod. "What's this?"

"I . . . I don't know," I answered numbly.

"It's a fishing pole! Isn't it?" He stooped closer, his darkness covering my face, and then the heavy rot of his breath. "And who're you, huh?"

"I just thought, maybe . . ."

"You're the Stein kid, that's who you are. That Stein kid."

"I guess so."

"What're you doing here, a kid like you?" He tried to clear his throat and seemed about to spit.

"I don't know," I answered.

"Don't you have no respect? There's a dead man in there and all those people feeling bad. Well, what d'you got to say for y'self?"

There was nothing I could say, not for myself or for anyone. I didn't know the words. I didn't know anything. My mouth moved but my tongue was thick and dry, choking on his close grunting and on the distant droning. I heard a break of voices in the room beyond, a growing babble. I tried to recognize a familiar voice, a friendly word, but the door swung shut.

POP

LORNE NOJUK PRESSED THE BURGER ON THE GRILL UNTIL IT HISSED. He watched it mottle into grey and flipped it over. When he topped it with a bun his fingers left a glazed imprint on the crust. Grease, he thought, rubbing his hands on his cotton apron. Everything here gets so damn greasy.

"Hey, Pop," a kid called from the pinball. "Where's my Coke?"

They all called him "Pop" though it made no sense to Lorne. He was thirty-three, slender, and as alert behind the counter as a young dog. He might have been mistaken for a kid himself if it weren't for his face – not that it looked old but it was gaunt and deeply set, hanging forward in furrows of distress.

Lorne Nojuk was called Pop, like the previous owner, like the place itself – The Popularity Grill. "We're going to the 'Pop'," the kids would say.

It's not a name at all, Lorne thought. It's just another noise. The name came with the short orders and the long hours and the kids who brawled and brooded here instead of heading home, kids like Jimmy and his pals who hardly had a home, who seemed to have nothing and to want everything. Lorne knew that it would only get worse at the end of the month when school closed for the summer. They'd hang around every afternoon while he'd have to serve them by himself. Lorne hated serving, it was such a thankless task, yet serving was the thing he knew most how to do.

"You want your Coke regular or large?" he asked.

No answer. The kid swayed and lunged, working the pinball flippers in the same puppet dance that caught him like all the others and held him to the game, eyes and hips swinging in a tight arc, nerves fused to wires as the bright maze flashed, banged, whirled in front, and the silver ball hurled on to drop, as always, into the gutter between his hands.

What a joke, Lorne thought. A pimply-faced kid plays a box of junk like he's got the world at his fingertips.

Lorne frowned at the jukebox in the corner. A song was just ending and the metal arm lowered and turned, rose and turned again to remove the 45 and select another. Soon it began to wail again.

> *I couldn't sleep a wink last night*
> *Just thinking of you, baby, things weren't right.*
> *I kept on tossin' and turnin' and tossin' (and turning)*
> *Tossin' and turnin' all night.*

This whole place is just a box of crazy boxes, Lorne decided. The cafe was a long open room of fluorescent lights and stainless steel, bright curving counters, stools, chairs and tables. Lorne took his position at the drink dispenser and pressed the lever. Waiting for the glass to fill, he stared out the window at the store signs, traffic lights, the cars that roared and fumed, flashing long blades of chrome under the glaring sky. "Damn street," he muttered. "It's just more of the same." The drink foamed over the rim of the glass. Lorne released the lever.

He carried it dripping down the aisle, around the curved counter, past the jukebox, across the floor to the pinball, and banged it onto the glass top, blocking the kid's view.

"I suppose you want credit, right?" Lorne asked.

"Hey! What?" The kid slid away the drink, too frantic even to swear. He saved the ball by fluttering it to a side bumper, then clipped it to the rollovers at the top, where it jingled madly between two rubber banks.

"Well, you're the last one getting it. Understand?" Lorne stalked back to the Formica counter, running a damp cloth along its edge, straightening the already straightened jars and shakers before heading to the phone beside the till. It was two o'clock. Time to check on Genie.

Then he remembered the burger on the grill.

Burnt.

Kids don't care anyway, he decided. Cast iron guts. Brains on tilt. Why keep going out of my way when they don't even notice? Nevertheless, he slipped the patty off the grill and trimmed away the scorched part. He began slicing the onion, one of the few tasks he enjoyed. The precision of cutting made such sense to him; the rounded paring knife was the simplest, the most perfect instrument and the onion itself was so cleanly constructed into segments as if to prove there was an order in the world. It seemed strange to Lorne that cutting could also cause his eyes to tear.

He thought of Genie's eyes. Always dry. And of her hands, moist and red as if she cried through them instead. He recalled how she'd rubbed her hands on the gatherings of the bedspread the night before as she stared through their bedroom window. "Sure, Lorne. Why not?" she'd said. "Get out to a movie. It'll do you good to get away from me. God, I wish I could get away from myself." Thinking of her hands, Lorne had stayed.

Genie's hands had begun trembling with the last change of medication and seemed to have taken on a life of their own. He'd first noticed them on the night she'd pleaded that he return to his night course in engineering. "You can't quit," she'd said, her arms tightening across her chest. "You can't let me ruin everything." Her hands gripped her upper arms, pale fingers pressing into flesh.

"Quit?" he'd answered. "What are you talking about, Genie? I'm no quitter."

"You need the degree. For us," she'd said. "You'll get out of the cafe. And I'll get better. Either these pills will work or I'll take more shocks." As she talked on, her fingers sought another part of her arm, a part she had not yet bruised.

The next day, Lorne quit the course.

The screen door slammed. Blackball and Mick sauntered in, both sixteen with the same black leather jackets, boots and sullen stares, both spinning stools as they headed to the pinball. Mick held a portable radio shoulder height, blasting "Twist and Shout" as if to make war on the jukebox.

"Shut it or lose it," Lorne snapped, jolting Mick from the rhythm of the song. The boy switched it off, was about to mumble some excuse when he stopped, hearing the screen door open and Jimmy's metal cleats strike the linoleum. His face sank back into a mask.

"Jimmy," Lorne said to the boy at the door. "Don't come in here if you're skipping school. I'm setting down some rules."

"Maybe I'm on a spare." Jimmy straddled a chair at the front table, modelling for the others, hair coiled over his forehead, head cocked, mouth set in a perfected sneer.

"Jimmy, I know how you're feeling . . ."

"Sure, Pop, you know everything."

"Don't you give me that tone," Lorne said. "You've been expecting way too much from me. I was trying to make allowances, trying to be friendly . . ." He was waving his vegetable knife as he spoke, becoming angrier as he realized how foolish he must look. The others watched, letting Jimmy speak for them.

"I never asked you for anything, Pop! It was always you with the big welcomes, the long talks, always cooking me your scraps. I told you private stuff and you spilled it to Debrone!"

"Jimmy, Mr. Debrone's the guidance counsellor. It was for your own good . . ."

"You did me good, all right. 'Deadbone' called me in and said, 'Mr. Nojuk told me about your problems. Why don't we have a little chat?' "

"Jimmy, you don't seem to appreciate how I've been trying to help you."

"So I tell Debrone what's bothering me. Especially about him. Now he's made sure I'll never skip again – 'cause I'm expelled."

Lorne turned away, feeling resentment rising sour from his guts.

Jimmy's voice followed. "I don't even care. I never cared. But you suckered me in with your 'heart to heart' and 'man to man.' Well, just get off my case!"

Lorne gazed through the window across the street at a heavy woman in a bright purple shift with a large paper bag of groceries. She was talking with her head bobbing from side to side, explaining something to the small and delicate girl she was leading by the wrist. The woman stopped in front of the butcher shop, still chattering on as the girl dawdled. She shifted the bag onto her right arm, still holding on to the girl with her right hand as she reached into the bag and drew out a long string of red licorice. The girl grabbed for it. The woman lost her grip, first on the bag, then on the girl. As the bag began to tumble, the woman slapped her. It seemed slow motion to Lorne – the slap, the girl cupping her hands across her eyes, the cans and jars rolling down the sidewalk.

The boys were snickering. One whispered, "Hey, Jimmy. Pop's blown a fuse."

Mick said, "Jimmy, how about those fries? Come on, where's your pull?"

Jimmy's voice was clear above the pinball and the jukebox. "You want fries on the house? Just act real cosy. Tell Pop how your old man knocks you around or maybe how your sister's such a slut, then he'll give you fries. But if you let him whine, you know, about his old lady and all, he'll give you a Deluxe Burger and pie à la mode."

"Get out!" Lorne shouted, his anger blazing in his eyes.

"What's the matter, Pop?" Jimmy asked. "Trouble at home?"

"Out! Right now!"

"I know a terrific counsellor. I'll bring my sis and you bring Genie. It'll be like a double date."

Lorne came from behind the counter, his hands balled into fists. Jimmy swaggered past him, kicked away a chair and slammed out the door. The others edged past Lorne to join Jimmy on the street. Spectators. Celebrants.

"You're barred. All three of you!" Lorne locked the door behind them. They jeered through the window, drummed on the door, while Lorne stared past them at concrete, at brick. They flung out their repertoire of curses and kicked the door with the pleasure of their daring. Finally they strutted down Main Street, all in a glorious roar. Lorne kept staring off as the sky turned to stainless steel.

It took a dozen hard heartbeats before Lorne felt the sharp throb in his hand. He looked down. His fingers, clenching the blade of his paring knife, were dripping blood.

"Damn! God damn!" He rushed past the boy staring from the pinball and shut himself in the back room. He ran cold water over the cut, which wasn't deep though it was messy, and he dabbed it dry with towels. He applied a bandage but it wouldn't grip his greasy skin so he tried washing the cut with soap, then detergent. Finally, he reached behind the gallon jars of mayonnaise and mustard for a dark green bottle of Scotch whisky. He poured the whisky over the cut and pressed down with a dish towel.

He watched the cotton blossom with his blood as he took his first deep drink. On the second drink, a warmth rose through his chest. The third shot was slow and he stayed with it until the room became solid and still. He imagined camera lenses, not clicking shut but opening one after another inside his brain.

When the phone out front began to ring, merging with the noise of pinball, he knew it was Genie. The ringing jangled through him. The twelfth ring was the last but the jangling continued. "No more grease," he said peering into the bottle. "This time I'm getting out clean."

He wrapped the cut with his handkerchief. He changed into his good set of clothes that he kept covered in dry-cleaner's plastic and dropped his soiled shirt and pants on the floor. Covering them with the bloody towel, he allowed himself a pale joke about the tragically departed.

First the cash register, he told himself. Concentrate.

He passed the kid still playing the machine.

"We're shutting down," Lorne said.

The kid glanced up uneasily. "What?"

The cash drawer sprang open; Lorne sorted the bills, queen's head up and to the right, in ones, twos, fives, tens and three twenties stacked and bound at each end with a rubber band. He slipped the pile into a Royal Bank deposit bag. "We're shut," he said. "We're out of service."

He turned the Open sign to Closed. Turned off the grill, the coffee-maker, exhaust fan, air-conditioner, illuminated displays, fluorescent lights, cigarette machine, jukebox, pinball.

"Hey, I'm playing that!" The kid cried out. "And you lost my replay."

Lorne stuffed a two-dollar bill into the kid's empty Coke glass. "Here, you just got lucky. Go play the dryers at the laundromat."

The kid pulled out the bill. "How come you're closing in the afternoon?"

Lorne drew the plastic curtains. He lowered the blind behind the door. "There's a death in the family. Pop just popped off in the back room."

Lorne was right behind the kid as he left. He was about to lock the door from the outside when he heard the muffled cry of the telephone. He waited fifteen rings before it stopped, turned the key and walked towards his car. He smiled at a candy wrapper that was sailing the pavement on a dusty wind.

TRAFFIC WAS A TOOTHLESS ROAR beyond the rolled-up windows. Lorne Nojuk was making good time, darting through the gaps, shrugging off the horns. When the bank clerk had asked why he was cashing half the account into travellers' checks, Lorne had smiled until the clerk became flustered and counted out the checks. It was that same thin smile he offered the store signs and billboards.

He tuned to one radio station after another but all the songs seemed to cry for something he no longer cared to recognize. He spun the dial across the band, amused by the shriek and sputter of voices, then switched it off and listened to the car.

This was something he used to do when he had first bought the car. It almost like a meditation, mentally tracing the components of one system and then another: electrical, fuel, exhaust, cooling, but most of all the power train with its engine – a Mercury V8 368, each separate piece joined by logic into a harmony of movement. He tried to recall the touch and shapes – he'd once dismantled an old Ford with his brother. When they'd reassembled it, a half-dozen pieces were left out, yet the car seemed to run just as well without them. That miracle of compensation had shaped Lorne's faith in the mechanical world – a faith he was never able to extend into the world of humans whose missing parts were not so easily overlooked.

LORNE RECOGNIZED RITA'S HAND draped over the edge of the third-floor balcony, swinging limply to a song on her hi-fi stereo. The words drifted overhead as he came up the apartment walk. They echoed in the stairwell.

Near the village, the peaceful village, the lion sleeps tonight
Near the village, the quiet village, the lion sleeps tonight.
Hush, my darling, don't fear my darling, the lion sleeps tonight.

He climbed swiftly, focussing on the steps, the railing, the pattern of the cinderblock wall. Only the open door made him hesitate.

She doesn't give a damn, he thought.

He set the door ajar so the draught would catch it and he moved silently to the balcony where she lay sunning on her stomach, swaying slightly side to side to the throbbing of the speakers. The sweet musk of coconut oil rose from her body on the breeze. The breeze swelled. The front door slammed.

"What?" Rita startled up to her knees to see Lorne standing above her. "Pop! . . . I mean, Lorne. God, what are you doing here?"

"Better keep the door locked, Rita. I could have been anybody." He lowered the volume on her stereo.

"Well, maybe you are just anybody." Seeing the hurt on his face, she laughed it off and rose for her mickey of dark Bacardi rum. "Who's watching the cafe?"

"I had to see you, Rita."

"I'm working the supper shift," she said. "You can see me then."

"I want to see you now."

"We *get off* at midnight, Lorne. That's the *policy,* isn't it?" She rested on her arm. "What's the problem? Is Horney Lorney getting too hot behind the grill?" Rita rose chuckling. She leaned against his chest, her fingers playing at his collar, her lips at his neck and throat. But before he could respond, she withdrew, slipping into her kimono, letting it trail open as she searched the living-room for a cigarette. "Lorne, now that we're lovers, I'm spending twice as much on smokes and half as much on food. So what do you figure, boss? Am I coming out ahead or what?"

He studied her face, as he did so often when she began like this – simple features that now, past thirty, might have settled into a vacancy except that she exercised her face constantly, training it with expression. It was the same with her voice. Rita tried on characters like odd hats, masking the frailty of her voice with exaggerated accents and wild words. She kept working everything, including what she had with Lorne – "articulation" was what she called it – keeping on the move, her borders constantly shifting, pushing him away, only to pull him closer somewhere else, but never too close. All the while, Lorne knew that she was camouflaging that part of herself that powered all the rest – her ravenous need, though for what he didn't know. Just as he didn't know what drew him to her – her courage or her fear, or the way the two came together in some mysterious mechanics of the spirit. Certainly, he was drawn to her spontaneity – she seemed so free that Lorne felt it like an ache.

Rita dragged on her cigarette, avoiding his gaze by

distracting herself in a mirror. He understood that this, too, was a performance, self-conscious and ironic. She drawled in the pose of a jaded vamp, a character she mocked so often that it had become a permanent part of who she was. "Jesus, Lorne. Now it's afternoon kicks, huh? You're a real late bloomer."

"I've come for you because you're the best thing that I've got."

"Got? I didn't sign any contract. All you *got* is me slinging dishes, forty hours a week with weekends off."

"You know what I mean, Rita."

"Maybe I do but do you know what you mean? You're very strange, Mr. Pop. Mr. Boss Nojuk. You're a stranger getting stranger."

"You've known me for two years."

"Oh sure, working lunch and supper, slinging burgers right beside you. And all that time you didn't say squeak. I figured, how many five-star knockouts is this guy going to meet? I was checking the bathroom walls to see if I was listed for a social disease – not that it would stop all those others from sniffing around. Then, four days after my uncle dies, you grab me like I said some sort of code word . . . Jesus, of all the times for you to get the hots. I was like a dishrag . . ."

Lorne let her talk, waiting for her own words to entangle her. Her hands darted like trapped birds, reaching for a drink, butting her half-smoked cigarette, piling up magazines, stacking records on the stereo. There was still no way to reach her through all her subterfuge.

"Or maybe you like your women in black crêpe?" she asked. "No? You sure? Because I can fix up a wicked little waitress outfit, a midnight special with a black veil and panties, and just a dash of eau de French fries." She slipped into the pose of the dumb blonde, a record poised in one hand like a cocktail platter. "I just want to know what to expect, that's all! I mean, gosh golly gee, Mr. Hefner, I really appreciate all you're doing for me! First you hire me as a Playboy bunny serving tables twelve to twenty-four. Now you're giving me free photo sessions." She bent her knees together, lifting her hands in mock astonishment, the platter raised to just below his chin. "You sure know how to take care of a girl!" She paused – the hesitancy he was waiting for.

Lorne took her by the arm and drew her close. She was about to rally with some clever phrase, but he ran his hand along her shoulders, probing, soothing her tension. He kissed her throat. Her voice weakened into a murmur of refusal and they sank together onto the cushions on the floor.

Lorne touched her slowly, exploring, whispering along her breasts and thighs, seeking points of pleasure, vulnerability. Her nipples hardening, she scratched lightly at his chest. He tried to hold his distance, to observe, to manipulate their passion. Instead he was aroused, and as always, driven to confusion by her shifting gestures of refusal and enticement.

A sudden desperation and all strategies collapsed. His lovemaking blurred into something between a hunger and a hurt. Lorne bit at her, bit himself, losing the boundaries of flesh as she cried out, held and directed him. Finally, at her call, he burst heavily within her. Yet Rita kept coming, releasing as he was already tightening back into himself. She shook raggedly, and again with weakening cries that left him feeling even more distant than before, empty and envious.

She pulled the scattered pillows to make a nest around them, dragged a Mexican blanket off the couch for a covering. "Lorne, sometimes you scare me," she said.

"Why?"

"Because you're always looking and listening." She curled inside his arms, her head upon his chest. "You get me feeling so wild – I don't know if I'm animal, vegetable or mineral. But all the while, you're holding yourself back, you're not showing anything at all."

"I'm going away."

"That's the trouble, Lorne. You're always off somewhere in your head."

"I mean I'm leaving town."

She bolted up. "Oh yah vold, herr general! You go and I vill guard ze bunker."

"I'm not kidding. This time I'm really going." He stared into her eyes, trying to summon that part of her that would take him seriously. "And I want you to come with me."

"Where?" For an instant her lip trembled.

"Anywhere you want that's far from here," he told her. "You're always talking about places. Name one and we're there."

She grinned, locking her arms and legs around him. "You vill stay here, mein prisoner. You von't escape! I have zee machine guns in every tower! You vill make love mit me forever!" She tightened her grip as he tried to rise. When he broke away she sprang up after him.

She circled as he pulled on his pants, sauntering in a parody of a cowboy. "This here bed is big enough for two of us, partner. But it's way too big for just one of us."

"Don't do this, Rita. It's not funny."

He could sense her losing the character, becoming grotesque. The fear was winning. "And if you try to hightail it," she ranted, "I'm going to get you. I'll jump right off this here balcony, partner. Splat onto your car. You'll be scraping me off all summer! Or maybe I'll corral myself inside your cafe and make myself a barbecue, and I mean myself. You want to hear a cowgirl's torch song all soaked in gasoline? . . . I'll . . . Lorne? Where are you going?"

He was grabbing the rest of his clothes, dizzy, breathless.

"For Christ's sake, Lorne, will you say something!"

"Forget it. It's a stupid idea. Stupid." A sock was missing. He left without it.

"We can't just skip town. What about your wife? Oh, God! Lorne, is that why you're upset . . . when I said that thing about jumping . . ."

"Figure it out, Rita. We're not leaving. I'm leaving." He headed to the door, his shirt clenched in his fist.

"Just cool it, Lorne. I didn't ask for this crap."

"You think I did?"

Waiting on the balcony as he got to his car, she shouted down, "What about work? Should I go in or not?"

LORNE NOJUK SAT PARKED outside his house for ten minutes before he turned off the ignition. The engine ran on, shaking the car until it sputtered out. Lorne frowned, cleaning the glass of the mileage gauge. He still believed his car, a Mercury Turnpike Cruiser, to be in top condition. The engine just needs a clean-out on the highway, he told himself. And so do I.

He waited another five minutes, still holding the steering wheel, his mind an open road. It had become his habit to stay in the car for measured periods, postponing going home, letting the silence fill the car's compartment like a sealed tank. He ran his hand across the dash, a display of his fetish for gauges and accessories. He tapped the clock and set it once again. Finally he unlocked the glove compartment filled with road maps he had never used. "This time," he said, savouring the words, as if to draw out some rich pleasure.

A high choking yelp broke through. It was Shadrack, his black hound tied in the front yard, calling out to him. Lorne hated Shadrack's barking as it if came from the house itself, demanding his attention: the rotting steps, the cracked window, the attic infested with a horde of pigeons, the blue paint job he had started four years ago that rose almost to the peeling gables, then stopped unexpectedly like a high watermark.

"What're you barking about?" Lorne scolded. "You got more bad news?" Shadrack yowled at his approach, straining at the chain. "Sit!" Lorne's tone pressed Shadrack to obey. "Roll over! Now crawl!" The dog moved through each command, eyes steady on his master. "Good." Released by the word, he leapt at his master's face, licking, groaning in low tormented vowels.

"Hush." As Lorne settled the dog, he surveyed the house for movement. He decided that once he was on the highway he would phone. Not Genie but her brother or the doctor. He'd explain, he told himself; he wouldn't make excuses, or ask for understanding, he'd just communicate the facts.

First, he must move quickly. He entered the house, braced for her surprise. There'd be questions, then tears or accusations. If she tried to block him? He would not let that happen.

He stormed through the hall to the back storage room. He found his suitcase under a pile of discarded clothes, laced with mildew. He slapped it clean and hauled it to the living-room, where he threw in his old engineering textbooks and a few favourite records. In the bathroom, he fixed on the order of packing: toiletries, towel, face cloth, toothbrush, toothpaste, razor, shaving cream.

Don't sort, he warned himself. You'll have time later.

Her pills were on the edge of the sink – two less than in the morning.

It means nothing, he thought. She could've flushed them. She could be hoarding them.

The house was heavy with her silence. And dim. The dying light seeped through the blind, drawing a faintness from the walls. The bedroom was so dark, the air so stale, he hesitated at the door. "Genie, are you in there?" The bed was empty, the blanket a twisted pile on the mattress. A glass lay broken on the floor at the end of the bed.

Lorne found her on the floor on the far side of the bed, a sheet wound around her body, revealing only her legs and her long hair spreading like an auburn stain.

"God! Genie, you didn't!" He crouched, sensing her as someone floating beneath him in a void, eyes marble white, mouthing an icy wind. He kept calling until her body spiralled up towards him.

"Lorne . . ." Her voice was thick, remote. "Lorne, I tried."

"Did you take something, Genie?" He steadied himself against the dresser.

"No." She was groggy. For a moment she tried to loosen the ravelled bedsheet, then gave up. She leaned against him for a long minute before her breathing deepened. "I wanted . . . to change things, that's all. But I couldn't."

"Have you hurt yourself?" He felt distant anger gathering in his chest.

"Nothing like that," she said. "I promised you, Lorne. I thought about it. But . . ."

"Get up. You shouldn't be on the floor."

"I've got no right to be like this," she mumbled. Her hand wavered toward the edge of the bed as he lifted her onto it. "I was going to change things, Lorne. To make a dinner, like before. Fish . . . I'd bake fresh salmon. We'd have artichoke hearts and wine . . . and tarts like the ones your sister sends. It was me who showed her how to make them . . . remember? That was before this . . ." She searched the hollow of her hands. "And I'd go to the Farmer's Market and the Ballerina Florists for carnations. I'd use the lace tablecloth from our anniversary. It's on the top shelf there, still in its wrapping paper."

"None of that's important." Lorne held her as she traced the dryness of her lips, the fawn mist of her eyebrows.

"It is important," she said. "That's why I can't do it. I kept thinking but not getting up. Then I remembered that I can't have wine with the medication. I'd planned for days and I still forgot that I can't have wine."

"Genie, you're making it worse. You should only think about what you can do."

"Doctor Reimer tells you to say that. But what if the stores won't let me cash a cheque? Or if Mrs. Slawik's out in her yard and starts asking questions? Or Mr. Werner? I went out for the mail and he was walking by. He looked at me so sadly, like he knew everything. Oh God!"

"You can't . . . let people scare you." He stared into the closet, telling himself, grab some shirts, pants. Throw them in the suitcase. If she follows you to the car, she'll be barefoot. Lock the door, turn the ignition, shift into drive. It'll only take two minutes, maybe three.

She faced the wall. "People don't frighten me, Lorne. I look out at them on the street – they must feel this, too. But they remember how to keep moving and talking. If it gets too quiet, they just talk more, and if things feel too slow, they get busier. They know how to cover it up or push it away. It's only me – I don't know how to do that anymore."

As she kept talking, staring at the wall, Lorne rose to pocket his tie clip from the dresser, to place his housekey and wedding ring in her jewellery box. He gathered a pile of socks and underwear with caution but she stayed a shadow by the bed, a voice seeping into fading light.

"I tell myself, 'Act busy, talk to people. The words don't matter, just use them to keep going.' But the spaces between the words get bigger . . . harder to fill. And so do the spaces between me and them. Spaces between everything. So everybody's separate and there's nothing to even touch . . ."

Lorne grabbed her by shoulders. He pushed her backwards on the bed and yelled down at her, "Stop it, Genie! . . . I can't hold the world together for you." He felt like he could strike her but she was so limp, lying there on the bed.

She rolled her head to face him, exposing the thin blue veins along her throat. "Help me end it," she whispered. "You want to, you know you do."

"Don't ask me that. You promised."

"You can do whatever you want – I can't do anything."

"Please don't, Genie."

"Then you have to hold me."

Lorne felt himself collapse in stages, first his face, his shoulders, then he sank beside her. She clasped her arms and legs around him.

So tired, he thought. It's like I've always been this tired.

The barking began in short bursts, gradually stretching into howls as they lay motionless. Finally, Genie spoke. "That dog isn't going to stop. Sometimes I think he's going to kill himself on his chain, the way he fights it. I want to let him loose, but I'm afraid he won't come back. He could run and never stop and kill himself that way, too."

Lorne hardly heard his own reply. "He might get lost. Or maybe run for a couple blocks and come right back, afraid to leave his chain. It's easy for a dog to act brave when he's all tied up." He rose from the bed. "I have to make supper and you have to get dressed. In half an hour it'll be time for your next pill."

Genie stared at the closet until Lorne picked out a housedress. He collected the pieces of broken glass, cradling them in his hands as he carried them to the kitchen garbage.

He took the suitcase into the back room. He was piling the old clothes over it when Shadrack began to bay.

Lorne found the dog at the end of his chain straining to reach a boy about ten years old who was backed against the fence. Someone hooted from across the street; the shadow of a boy crouched with two others behind a truck. Lorne thought of Jimmy and his pals, but these were younger kids, still awkward in their wildness.

"Did those guys chase you in here?" Lorne startled the boy.

"I . . . I'm not scared," he answered with a quaver in his voice.

"Shadrack won't hurt you. He's a good dog." Lorne slipped the chain from the stake and guided the dog to the boy, who was almost featureless in the dark but familiar, like the paperboy or some neighbour's kid. He could be any boy at all, Lorne thought, remembering how he'd once stumbled on his old kindergarten class photo and had shown it to Genie. She'd stared at it unable to guess which face was his.

Shadrack licked the boy's fingers and lay down, stretching on his side, scraping the ground with his paws. All the while the boy stared up at Lorne.

"He wants you to pet him," Lorne said. "Go on. He won't bite."

The boy scratched under the dog's ear. "I know Shadrack. Poor old fellah."

"Then what are you scared of?" Lorne asked. "Come on, you can tell me."

The kids across the street hollered, "Run! Run! While you can!" The boy's face went slack, looking at something over Lorne's shoulder.

Lorne looked back. It was Genie the boy was seeing. She was in the window, worn, haggard, her fingers fretting at a lace curtain as she retreated into the darkness. The curtains closed in front of her.

"Too late. Too late," the others chanted from the impossible distance of the street as Lorne reached out to comfort the boy. "You're cursed!" they taunted and shook their fists.

"Let go, damn you!" the boy cried out. He struck away Lorne's hand and stumbled through the gate, shrieking wild words as he ran down the street.

Shadrack broke into a wild halloo, trying to follow. Lorne held him back with both hands on the chain, but was lurched forward with every lunge. The rusty chain tore at his cut. His hand became warm and slippery. Like grease, Lorne thought. Still, he did not let go or tie Shadrack to the stake. The pain seemed to him to be such a clear, simple sensation; something he could focus on, letting everything else flow through.

Even when the voices trailed away, the dog still barked and struggled, though no longer after boys or cars or strange movements in the dark. Lorne held on, though he yearned for Shadrack to break free, imagining the dog leaping across great stretches of grey earth. Shadrack was very strong and would not stop and Lorne's hand, his arm and shoulder had become a full deep ache.

DEAF MESSENGER

RITA, STILL IN HER KIMONO, WAS TOSSING CUSHIONS ONTO THE couch when my parents and I peered through her open door. "You're such a scandal!" my mother sang out, delighted. Although it was after school and after work for us, it looked like Rita's day was just beginning. We ignored the fact that she worked an evening shift at Mr. Nojuk's cafe. Our Rita wasn't bound to the dreary world that held us in. Our Rita was a scandal.

"We won't stay long," my mother chirped. "I know you've got a thousand things to do, but I had to see your new apartment."

"You're just in time for the five o'clock tour," Rita quipped. "And the five o'clock drink. Mine's a double 'cause I'm taking the night off."

I wanted to say, "Rita, you promised me I'd always be your Darling Danny but you never even visit." To say, "Now that you've switched from working at lunchtime, I don't ever get to see you." She'd answer, "I'm sorry, Danny. Jeez, I've missed you. Let's go on that date!"

But I pouted in the doorway with all the resentment an

eleven-year-old could muster until my mother pulled me inside with her. She was dazzled, especially by Rita's white vinyl couch. It was so frivolous, so daringly impractical – oversized, overpadded. Overpriced as well, according to my father. Rita had bought it from a short, stocky man in a cowboy hat, famous for hollering "Come on down!" Texas-style on television.

"Ooh, Rita, it's so . . . splendid!" My mother cooed, running her hands along the vinyl, admiring the modern contours. "I can just see you lounging with champagne. Oh, look! You've even got a matching love-seat."

"Love-seat?" my father laughed. "That little thing?"

"Rita, the colour goes perfectly with those drapes. And you've got a balcony. That's so classy!"

My dad lifted the love-seat at one end. "There's hardly anything to it. Hey Rita," he smirked, "do you think it'll take the wear and tear?"

I thought of Rita dancing on the love-seat all alone, with the moonlight flooding in.

"Hey! You said you'd call me to help you with the move." My father looked wounded, his large hands open and empty at his sides. "You didn't pay somebody, did you?"

Rita tightened her silk sash, its Chinese letters knotting into one another. "Murray, you just don't get it. I wanted to be moved by my birthday, not by Christ's birthday."

"Aw, come on, Rita!" he said. "I wouldn't have stood you up."

"It didn't matter. There was hardly anything left to haul. Moving it was easier than setting it on fire." Rita swept off to the galley kitchen. "Come on, Danny, let's stuff our faces till we're sick!"

But her fridge was a wasteland – a half-empty Coca Cola, leftover cartons of Chinese takeout, three Black Label beer, a tonic water, and a crusted catsup bottle without a cap. She threw open every cupboard. "Jeez, Danny, I guess we'll have to cook the cat. Oh wait, here's something." She rummaged through a cardboard box still packed with dishes and drew out a tin of candies.

"Is today really your birthday?" I asked her.

"Why not?" Rita answered, watching my father edging into the kitchen.

"Ask Rita how old she is," my father nudged. "I bet she's almost as old as your mom."

Rita winked to me. "Never tell anyone your age, Danny, because numbers lie. Your real age is how young you feel. Isn't that right, Murray?" My father nodded expansively. "And how you feel depends on three things," she added, "who you work for and who you sleep with and never getting those two mixed up!" She wagged her finger at him. "Of course, I always get things mixed up. 'Cause I'm one mixed-up tamale. Olé!" She rattled the candies past him like a tambourine. The crimson dragon on her robe shimmered after her into the living-room. My father's face darkened as he poured himself a beer.

I scrambled to join Rita on her couch and pried open the candy tin.

"Grab a handful, Danny," she said. "Go on, be a greedy guts!" These were her Aunt Beatrice's Christmas candies, the ones her aunt picked over every evening, taking one and only one just like medication.

"Rita, the boy's cramming them in like a squirrel!" my mother called in mock complaint as she stood in the sunlight of the balcony. "Your Aunt Beatrice would take a fit."

"Beatrice was straight as a rod, all right," said Rita. "And she could swing one, too. It was the only thing she never seemed to spare me."

It felt strange to think that Beatrice's candy tin could have outlasted her – she'd died in March just three months ago and Alec so soon afterwards. Whenever we'd visited, Beatrice brought out that same round tin, raised it over my head and had me recite her catechism on hard candy:

I take one and only one
Hard candy every day
So my candies last till Christmas
When a new tin comes my way.

"Beatrice sure loved her sweets," my father said, joining us on the couch. "Though she'd never own up to it."

"And her pies!" my mother added. "I begged her to show me how she made them. But no, 'I'll never tell,' she'd say. 'If I give away my secrets, I'll lose my visitors.' Rita, I hope you saved her box of recipes."

Rita was heading back to the kitchen. "Seems like I'm out of everything but good looks and bad luck. How about that drink?"

"How about that tour?" my mother asked, all the weariness of her day dispelled, charmed away by Rita. It was like this whenever she was with her. The next day my mother would shop for some perfume that Rita had been wearing or for Rita's latest favourite record, though my mother never played it more than once or twice. She said the songs never sounded half as good at home.

"Give us the tour, Rita," my mother called, peering down the hall. "I've been dying to see how the other half lives."

"Half what? Half dead? Half crazy?" Rita actually sneered, not in a joke or jibe. She bared her teeth and my heart jumped. Had we damaged something? Insulted her?

Yet my mother kept smiling, my father grinning, stretching his arms along the couch. Two more heartbeats. Rita laughed back into herself again. "Okay. Come on. Let's get this show on the road!" And she trooped us through the apartment.

There was only the pantry, the bathroom, and then her bedroom. I peeked between my parents, too shy for more than a glance. The window was heavily draped so the only light was a red lava lamp on a blond veneered night table. On the other side was an Oriental screen and a mirrored vanity. Between them was the bed – satin with a matching upholstered headboard that fanned behind it so the whole thing looked like a nightclub stage. Everything was new – there was nothing of her aunt and uncle's.

"I wanted a clean sweep," she said. "When I moved out, I sent everything to auction. All that heavy oak and clutter – I couldn't breathe!" She poked another cigarette between her lips and snapped her Ronson lighter. Smoke wafted over the furniture like incense. "I bought this all in one shot – a package deal. The day the house gets sold, I'm getting a lipstick-red '62 Corvette convertible and I'm driving south till the money's gone."

My parents nodded with surprise. They wanted to know when and how and how much but I could only stare, wanting Rita to wink and grin, to say that this was just another of her jokes. How could she take everything that belonged to Beatrice and Alec and trade it all away? It was as if she were becoming some kind of Bizarro Woman from the comic books, a monstrous distortion of the Rita that I'd always known.

When she was alone, fixing martinis in the kitchen, I tried to talk to her again. She made herself so busy with her drinks and cigarette and moving things around that even when she finally paused, to press an ice-cube to her temple, all I could do was ask her silly questions. "How'd you get the day off, Rita? Did you make some excuse to Mr. Nojuk? Are you going to a party?" She shook her head as if holding back some wild laugh. "You know, Rita," I kept on, "I went past the cafe and it was all closed up. I bet Mr. Nojuk figured that he just can't get by without you. What you think?"

"Nothing. I don't think nothing, okay?" She waved me away, fumbling with the bottle. Gin spilled on the checkered tiles.

By the time I fetched a rag she was down on her knees soaking up the spill with newspaper from a packing box. I touched her shoulder. "That's no good. Wipe it up with this."

"Let go, damn you!" she yelled.

I stumbled back, horrified. Rita had sworn at me.

She stayed on her knees in front of me with her head down and her hair cloaking her face, making me afraid that she'd spring up to swear again. But her shoulders slumped and she breathed out, "Look, just give me some time alone."

I retreated to the balcony and gripped the railing. My eyes were throbbing as I frowned at the traffic down below. I used my mind to steer cars onto side streets, to make them turn or brake, to snarl them in a jam. I blamed this strange apartment for making Rita act this way. I wanted her back in the old house or back serving lunches at the cafe where she'd always save me my favourite seat and bend to whisper jokes and silly gossip in my ear.

My parents' voices pulled at me.

"Murray, tell Danny not to lean against that rail. What's gotten into you, Danny?"

"Deborah, the boy needs air. Rita's smoking that Yankee mule crap again."

"I'm only smoking one at a time, out of respect for present company," Rita joked, pretending to be herself again. "But you know me, where there's fire, there's always smoke."

"Let me try one, Rita," my mother murmured. "I bet they're not so bad."

I didn't want to hear them anymore, not now that I could see that they were showing off, teasing, hiding who they really were. I concentrated on the hollow roar of traffic so that all their words broke into empty syllables.

Above us, in the clouds, a clownish face was tumbling off an erupting thunderhead. I thought of Aaron, the deaf messenger – he wouldn't be bothered by what anybody said. Mr. Werner had told me stories about Aaron, the poor rabbinical student in his Old Country village so many years ago. Aaron made his living by reading letters for the illiterate peasants. He always covered his ears as he read the words out loud so he would not violate the privacy of the message. Mr. Werner thought this showed that Aaron was the most humble, pious person he'd ever known. This had made so little sense to me that I'd snickered, wondering who was dumber, the peasants or Aaron or Mr. Werner. For Rita always said, "If you can't tell who the dumb one is, then probably it's you."

Yet there I was on that balcony, as Rita and my parents talked on, wishing for Aaron's mindlessness, for his art of understanding nothing.

"HE'D KEEP SAYING I wasn't respectable. Well, maybe I didn't want to be. How about that? Maybe I didn't respect being respectable." Rita was on her third drink of the evening.

"Your uncle was just concerned for you, that's all," my father answered. "He was cut from the old cloth and so was your Aunt Beatrice. I sure miss the fun we had."

"Fun?" Rita snorted. "A couple of sofa polkas, some tea and sweets, then off to bed. Not me!"

"Those two lived for one another," my mother said. "Didn't they, Murray?" She moved closer to my father on the vinyl seat. "They'd tease and complain, but when all was said and done, they were just a couple of old-fashioned love birds."

Rita settled awkwardly on the red leather hassock by the hi-fi. "I couldn't keep him going after Beatrice died," she said with a slur that came from gin and weariness and maybe something more. "He wouldn't even let me call the doctor, he'd just say, 'Life's not worth the price of the fare without my Beatrice.' And if I'd argue, he'd shout one thing or another that Beatrice used to use on me – like he was being both him and her together."

"They knew each other better than they knew themselves," my father expounded. He leaned back on the vinyl love-seat, preferring firm support while he was being philosophical. "Well, you know, a person gets changed, living all those years with someone else. You even start to look alike."

"No matter what I did or said, it was all no good," Rita went on.

"Now don't you start feeling bad about yourself," my mother cautioned, coming over to stand by her. Her hand hesitated, trying to find some spot to comfort. "You're still in a period of adjustment – after all, poor Alec only left a couple months ago."

"I guess I've just got bad luck with guys." Rita laughed. She was mistress of the rueful laugh.

My mother took this as a cue for perkiness. "Well, how about a cup of tea? Now don't tell me, let me guess. Where do you keep it?"

Rita's mouth pursed, "Oh sure. All I need is another cup of Beatrice's Red Rose orange pekoe! That'll make everything dandy! Well, I'll pick my own poison, thank you!" She was back on her feet first to the bottle, then to the hi-fi, slipping the dust cover off a 45. "Murray, let's get this wake awake. I'll spin a record and you spin me!" She kicked the rug against the wall and turned up Elvis Presley's "Jailhouse Rock."

The band was jumping and they began to swing
You should have heard those knocked out jail birds sing
Let's rock. Let's rock.

I stared into a vacant corner. I was remembering Alec and Beatrice, dead and buried. Alec's accordion lay dusty in my mind beside their empty fireplace, Beatrice's tea caddy, her silver set and bric-à-brac. All lost with them. It seemed impossible that Alec and Beatrice could be so completely gone, that their bodies could be rotting even as we spoke their names. I tried to bring them back through memories, to relive every moment that we'd shared, but I could only recall a half-dozen broken scenes.

Yet Rita seemed eager to be rid of them, as if she were trying to drive them off with the very songs they hated. I watched her record spin, her needle cutting along the grooves, but I wouldn't listen to her song. I hummed furtively over it, trying to unwind her music with their favourite tune, "Greensleeves," the tune that Alec played on his accordion while Beatrice served her bitter tea in flowery china cups. I could almost see them in their parlour, I whispered out their names, "Beatrice McKay! Alec McKay!"

Nothing happened. Or rather, something unexpected happened. A cuckoo clock began to call out the hour. Alec's clock. No one else noticed. So as they danced I followed the calls to Rita's bedroom. I knew I wasn't allowed in there alone but the bird seemed to promise some woody scent of Alec's pipe, a taste of Beatrice's bittersweet pies, as if inside the clock

I'd find a chamber on the other side of time where Alec still played his accordion and Beatrice sang along.

I eased the bedroom door shut behind me. The cuckoo ceased as I entered and I couldn't see it. I waited, thinking of how Alec would rap the table to make a point or how Beatrice's rocker creaked fast time when she grew impatient with his speeches.

I heard it – a hard heart ticking from the closet. The clock was inside, askew on a hook, its weights and chains strung over a wrinkled negligée.

I thought of Alec's pet theory that twenty minutes to and twenty past each hour are the lulling times when minds and spirits have to rest. "But what happens at the top of the hour?" I would ask. A howl of laughter rose from the living-room. What happens now?

I lowered my eyes and recognized the carpet at my feet – another remnant of them. Beatrice's India carpet – a flowering maze in auburn, wine and green that I used to play on when I was smaller, crawling under their dining-room table, tracing each pale green path to the gold star at the centre.

Rita's new bed was covering the star – a bed of pleated satin glowing crimson under the lamplight. I'd seen this kind of bed in the movies; I understood that it was for kissing and touching, for unmarried men and women to wrestle and press together as if trying to force something from each other. I wondered, did a bed like this make them strong or weak?

The bedcovers weren't made up and I could still read the impression left by Rita's body shaped in waves of satin, more disturbing than her lipstick on a glass. I wanted to lie in the hollow where she'd slept, to fill the ghostly moulding of her body and know her heat, her smell, to dream in the residue of her dreams. It wasn't really Alec or Beatrice whom I'd wanted, it was Rita, and I must have known it all along.

She grinned at me from a dozen photos on the wall: Rita in a nightclub booth at New Year's crammed with a dozen other celebrants, their party horns and blowers unravelling long paper tongues. Rita at a race-track wicket with two soldiers

tossing betting stubs like confetti. In one picture outside a
fortune teller's tent she was pointing at her outstretched palm,
pretending to faint into a clutch of friends. Always joking.
Always in a crowd.

Everything spoke of Rita: her cones of Hindu incense, the
brandy snifter full of matchbooks, a gutted scarlet candle, an
embroidered handkerchief, a pair of velvet gloves that
blossomed from a shimmering evening bag.

It was her mirrored vanity that drew me to its shrine of
perfume bottles. I fingered a flat bottle bound in pressed
leather that showed a relief of a dying bull and a matador half
hidden by his cape. The matador's sword was thrust into the
animal's fleshy throat as the bull's horn curved up towards his
heart. I unscrewed the bottle cap. It smelled of rum.

A strand of beads led me to her drawers stuffed with
scented soaps, nylons, and black lacy straps and twists. I felt I
was coming closer to her, excited by her private things.

"Why you little devil!" Rita at the door startled me. I turned
so as not to face her and glimpsed my reflection in the mirror.
That reflection couldn't be me, I thought, not Danny – that had
to be someone else in there – someone horrible, lurking with
his hands inside her drawer.

"God, they're starting young!" she huffed, as if gloating
over her own outrage. "I've got you boys coming and going,
don't I? Well, don't I?"

"Danny, shame on you!" my mother scolded.

"He didn't mean anything," my father said. "You know how
boys are." He was standing beside my mother, both of them
hesitating at the threshold, respecting the privacy that I had
violated.

Rita jeered, "You bet I know how boys are! Let down my
guard and they creep into my underwear!"

I was weak, wanting to escape through the mirror, under
the bed, to be an insect crawling into a crack.

"Danny," my mother said, sounding crushed herself. "Tell
Rita that you're sorry."

My mouth opened, but I couldn't speak. Rita began pulling

things out of the drawer, her teeth clenched in a smirk. "You like to feel them, Danny? Which ones? The stockings? The panties? Not the slinky stuff, oh no! You'll need a note from Daddy for that." She went rummaging in the closet as the music blared from the living-room and those other two, no longer my parents, kept their place as witnesses. The mirror was empty. Whoever I'd glimpsed in it was gone, leaving me alone, a pathetic boy, to take the blame instead of him.

She drew out a man's suit. "How about this? If you want to be the big man, you'll have to wear his clothes."

She prodded me into the jacket. I was numb and wooden, my arms jerking into the sleeves.

"Rita. A joke's a joke!" My father sounded miles away.

"I thought you liked jokes, Murray. I had another 'joker' who kept a change of clothes in here – a real quick-change artist. Make a joke out of that, Murray."

"Don't start on me, Rita."

"Not on your life, I'm starting younger," she snapped back. "Danny's my new dancing partner! Come on, one, two, three!" She sang out the lines to "Lady of Spain," gripping my wrist and side, jostling me around the floor. My face was pushed against her breast, and her smells of smoke and perfumed gin. " 'Lady of Spain I adore you, / Right from the night I first saw you . . .' "

"Rita!" My father's voice was firm. "You're scaring him!" His broad hands moved me away. "Danny, say you're sorry. Then we'll leave."

I nodded dumbly. It was over. Rita wavered, then slumped onto the bed, her hands hiding her face as my mother rushed to her side. "The guy dumped me, Deborah," she said. "Just before you came. Big Boss Nojuk! Mister Short Order! Why do I always fall for the bastards? He'd come when he wanted and take what he wanted like I was his goddamned slave!"

My mother drew the handkerchief from Rita's evening bag. "Dear," she whispered, "do you want to be alone?"

She clutched my mother's hand. "You know what he said once? He said, 'You just go after guys who you can't have but as soon as it gets real you fold right up.' " Rita struck the pillow. "Damn him! I'm too honest, that's my problem. I gave him stuff to use against me."

My mother signalled us out.

"Don't go, not yet." Rita forced herself to smile at me, but the mascara made teary bruises under her eyes. "Danny, I'm sorry. I don't mean to be like this. How about we forget it happened?"

"Okay," I mumbled.

"It's not because of you. I'm just having trouble with one of your big brothers."

"I don't have brothers."

"They're all your brothers, Danny. Every one of them with an itch in his pants. You'll be itching, too, sooner than you think."

I lowered my head in confusion.

"Oh God, what am I saying? Look, we're still pals. How about it?"

My father's hand guided me out, closing the door softly behind us. We stood in the living-room trying not to hear the muffled cries, the soothing words; then Rita wailed, "I don't love him, Deborah, I swear it! But I can't help myself – I want him back. God, look what he's doing to me!" My father and I could not face each other. We, too, were brothers.

My mother came out to confer with my father in the hall. When she stepped back inside, my father told me, "Your mother and I have to stay. Do you think you can walk home by yourself? As soon as you're inside, you lock the door, wash up and get into bed."

I KNEW MR. NOJUK'S HOUSE with the leaning fence. I knew his huge black dog, Shadrack, that was always chained up in the front yard. But I didn't know why I was running there instead of heading home. I should have been glad to get away from Rita's, scared to disobey again, but I kept heading to his house, feeling only my shame like an awful weight that I didn't know how to drop, not looking up even when three boys on the street tried to block me.

"Hey, kid!" Riley, the red-haired boy, stood in front. He was from my school and a year older though no bigger than I was. "I know you," he said. "You're from that store on Main Street. Where do you think you're going?"

"To Mr. Nojuk's."

"Ha! His dog will tear you to shreds." He poked my chest. "If you're lucky, you'll die quick."

I pushed past them, rushed across the street and through the gate. They didn't follow but jeered from behind a parked truck. I heard a whining and a drag of chain; Shadrack stretched towards me in the dirt.

"Hiya, fellah. There's a good boy," I told him, offering my hand to lick and nuzzle.

Rita had told me all about Shadrack: "You should see Pop Nojuk's big old hound," she'd said. "He's such a softie, I could stick my head inside his mouth and he'd moan like a sweetheart. It's those little moody dogs that do the damage, isn't that right, boss?" She'd glanced at Mr. Nojuk who was listening from his grill, but as always he kept looking down.

Shadrack groaned, begging for me to stroke him. "What's wrong, fellah?" I asked, wondering how it felt to be a dog tied on a chain with Mr. Nojuk for a master. The yard seemed to be closing in, the fence like broken teeth, the old house darkening over me. I should have gone straight home, I told myself. I was crazy to have come. I edged towards the gate, but Shadrack followed, pawing at my side, and when I stepped beyond his reach he began to yelp and strangle at his chain. "I can't help you," I pleaded. "I can't." But I stayed with him in the yard, soothing, letting him lick and chew my fingers, hoping that it would be enough, that something would be enough, though I sensed that once I was gone there would be no comfort left.

I heard a creaking as if the house was stooping closer and I backed away from Shadrack into the corner of the fence.

"Did those kids chase you in here?" It was Mr. Nojuk filling the shadow of his porch.

I felt I had to stare him down or he would get me in

whatever spell he'd used on Rita. And on Shadrack. "I . . . I'm not scared," I told him, staring hard.

He descended, heavy with darkness, coaxing me with words about the dog and how I needn't be afraid and how I must think only about the dog. I listened, just for a moment, then another, lulled by his soothing voice, his deep, steady breathing and by the furry yearning of the dog.

"I know Shadrack," I said. "Poor old fellah."

"Then what are you scared of?" He was closing in with questions. "Come on, you can tell me."

"Run!" the boys hollered from across the street. "Run while you can!"

I looked up past him and saw a woman in the window, frail, shrunken – Mr. Nojuk's wife. I'd heard about her only in hushed words, veiled looks, but there she was, behind lace curtains trapped inside the house; he must have the same power over her, I thought, as he has on Rita.

"Too late!" the boys all cried. "Too late. You're cursed!" even as he reached out for me.

I slapped away his hand and yelled something at him, I don't know what, but I know that it was Rita shrieking through my mouth: her words, her voice, her fury. Mr. Nojuk stumbled back as if he'd heard her, too, and felt her striking him.

I bolted out the gate with Shadrack leaping and barking me on, past the wildness of boys, racing up the street, my arms flailing, breaking free. Away from all of them and from the darkness of that place.

I was flying, singing out in words that were not mine.

CITY BUTCHERS

DEAN LAY BESIDE HER WATCHING. HER PREGNANT BODY HEAVED IN sleep, struggling with the sheet like a creature trying to shed its skin. He felt painfully close, lying naked beside her on the bed, both of them drenched in the red spill of neon from the sign outside their window. Its border of lights flashed white. Their skin glimmered, then darkened again in the bloody wash. The sign read CITY BUTCHERS.

Had she woken him? he wondered. Or had the dream? His mind still ached from its thunder.

Dean was rushing out of his old school yard; it was seeding time but he couldn't find the school bus to take him home. As he glanced back, the school turned into City Butchers here in Winnipeg with Janet on her knees inside taking confession from her priest. "One body," the priest was whispering in her ear. "When two people marry they become one body." Dean began to run then fly toward a throbbing light far up the street, his toes dusting along the ground, his voice rising higher, trying to reach the light's clear sharp pitch while the shops of Main Street shrank on either side into garish booths crammed with faces. His boss, Roberto the butcher, appeared in his path, lifting a leathery flap that opened into darkness. Dean couldn't stop; he crashed through, and was swallowed by a crowd that sang as its thousand arms carried him overhead towards a wooden block while Dean screamed soundlessly into the roar.

"Damn dreams," Dean whispered. His breath felt hot against his skin. He reached across Janet to the cafe saucer he used for an ashtray. He found a butt and struck a match, then he lay back again and blew smoke into a white stream, watching for it to be caught in the next pulsation of red light.

Janet turned slowly on her back, her leg crossing his, an arm drawn along his front. Her hand came to rest upon his thigh.

He thought, maybe she's not asleep. Maybe she's faking, wanting more than she can ask for when she's awake.

Her arm seemed to stroke dark currents, calling to him.

He decided it was the baby who'd woken him, restless in its womb, making both of them restless. More than once, he'd felt it, Janet pressing his hand against her swollen belly and having him wait, smiling, and he trying to smile until it came – a blow from deep within.

She'd say, "Feel the kick? Our baby's trying to stretch."

He'd think, it's growing, that thing inside her.

Dean moved her arm, slipped away from her. He rose to drift with the smoke, watching it curl through the window screen, as if both he and it were drawn to the glimmer of the sign. A breath of wind – the smoke was gone.

"That's where dreams go," he remembered his mother telling him. "Out the window. And they don't come back." Dean's bedroom window on the farm had been filled by field and bush so dark and far from town that he would strain to hear the whisper of the highway, hoping for the faint down-gearing of a car that might mean a visitor.

He gazed past the sign's twisting tubes of neon to the gleam of the street. Main Street fed him light. It fed him cars and buses, and trucks whose lights high-beamed all night long across the bedroom walls.

"Rock, rock, rocking this firetrap down," he sang to the sign, running his finger along the screen's old wooden frame. Paint broke off in yellow scabs. The rusty screws were loose as rotten teeth.

"Rock and rolling it to the ground." Tapping in fast time, leading into his song:

Living on Main Street.
Rocking a mean streak.
Keeping a hard beat,
Rock and rolling this street.

The first song that he'd written here.

Yeah, yeah, he chanted to himself. I'll turn this noise into a beat, the beat into music to take me where the lights lead, and the cars rumble and groan; pistons, tappets, mufflers, tires and everyone inside; the Impala and the Fury boys with hungry hands drumming on the dash, the mamas in their station wagons with kids crammed in the back, screaming through their mamas' chore lists, grocery lists, phone numbers and appointments, blowing every fuse; and the old croaks in their old Pontiacs, wheezing behind the wheel. I'd put on more miles, get more sparks than them with all their burnt-out plugs. And that sunglassed woman in her open Thunderbird, a slow sighing, heat glazed woman who shifts and shifts again with dark glasses and dark thighs on a vinyl seat.

Janet groaned from the sheets, "Dean? What's the matter?"

He frowned to the burning tip of his cigarette. "Just don't feel like sleeping."

"You getting those dreams?" she asked.

"It's the heat, traffic, that greasy hamburger."

"You didn't even touch your supper. You get meat free from work but you don't eat. You don't sleep, either. Dean, you're going to get sick."

"Just sick of meat," he answered.

"Honey, come on to bed."

He waited as Janet's breathing deepened into sleep.

Outside, two toughs were strutting up the street and Dean watched his perspective of them change as they approached. At the point they walked directly beneath his view their heads appeared to be twisting off their shoulders, their shoulders twisting over their legs, as their laughter tumbled ahead like an empty can.

"Ha! I got ten bucks right here, man!"

"Where'd you get it, Jimmy? Your old man's wallet?"

"You want to know or you want to go?"

"He'll beat you to hell, again."

"I don't care. Let's blow it at the Ex."

"Ten bucks goes nowhere."

"Then what else? Eh? What else?"

"Losers," Dean pronounced upon them. "You don't have it."

Mrs. Klatt, from the movie house, she didn't have it either as she hesitated on the curb outside St. Joseph's Bingo Hall pleading, "Wait. Wait!" to her friend hobbling across the street, both of them terrified of the cars revving their engines at the traffic light a block away.

And he could see that Murray Stein didn't have it, as he shook the locked door of his clothing shop, testing it again and again, punishing it because his store was not a pool hall on Selkirk Avenue or a poker club where he could slap backs and watch others win and lose. Stein would never have it, Dean saw that clearly. Or even Stein's good-looking wife who'd forget to lock the door at all, as if wanting to be robbed, to be cleaned out by some crazy storm. Dean had seen them, heard them all, from this second-storey watch.

Dean smiled, remembering how he'd once confused the Stein woman with a mannequin. He was on his way home with groceries, after one of his first days at the butcher shop, wanting a beer or a scalding bath, or anything to wash away the smell of meat that made him a brother to what he had to scrape and grind. She was standing in her shop window beside two mannequins. He realized later that she must have been dressing one of them and had paused just before he'd glanced up. Mistaking her for a mannequin, Dean admired the indifference of her eyes, her smooth skin, the arch of her throat – forever perfect. Until she moved. Dean stepped back, amazed. He lingered, letting the full disappointment sink in that she was just another artful display of frail flesh.

What about those mannequins down there? Dean wondered, sucking deeply on his cigarette, holding in the smoke. Do they have what it takes? They don't feel this heat. Or want to eat or sleep or to be anything they aren't already.

They were gleaming in their spotlight, three of them, two complete figures and a torso, poised as if they were listening to his thoughts. The two figures had their long arms raised and he imagined them stretching out to him, their cool touch like a current. Just plaster and paint, he thought. But Jesus, they do it to me.

The heat of his cigarette burned toward his fingers. He waited for a moment beyond discomfort, before crushing the ember against the screen, against the night sky, to complete the mannequins' spell with a fall of stars.

Fireworks, he thought. The carnival's in town.

The annual summer exhibition was having its ten-day run with a full midway and rides. Tomorrow would be Saturday, the last night. Dean had talked every day about going but Janet was always tired or worried about one thing or another or they'd get stuck in some argument. So every night they'd stayed at home.

"Getting nowhere. Being nowhere," Dean told the dead butt of his cigarette. "I shouldn't be here. Not at twenty. Not with her."

Janet had been just one of many young women he'd met through his music but she'd been the one who'd followed as he and the band moved from small towns to bigger towns and larger halls, getting an agent, planning a demo record. Then the band broke up. Still she stuck with him even when he moved on to Winnipeg and to this job that was only meant to keep things going until he found another band, but he didn't find one and everything seemed to stall. She became pregnant, they got married, he kept working nine to five, six days a week.

Now how do I get out of here, he wondered, with her and with that thing that's moving inside her?

He looked at his electric guitar, a Fender Stratocaster, leaning in the corner. It was draped with laundry – a work shirt, a blouse, a knot of sweaty sheets.

This wasn't the way things went in the songs he played.

"Dean? Baby, I need you." Janet was stirring again. "Come on, baby. Come back to bed."

THE MORNING GOT HOT FAST, especially in the blaze of the white stucco wall behind the butcher shop. Dean came out to dump a tray of fat and bone, holding his breath before he opened the steel drum. The flies, resonating within, were clotted over entrails and genitalia, and over the bloody head of a goat; the unused parts of 'the butcher's special feature.' As Dean dumped the tray, a black storm of flies burst into his face. Fumbling the lid shut, he scraped himself. In a sudden fury, he slammed the lid down. The drum hummed with menace.

"Bugger off!" he shouted and sat on the back step at a wary distance. His match shook as he lit his cigarette. He sucked in too fast, tasting sulphur.

What a lousy day, he thought. This heat. And the butcher shop's so crowded on a Saturday. "You damn flies, this is just how you like it," he spoke aloud. Bad sign, he thought. Talking to myself. Talking to the flies – that's worse.

The drum seemed to quaver in a laugh. A rich joke for the flies. Dean thought of them chuckling, humming into the wastes of flesh, crawling over each other in the dark. The flies enjoyed so many jokes.

He rubbed his scraped knuckle. The torn skin looked like another of the shreds of fat sticking to his hand. A fly landed on it and began to probe.

Flies don't know the difference, he thought. Or they don't care.

Dean had tried killing them. He'd once spent a lunch hour outside, swatting them on the back wall and windows, even in the drum. They died fast. At every stroke, one or two twisted dead. He'd kept a count, one hundred and twelve. But at the break, he'd heard the drone again. Stepping outside, he opened the drum. They were all back, maybe more, feasting on the dead ones.

"Nuts," he muttered, rubbing his hands with his apron. "Everything here is nuts."

Like the Maria number. When Dean started working as a boner, stripping meat, he had been confused by everything: the equipment, the rules, but especially by Ruis and Roberto shouting in Portuguese. Angry or joking? He never knew which. Until the first time the sides of beef were delivered – like a saints' procession swaying out of the refrigerated truck. Roberto ran to the first carcass coming down the plank. He caressed it, moaning, "Maria! What did they do to you, Maria?" Dean could laugh, relieved that this, at least, was something he could understand, something that was supposed to be funny. Even Ruis, who knew almost no English, loosened into a sneer as Roberto cooed, "Maria! You talk to me! Where you hurt, Maria?"

This turned out to be a ritual performed at each delivery. Everybody laughed, even the worker who huffed the carcass off the truck, his white coat bruised with the blood, his face gnarled by the weight. And they had all kept laughing, except for Dean.

"*CARNE.* WOMEN." IT WAS RUIS, lowing at him from behind the screen door. He'd come to fetch Dean for Roberto.

Dean flicked his cigarette at the steel drum. *Carne,* Dean thought, that means meat in Portugese. "What's-a-matter, Ruis?" Dean asked. "You chop off something that you need?"

"*Carne!* Women!" Ruis gestured to the front. There were women wanting service.

Dean first changed into a clean apron in the bathroom. Wash carefully, he told himself. You've got to look good for the customers – that's what Roberto says. Check your nails, your shirt, your hair. Smile in the mirror.

But something was off beat, jangling through his head. Dean stared. Don't, he told himself. Don't stare. Seeing past his skin, to the outline of cheekbones, forehead, skull. He glared, "Get it together, man." The pupils of his eyes were quivering. His mouth shaped an answer, Rot in Hell.

The front was crowded. None of Roberto's regular sweethearts, either, but mostly older women, dark pigeons pecking the glass, and a hard-faced younger one, scowling through her rouge. A couple of old guys were lost at the back, dogging at the edge for some way in.

"Yes, ma'am? Something for the weekend? Going to the midway?"

"Hey, I been here first!" the young woman called out. "I want four pounds of chicken breast. And fresh. I know when you freeze it."

Roberto stepped in, nodding to Dean, *this one belongs to me.*

Although young, her body was loose and wide, slumped into tight pants, balanced on high heels. "You want breasts, lady?" Roberto cooed. "Did Mama send you for some nice big breasts? Why you laughing? What's your name, laughing lady?"

"Mary Anne."

"Maria! Dean, hey Dino, you hear that? She's my Maria!" Then quietly, "Dean, you take the one with the pork shoulder." Dean nodded as Roberto stepped onto his special ledge running behind the counter, the ledge that raised him up a full head taller. Roberto was a small man who liked the large, a lean man who loved the fat, who clicked his tongue approvingly at the width of this woman's thighs and at how they pressed against the glass window of the counter as she inclined towards him.

Dean tried not to stare at Roberto's bony fingers prodding the chicken's breast, raising it like a gift. Or at the woman's pale sausage fingers, almost touching Roberto's as they played upon the meat. They hesitated, posed like figures Dean remembered from a vase: a lord and lady dancing around each other, lovers yearning towards, yet never touching, their hands joined by a length of handkerchief. Only this was not a handkerchief, it was the flesh of a dead bird.

"Hey, good-looking, how about me?" The call of the pork shoulder woman.

"Yes, ma'am. Whatever you want," Dean said, sliding open the counter door, bending over the meats. Her face blurred in the foggy glass, her voice muffled, "I want a big one." Clack. Her fingernail struck the glass close to his ear. "No, no . . . that's all bone." Clack. Clack. Dean grew heady with the smell of chilled blood, the glaze of meat; he felt an impulse to crawl all the way into the counter, onto the mound, to sink into dank oblivion. On the other side of the glass, the crowd was closing in, calling, pointing.

"You got a rump roast? I want to see it."

"Headcheese. You got some? What's wrong, you don't understand? Maybe you call it potted head."

"Last week, I fried your kidneys. They were awful, all dried up." Fingers pressed against the glass, turning bloodless white, marking a foggy trail.

Dean pulled himself up, swaying before them. They were changing, shifting. His face felt like it was shifting, too. He was grinning hard at the woman's porky shoulders rubbing inside her dress. Grinning so hard it hurt.

Don't, he warned himself. Don't do this.

But he couldn't stop grinning at the hocks and jowls of these hungry sisters. Flanks wrapped in polyester. Sides dressed in acrylic. And at their grisly brothers with thin shanks in checkered pants and stretched out nylon socks – all creatures out of cartoons. Noisy cow and pig women, pecking chicken and turkey women. Scrawny mongrel men snapping for some scraps.

"How much is your liver?"

"What you got in your sausage?"

Their words streamed through his chest, filling his head as if it, too, were a balloon. Fat brisket faces glowered. Lean faces tightened around their eyes and teeth. He could not understand them anymore. He could only nod and grin.

"Roberto! This kid's deaf or something."

"Dino, give the customers what they want."

"I . . . I don't think . . ."

"You don't got to think, Dino. Just get more hamburger from the cooler. I'm taking over."

"Yeah, the cool room," Dean whispered to his hands, groping to untie his apron. "Get it, man. The walk-in cool-down room. A little room for being cool."

The door sealed behind him. He giggled in the chill, "Step on in to The Moo Moo Morgue, The Rest in Pieces Pork Chop Lounge." He smirked at a carcass on a hook, "Glad to meat you!" Shaken by rips of laughter, he held it for support. "Hey, sweetheart, sweet liver. Hey, sweet kidneys!" he crooned as he swayed with it. "Save your last dance for me!" He spun and caught it. "That's hysterical! Hysterical!" he cried, slipping down the carcass to the floor, trembling as he gripped a tray of hamburger.

Holding back his breath, he focussed precisely on the mound of hamburger, shaping it into a perfect heart, pressed his ear against it and listened. "Sorry to have to tell you," he whispered, gritting his teeth to stop more laughter, "but you're dead." He slapped the meat together into balls and pelted them at the door. Hamburger snowballs, he thought. I'll make hamburger snowmen. Meatmen with meatballs. And big hamburger mamas. I could bring a little burger baby home to Janet. Won't she be surprised.

He wiped his tears, imagining the warm, fleshy thing inside his wife, already prodding, testing with small and bloody fingers.

He felt the cold sweeping through his heart. No more jokes, Dean told himself. Or being a joke. Not now that Hell is freezing over.

DEAN SQUINTED AT THE FERRIS wheel, a black skeleton blazing in the sun that was lowering behind it.

Big wheel, he thought, I've got your number.

Leaving had been simple, like something happening to someone else. Janet was out. Dean packed a duffel bag, hitched downtown, and stowed the bag in the bus depot locker. The

Exhibition was a single easy hitch straight down Portage Avenue.

Once I make it big I'll send her money, a ticket, whatever she wants, he told himself. I'll make it up to her. He knew he could believe this long enough to get him through the night.

He found the radio booth near the front gate with a banner raised above it twice its size. It read CKY STAR SEARCH '62. The same words in the same block letters were on the top of the registration form, followed by two more lines in red.

ALL EXPENSES PAID TO HOLLYWOOD
AUDITION WITH TOP TALENT AGENCY

Dean pushed to the front of the stage to watch the other contestants. Some fat, ugly man told jokes about being fatter and uglier. A trembling girl lip-synched from an Italian opera, pretending to cry.

I can't wait here, he thought.

He gripped his guitar case and joined the crowd surging to the midway, his song beating in him with a hard fast pulse. Two more hours, he told himself, then he'd release it to the crowd, move them, shape them until they'd cry and cheer for him and him alone to become their star.

The carnival swirled around him, greasy fries and plastic toys, kids shrieking, carnies barking pitches. Two boys in Cuban heels slid under the fence while their buddy distracted the security guard in an argument. They dashed past Dean, proud and hot with fear, pulling out their money for the Crown & Anchor game. They started losing fast.

At the Spin-a-Fortune booth, a woman with a huge plush tiger was arguing with the carnie.

"What you talking about?" she spat out. "I bet double zero. You owe me thirty bucks."

"No way, doll," he answered. "Your bet wasn't down when I spun the wheel."

A sunburnt man in a cowboy hat barked at him from the other side. "It was, damn it. I saw it."

"You think I'm stupid? You two are in this together. You ain't even supposed to be playing. You're employees."

"I saw her place that bet," said Dean. Both the carnie and the cowboy stared at him. "You aren't supposed to be taking bets that big, are you?" Dean spoke coolly, avoiding looking at the woman. "Maybe you'd better shut the game while we talk it over with the cops." All the while Dean wondered, why should I lie for her?

Her face was pretty but empty, impossible to read. She seemed restless, sullen in her high heels, tight vinyl skirt, pale glazed lipstick.

I've known lots like her, he thought. Except for her eyes. Their crystal blue astounded him, as if they weren't meant for the sights of this world at all. He thought of jewelled planets, rocket ships, bodies suspended in time capsules.

The carnie tossed two ragged tens onto the counter. "That's all you're getting. Now take off. I don't need your trouble."

"And I didn't need your dirty come-ons," she said, snatching them. "I ain't nobody's prize doll."

Dean knew not to follow her closely, but to stroll in the same direction, and to look up when she glanced back so she would understand. He watched her wait between two shooting galleries and meet with the man in the cowboy hat. They divided the money, they began to argue, their faces pressing close, words wrestling together. The man seized her wrist, she slapped at him and, abruptly, broke into a kind of angry jig, kicking dust on his snakeskin boots. The man backed away, confused, swore something and stormed off.

As Dean approached, the woman's eyes were buzzing an electric blue. "Damn animal – thinks he owns me, owns the whole damn show!"

"You still got your share," Dean said.

She laughed without a smile. "Yeah, sport? You figure that's what got him hot – he didn't like the split? So what else do you figure?"

"I figure you didn't win that tiger," Dean told her, his own eyes calm and steady.

"It's bait to draw some action on the games. I get paid to lug around big prizes – show off the plush, so it looks like an easy win. Get the crowd heading for the punk racks, you know, those knock down games. Especially single guys – they blow their brains out."

"How about the single women, what do they do?"

"Whatever they can, as long as the jerks keep playing games. Me, I'll play the other side – I'm going to be a carnie with my own booth. And I won't get suckered in, not like that slob at Spin-a-Fortune."

"What do they call you? Plush? Tiger? Maybe they call you Trouble."

"You can call me Candy."

"So, Candy, how about a drink?"

"As long as you're paying."

Candy knew her way around; she cadged drinks from the beer garden, coaxed the ride jockeys to get them on for free. She had a sharp cool edge, unfazed by the roller coaster or the House of Horrors or Gravitron dropping its floor and spinning them against the walls. She polished her boredom like her fingernails and smiled only at someone else's surprise. The only game Candy seemed to like was how to spot the fix.

They gambled until Dean lost nearly everything. He flung his last coins at the Toss and Pitch, laughing, "Take it all. It's a gift from me to you."

"Here," said Candy, giving him her plush tiger. "You just got lucky. Come on, I've got a place."

"No time, I'm on stage soon. And I want you in the crowd, watching . . . and waiting for me." Her eyes narrowed and he knew she understood him, probably too well.

"How about the Ferris wheel?" she asked. "It's wild up there. The whole midway only runs as long as the wheel keeps turning. We can look down at everything and still be alone. It'll do you good before a show."

He took her by the arms to kiss her but she stiffened and when he pressed against her, she bit his lip and ran off. As he pursued her, he dropped the toy tiger. He stopped to pick it up and recognized someone turning away. It was the shopkeeper from Main Street, looking as remote as the time he'd seen her

135

in her shop window. He felt a nervous impulse in his hands like a mild shock of crossed wires.

Deborah Stein stood with her back to him looking up at the House of Mirrors, its windows revealing a half-dozen men, some bumping against the panes, others clowning or swearing, one flexing his muscles in a show of strength. A boy jumped up and down as if trying to climb out of a glass cage. The strains of music, machines, voices, jangled in Dean's head; the bodies seemed to twist as if on hooks and he felt the chill of the meat locker. He picked up the toy tiger and ran.

When he reached Candy, he was so desperate with apologies that she smirked and clapped as if it were an act. The faces of the crowd, the painted facades of the lesser rides fell behind them as they pushed towards the Ferris wheel which grew more massive and brilliant with their every step.

Yet Dean was not surprised when he was tripped, and he landed almost gracefully with his guitar jangling by his ear. Rising on one foot, he recognized the sunburned face, the cowboy hat. He was about to speak when a fist struck his temple, another cracked his rib.

Candy shrilled from behind, "Don't, Wolf! Stop it!" Legs and faces spun as Dean twisted from the first kick of the boot.

When he managed to open his stinging eye he was looking through a maze of legs. Just beyond, the cowboy was pushing Candy off the midway into the darkness behind the booths.

DEAN SCANNED THE BACK LOT closed in by plywood walls. It was a mess of mud and cables. At the far end, powering the Ferris wheel, was a dragon's nest of generators fuming into blackness.

They aren't here, he told himself. No one can be here.

He called out, "Candy?" alarmed by the cracking in his voice. Then, beside the generators, a frenzy of shadows. Candy was kicking at the cowboy; he was grabbing for her arms, trying to pin her against a trailer wall.

Dean ran low across the field, his heart pounding in his

chest. He tackled him, and as the cowboy tried to rise, he hammered him down. And again. The man struggled to his knees, hat crushed on the ground, face clotted with mud. Dean had him.

"Don't hurt him!" Candy's voice was wild and crying but for the cowboy. She clung to Dean like fire, biting and tearing his scalp. He tried to ward her off, push away her tangle of arms and legs as he saw the man-shadow rising, saw it draw a brightness from its hip.

The flash-slash of a blade. A rip of cloth. Heat.

"Wolf!" Candy was screaming. "You knifed him!"

"Bloody right."

A wide throb in his abdomen. Dean hunched over the pain. Crazy, he thought, falling to his knees, balling up at their feet.

"You could do time for this." Candy's voice was hoarse above the roar of generators.

"You mess with anyone again, I'll cut you, too. I swear it."

"Shut up! Let's get out of here!"

SO CRAZY, DEAN THOUGHT, on his back unable to move or groan. Flesh becoming pain. His wound eating all his strength, gnawing for more. He could barely feel the mud moulding around him, barely hear the slip and splash of their feet running, or their words breaking against the midway. Yet he could understand that to be alone like this was worse and more true than any dream.

He felt something becoming real, felt it in his abdomen. Something like warm mud. He fumbled along the lips of a wound, his mind slowly comprehending what his hands already knew.

Mute, mouthing pain erasing time. No minutes. No seconds. No count to the breath or pulse or beat. Not even tears.

Then measured beats of footsteps, voices closing in with shadows – "get security . . . who's the kid? . . ambulance" – and one shadow hovering with a probing hand, its voice soothing,

"Take it easy . . . bad cut . . . you're going to make it . . . always looks worse than . . . it's soon coming."

Dean panted face up. The Ferris wheel rolled above him, blazing with bursts of light. Make this stop. Promise this will stop, he mutely begged the Ferris lights with its showering stars that burned his breath. He heard the ambulance's siren through the keening of the wheel and Dean cried out, "Baby!" Wanting the ambulance to be for Janet who was out there somewhere and for the baby who was coming. This was its time. Dean felt the baby inside of him. It was searching its way out, its heart beating through his, its veiled eyes seeking light. "It's coming!" Dean cried, into the exploding wheel.

THE PORTRAIT

THE BUS DOORS WERE STILL OPENING AS DANIEL BARGED THROUGH, his eyes fixed on the Ferris wheel.

"Daniel! Wait for us," Deborah called.

"That boy's like a horse to the post," Murray said as Deborah looked to him to slow Daniel down.

Reaching the entrance gate, Deborah stopped to adjust her high heel. Murray and Daniel kept going. It struck Deborah that the three of them had never learned how to walk together, not like the families in the ads, those perfect people who seemed to say, "Look at us – smiling, holding one another. This is what you look like when you are truly happy."

Daniel either charged forward or dragged behind her. Murray never held her hand. His hands were either dug into his pockets or dangling so huge and loose that Deborah wanted to poke him. And she knew how tired, how tense she often looked.

She thought, if only the business was better. Each day they pushed to make their sales and meet their debts. Each night they accounted for the day and planned the next. There was so little left of themselves to offer one another.

"Not tonight. Not even a word about work," Deborah had told Murray, as he punched the total on the register to cash out. "It's time we have some real fun together."

"How much can we spend?" Murray asked.

She studied the lines of his brow and named a figure between what she wanted and what they could afford. "It's Saturday night and we're going to the midway," she said. "Let's call it mad money."

Murray laughed on cue and grinned, trying to look suave as he counted out the cash. Still, Deborah couldn't help but notice that he'd developed a clerk's habit of snapping every bill so none were stuck together.

THE ENTRANCE TO THE MIDWAY was a barrage of hawkers with balloons, toys, candied apples, puppets dangling by their strings. Deborah and Murray let Daniel guide them through, waving his wand of cotton candy, and they laughed when he was spooked by a fortune teller who called to him from inside her tent. A pastel artist asked Deborah if she were French, and Murray, pretending to be jealous, bribed her away with the promise of a Ferris ride. Deborah heard herself giggling. But as they were funnelled deeper into the midway, and were pressed together by the crowd, Deborah gripped Daniel with both hands, trying to keep pace, steering past the games, pushing toward the rides.

"Wait a minute," Murray muttered and slipped away.

"Murray, come back," she called after him.

They found him at a game booth, spellbound by a wall of glossy pictures in gilded frames. At eye level was a picture of a cowgirl in a tight checkered shirt swaying a basket of bunnies from her hip. Beneath it was a picture of a tuxedoed playboy with a smoking gun and Jaguar. The top picture was Jesus bleeding on the Cross.

Jewellery and wallets hung from shelves of radios, clocks, food mixers and silverware. An old carnie touched the prizes one by one as he chanted out his steady pitch through the crackle of his microphone:

"Could-you-should-you-would-you do it, do it
For a buck you get a chance.
Could-you-should-you-would-you do it, do it
 For a buck you get a chance.
Heya mister, heya sister,
 Go on, take a chance."

He was smirking straight at Murray, a challenge in his bloodshot eyes. Murray straightened, as if to stare him down.

Deborah almost said, "Don't be a fool, Murray," but bit her lip.

"I could sure do with a good watch," he told her.

"Murray, just one game, okay?"

He gave the carnie a five, hardly glancing at the change. Deborah recognized his fixed look – he was concentrating his power of belief so that the darts would have to hit the star.

He still wants what's best for us, she told herself. It's just that he tries to get it in his way.

The darts flew wild. Murray bought another set and made two hits. Other men started games as well, building a cone of intensity with Murray at the head. He smirked, cajoled the fellows on either side, his team, his gang. Until the fourth set when he made all three hits.

The carnie called out, "Winner! We've got a winner!" and Murray raised both hands in victory while Daniel cheered. The carnie handed him a small plush frog which made Deborah smile, thinking how she'd hang it on her bedroom mirror.

"What's this junk? I was going for the watch," Murray said.

The carnie, making change for other players, didn't bother looking up as he spoke. "If you want the big prize, get all three darts inside the red." The target had two stars, a small red star inside a larger blue one.

"Murray," said Deborah. "The watch might not even work."

"It'll work fine, damn it." Murray glared at the target. "You called it mad money, didn't you? So don't go fretting at me."

She used to admire his stubbornness; how when they'd first met he'd kept joking, flattering until she finally let him have her phone number; again when they were setting up the

141

store and he worked a week with hardly any sleep. And that long ride to the hospital when she was in her labour, Murray spoke with such firmness, never wavering for a moment. It had seemed as if Murray could battle a path through the world while she would follow close behind, cradling what was precious to them. "Like I was carrying our hearts safe inside a golden box," she'd once written to her friend.

Things turned out not to be that way at all. Not with him, nor the world, nor with their hearts. Deborah waited through two more games until Murray pulled out his wallet once again.

She said, "Murray, I'm taking Daniel to the rides. Are you coming or not?"

"Go on ahead. I'll catch up."

MURRAY SHOWED UP A HALF-HOUR LATER at the bumper cars, looking sheepish. Daniel asked if he had won.

"All those games are fixed," he mumbled.

Deborah, pretending not to care, told him to take Daniel into the House of Mirrors. She stayed out front while the two of them lost themselves inside, bumping about the glass and mirrored maze, clowning for each other and for her, with every step becoming more confused and helpless. Deborah recognized at once what Murray was doing: he was apologizing by becoming unblameable. She felt flattered and glanced around self-consciously, ready to let herself laugh out loud.

When she saw Dean, the young butcher's helper, she stiffened. He was by the roller coaster ride pressing against a blonde woman in stiletto heels who was teasing at the opening of his shirt. As he moved to kiss her, Deborah pressed her fingernails against her own pale lips. Suddenly, as if he'd been bitten, Dean lurched backward. The blonde woman laughed and ran off in Deborah's direction with Dean following, calling after her.

Deborah turned so as not to be recognized but as Dean passed, she felt an emptiness yawning inside. He was cheating on his wife, Janet. Coward, she thought, throwing everything away, marriage, love, your whole future together. Wasting it on a brassy whore, a slut – words Deborah had never used before, not even in her thoughts.

Deborah imagined herself rushing to Dean and Janet's apartment over the butcher shop, describing everything to Janet, dramatizing every detail that would raise the young woman into fury, so the two of them might join in rage, grief, self-pity, every sort of passion that would fill that emptiness.

Yet she felt that Janet would fail her; as soon as she'd hear that Dean was with another woman she'd become numb, she'd curl up on a couch, or bed, capable of nothing but despair. Deborah understood then that she was aching with her own, not Janet's, hurt.

Deborah had been aware of Dean for well over a year, ever since he'd begun working at the butcher shop across from their store. He looked sensitive and open as if he'd just been delivered out of boyhood, and with such energy and poise – she was sure he was intelligent, passionate, not just some punk with a drive for wild music, but a singer, songwriter, an artist of the people.

Yet they'd never even spoken. Nor did she want to; it was only her "hobby" to study the colourful characters who passed beneath the window of her store – exotic immigrants and home-grown crazies, the lost and broken who scavenged in back lanes, the local gentry who managed banks or owned car dealerships, and all those others who found or lost themselves in the shout and jostle of Main Street. Deborah kept a mental note of whoever caught her eye, sorting and collecting not so differently from when she was a girl filling scrapbooks with cutouts of world leaders, criminals and movie stars.

Despite herself, Deborah had become preoccupied by Dean because of a single, unguarded moment. She'd been dressing a display window, and paused while positioning a mannequin's wig. She let her eyes rest on a line of telephone wires glowing in the setting sun. Suddenly she saw Dean gazing up at her as if fascinated. Deborah felt gripped, she couldn't move, not even breathe. An instant of vertigo, then, leaning on the mannequin, she recovered herself.

Dean stepped back in surprise and Deborah realized that he must have mistaken her for a mannequin. When she'd moved, the spell had broken. She grinned as if to laugh it off, excuse, explain that it was just a typical, human, ridiculous mistake.

At that point, another man might have played the fool or scoffed but Dean stood quietly and studied her with a sadness softening his eyes and mouth until it was Deborah who became confused. She fumbled the wig, tipped over a hat stand, retreated from the window.

For days afterwards that moment had possessed her – the twinning of their gaze, her giddiness, his sadness. She sensed some mystery had been revealed. Only it was some mystery about herself and Dean alone had understood it.

He's looked into me, she kept thinking. He's learned something about me that I've forgotten or that I never knew. He'll tell me what it is if I can only get close to him. At that point she'd stamp her foot or lecture herself. Who do you think you are, that stupid Alma Batiuk – writing perfumed notes to everybody's husbands? Or Genie Nojuk phoning neighbours, even strangers, to beg forgiveness for nothing at all? You've still got your self-respect.

Deborah disciplined herself with work. She organized a school fashion show, rearranged displays, began calling up unpaid accounts so that whatever had accidentally opened would close and seal itself completely.

Yet, during last year's April sale, when Dean came into the store with Janet, Deborah felt the giddiness again. She had to lean against a counter and stayed at the back of the store, letting Murray serve them. She glanced up occasionally, waiting for some gesture, at least a sign of recognition. Dean ignored her. He slouched in that scornful way some men have while waiting for a woman shopping. He spoke gruffly to Murray, who was trying to show him a shirt, and left before Deborah could approach.

Now it's you who's embarrassed, Deborah had thought. Maybe you can't handle what you've seen in me or in yourself. Well, at least it's ended.

Deborah still noticed whenever Dean passed outside but she expected nothing from him. She only wanted to know what he'd become; many young men grew so hard so quickly on that street. They'd act tough in public, then, at home, turn into spoiled, dangerous children. Careless and weak, they broke at the first setback and took to drinking, gambling, quarrelling over any point of their wounded pride – the common ways, it seemed to Deborah, that men give in to their confusion. They'd waste half their pay before they got it home, then take their failures out in blows against those who asked for love. The good-looking ones, like Dean, were often the most cruel.

Whenever Janet came in to browse, Deborah drew her into conversation, chatting as Janet looked at a dress. Eventually, they traded details of their personal lives through the curtain of the change room. Janet complained of Dean with the fondness of a lover; he was impulsive, moody, deep, the very things that drew Janet to him. She'd met Dean while working at the front desk of her small-town hotel. Still too young to be allowed inside the hotel pub, Janet had watched from the lobby as Dean took the stage. He'd formed the band a few months before in another town in the district, and could play every song from a beach movie that was showing at the local drive-in. A few nights of awkward lust and then, as if sex proved love, and love proved mutual destiny, Dean and Janet left everything and headed to the city.

THE LAST TIME JANET came into the store, just after New Year's, her complaints to Deborah had lost all their fond ironies. Neither Dean nor she had any family here, except for his uncle, who turned out to be a drunk, while the friends they'd made had come and gone, they were nothing like the people she knew in the country. Dean still had not found himself a band, only fill-in work at weddings when a guitar player called in sick. "I can't believe it," Janet said. "I mean, it's all got to be some kind of joke."

As she called Deborah into the change room to help with the dress, her voice began to fray. "Oh, God, what am I doing? I can't pay for this. I'm nuts to even try it on."

"I trust your credit, dear. Now let's see it on you." Deborah thought, sweet, mixed up Janet – skin so delicate a touch could bruise it.

Janet bowed her head, fretting at the buttons. The chain of her crucifix dangled in the way. "I can't get this on! God, I've been such a pig. I bet I'll need a size fifteen."

"You'll fit the twelve just fine. It's made for you." Deborah often marked the sizes down. This made a dress more attractive and Deborah knew that Janet needed something like a dress. She had that sinking look some women get when they've worn out all their dreams.

She cheered Janet along, buttoning the front, adjusting the shoulders, trying to keep a rhythm of joking and flattering that often led to sales. Deborah liked to think that she sold a mood, a change of personality. That's what clothing promised – the right blouse, the proper cut and colour could change things like a charm.

"Men think we dress for them," Deborah chatted. "As if clothes are just different kinds of lures. They don't know what they're even looking at. They always go after something cheap. Forget about what men like, if it makes you feel good, then it's the dress for you."

But the girl was looking worse and the dress was far too tight. "You see! You see!" Janet broke into a gasping laugh. "It's all a joke!"

Deborah waited for the tears. She had seen all this before, when some woman disrobed in the change room. It could be like a confession box.

"I don't know!" Janet dropped into the chair. "There I go again! All the time, I'm saying, 'I don't know,' like I'm some kind of dummy."

"It's just an expression, Janet."

"We still don't have nothing and we've both been working hard for so long."

"You can't save all at once," said Deborah.

"We even owe money on the bed. It's where we make love and even it doesn't belong to us. But that didn't stop Dean from borrowing on next week's pay just to fix his stupid guitar."

"Try putting away your tip money. If you can just save that."

"There won't be no more tips!" Janet flared as if she were arguing with someone else. "Not much longer. I can't wait tables once they see I'm . . ." Her tears broke and she hid her face in her hands. "God, can't you tell?"

Deborah gently brushed the hair from Janet's nape, watching her shoulders heave as she gasped. The girl's hands were so red and swollen and so tightly pressed against her face, they looked like a stranger's hands trying to silence her.

She's still thin from the back, Deborah thought, probably not yet four months along. She could hide it a little while longer.

"When are you going to tell Dean?" Deborah asked.

The girl backed into the corner, shaking her head.

"HEY, GOOD-LOOKING, what you got cooking? Yeah, I'm talking to you in the sugary blue! Where'd you buy that knock-out dress, Stein's Style Shoppe?"

Deborah froze beneath the laughter of the man and boy.

"Mom! Dad's talking to you."

"You are some pin-up! Hoo, hoo!" Murray and Daniel hooted from the balcony on the second floor of the House of Mirrors. Behind them was a gallery with a flashing sign that read The Attic of Crazy Mirrors. The top of the sign was a brightly painted head of a character with rolling eyes. The inside of his head was painted as a row of mirrors showing an assortment of freaks. There was a devil standing at one end and a clown at the other.

"Come on up, Deborah," Murray yelled. "There's these crazy mirrors!"

"Murray, stop yelling!"

"Then come up. We're having some fun up here."

Driven by their hoots, Deborah entered the House of Mirrors.

Immediately she had to turn, then turn again. She entered an airless, muffled hall of glass – some transparent, others mirrored. The glass walls were so streaked and smudged that she manoeuvred past them as if each handprint were reaching out to touch her. Then came the reflections of herself, each one suddenly appearing as if she were wandering unprepared onto a harshly lit stage. Further halls and then the same one again.

Deborah could hear Murray's distant laughter. At first she felt hurt, thinking that he was laughing at her, but soon she realized he was probably laughing at himself or Danny. She concentrated on his voice and followed it up a spiral staircase coming out upon a balcony that overlooked the midway.

"Oh, what a lovely view!" she said.

"We should see it from the top of the Ferris wheel," said Murray.

The Ferris wheel turned above them at the far end of the midway, reminding Deborah of a Hollywood extravaganza, a great wheeling waltz in a Viennese palace, cavaliers and ladies, diamonds and pearls. From this height on the balcony everything – even the carnies, rubes and gamblers, the Deans and bottled blondes – looked perfect and happy. She was about to turn back to Murray to say, "Yes, let's get Daniel some treat and we'll go up, just the two of us."

"Mom! Look at me!" Daniel was calling from the gallery of distorted mirrors inside. "You got to look!" He stepped towards the mirror and his reflection stepped toward him, a groggy head that wavered above a stem-thin body. Daniel moaned, "Wooo! Wooo! Wooo!" moving closer as the head detached, bobbing away into a smear of colour. "Wow, spooky! We should have brought a camera!"

"Get a load of this one, Deborah!" Murray twisted into a body-building pose. The mirror's image furrowed and then compressed into a madly muscled dwarf. "Step right up, darling. It's your turn, now!"

"I don't feel like it, Murray."

"Aw, Deborah!"

"Mom, no fair! We did!"

She hurried past the mirrors, trying not to look at them.

"Deborah, for Chrissakes, loosen up." Murray caught her shoulders. "Now take a look at yourself!" He turned her firmly. She looked at the reflection in front of her – a wide-eyed infantile face, a body that seemed to be a single swollen breast and beneath it an old crippled woman's legs. Her son and husband howled in delight.

"LOOK, DEBORAH. I ALREADY SAID I shouldn't have grabbed you. Okay, you got upset but you don't have to stay upset."

Deborah sat on a bench staring down the midway, trying not to listen to Murray, who seemed no more than a shadow on her periphery. Daniel, placed on a farther bench, was slightly more in view, hunched over his cone of rainbow ice-cream. As Murray talked, a nearby ride drowned him out with a rising chorus of screams and a ringing like a huge cash register gone mad.

Deborah noticed something sticky on the sole of her shoe, a lump crusted with dirt. She thought of looking for some sort of stick to pry it off but she didn't want to touch it. She didn't want to touch anything.

". . . and you're just making everything worse," Murray went on. "I mean, I said I'm sorry. What more do you want?"

"I want fifteen dollars," she said.

"What for?"

"Fifteen dollars."

DEBORAH STEERED DANIEL with her hand on his shoulder past the games and then past the food stands. Murray followed at a cautious distance. She stopped at the pastel artist. He was leaning forward, concentrating on his work. Behind him was a display of portraits: Marilyn Monroe, Marlon Brando, even

Jacqueline Kennedy as if they had really posed for him. He's very good, Deborah thought, especially with the eyes.

The man was blending pastel colours onto the background with a roll of paper, completing the portrait of a teen-aged girl. The girl kept glancing to her friends for assurance, who cooed and nodded and, as she got to see it, raised a gentle cheer. A young man stood beside her, scanning the crowd as if to ward off any careless word.

"Who's next?" the artist asked.

"I am," said Deborah.

"Do you want full colour? It takes half an hour."

"Yes. And could you, could you make it look . . . good?"

"Ma'am, it'll look more than good."

"But do you know what I mean?"

"I won't even have to try with you."

Deborah took her place in front of him on a low platform, trying to settle in a pose. She was not sure how to smile. "When I was seventeen," she told him, "I won a beauty contest in my home town. Of course, that's a long time ago."

"I bet it wasn't all that long."

Daniel sat next to her, chewing at the edges of his ice-cream cone. Murray stood behind the artist as he worked, concentrating on the picture, then on her. People paused to watch, they moved on, others came.

By tilting her head upward to her right, Deborah was able to avoid seeing Murray's appraisals or Daniel staring mindlessly at the passing crowd, ice-cream dripping onto his pants. Even the Ferris wheel softened to a blur. Finally, she told Murray he could leave and to take Daniel with him. "I'll know where to find you," she said, her eyes on a starry string of bulbs.

Once they left, she felt her breath deepening and the muscles of her face settling into a soft smile. She felt cared for, even more than at the salon, where Liz would rest the back of her head upon a towel and then the tender washing of her hair with warm and thick shampoo.

The artist, half hidden behind the easel, had the intense gaze, the swift hand of a stage magician. Deborah sensed him conjuring a beauty that her life had never quite released, a beauty that had somehow been held back from her. She imagined her portrait emerging as if he were sweeping away a stale white fog; first the eyes glowing in wondrous hazel, then the feathering of her eyebrows, the clear lines of nose and mouth. He would bring out the colour of the cheeks, her whole skin growing fresh and smooth. Next, with certain grace, he'd chalk the hair and brush it out with his finger. Finally, with the face complete and beautiful, a pink and blue aura would fill the background.

Deborah knew that her portrait would look more lovely, more happy than she had ever been and this was what she wanted. She would hang it in the living-room or in the bedroom by her mirror. Others would look at it and she would become transformed before their eyes. Through years of seeing it every day, the portrait would charm even Deborah's own memories of herself and take on a truth of its own. Knowing this, she could already feel the change.

SPIN MASTER

NO BRAKES. THAT'S HOW I'LL DO IT, I TOLD THE COUNTRY ROAD that blurred beneath my feet.

I spread my legs, feet free of pedals, and let my Raleigh glide. This time I'd show them all, especially my father.

I rumbled down the dawn-grey hill, gravel tearing at my tires. I didn't feel skinny at all. Or short. Or anything like a loser.

Not while I had my father's fishing rod aimed like a lance at the wooden bridge, my bridge, where I'd biked with just a hook and line every August morning, rising early enough to miss my uncle and aunt grumbling awake on the other side of the panelboard partition, and to miss my mother fussing over the cottage stove, burning porridge that my cousins would poke and my father would drown in cream, mixing it into a sweet soup; this day I'd risen in darkness, dressed in shadows, a shadow myself sifting cereal into a bowl already filled with milk, muffling the falling flakes, hushing shut the fridge door, the cabinet door, the screen door so I'd be gone before even my mother woke, my mother who said she couldn't sleep because of "nerves," who clip-clopped onto the porch in frayed pink slippers sighing, "Daniel! Are you going out again? I don't know what you're doing anymore."

My uncle's summer cottage was worse than home; I had to share everything with my cousins, which simply meant giving in, giving up, and constantly apologizing because everyone was cranky and cramped. I got so jumpy that I made even more mistakes: I tore the screen, bent the lawnmower blade, moved the candle to where it set the curtain into flames so that my aunt would chime at every chance, "It's a good thing your Uncle Steve was there to stamp it out. We could have all been burned alive!" And my uncle would grunt back, "We have to watch that kid every minute of the day. He doesn't have a clue." My mother looked to my father for some kind of answer and my father stared darkly over rows of cottage roofs.

It was better to bike away, past sleeping lawns and curtained windows. Only this time I had the Bradley Spin Master, the fishing rod that I gave my father for his birthday, bought with my own money from my own bank account.

"What do I know about fishing?" I later heard him ask my mother. "No one gets in shape by fishing and wishing and sitting in some boat."

Still, I'd pressed him into bringing it with us to the cottage. He warned me, "I'll pack it, Danny, but you're responsible for it." Wasn't that almost saying I could use it at the bridge?

I was sure the rod would do it. I had practised behind my parents' store with Mr. Werner, casting for pages of his Jewish Post. Kitefish, we called them as they fluttered in the wind, hooked and struggling to escape into the clouds.

The Spin Master was far better than my hand-held hook and line that only pulled in sour catfish. Or sauger. Or toss-away perch. The Spin Master would catch a fighting fish so huge, so heavy I would have to grip with both my hands to haul it waist-high through the cottage doorway shouting, "Here's supper, Dad! I got the Big One!" as my father, uncle, cousins, the whole lot would jump to their feet, astounded.

"No brakes, no brakes," I whispered, the bike shaking out

my words, vowing to the hill, the road, the tires – let hill, road, tires decide; my feet will fly or break on stones but they wouldn't touch the pedals. Not till I was there.

Just before grace and courage failed, the merciful hill levelled out, steadying my heart, and carried me onto the rumbling planks.

A single clap applauded from the river – the sound of a broaching fish, ten yards out.

"The next one belongs to me. I swear it."

I tested the rod in the air. It was strong, alive, eager in the rising sun. I gripped it between my thighs and tied on a red devil lure. The rod swayed, tip trembling in the air, divining for the Big One.

Another splash, rings widening from its bull's-eye centre. The rod couldn't wait. I cast the line. Reel whined, lure sang through sky toward the rings on water that were broadening in a welcome.

But the reel seized, clogged. The lure jerked and faltered. I choked a cry as it spiralled, dead, into the water.

The spool had become a snarl. I tucked the handle under my arm and worried at the line with both hands, feeding it out until it hung in a loose tangle at my knees. The more I tried to separate the loops the more it clenched into a mass of knots.

I felt a familiar scurrying in my chest, a draining in my limbs that told me this day was already ruined like so many others and I would not free the line and if I did I would not catch a fish, and if I did catch a fish, something else would go wrong, something I should have seen coming from the start.

I lifted the tangle, a mad cat's cradle that netted sky, bridge, river, everything. "Not fair!" I moaned.

Not then and there. Not after school was finally over and I was free of fractions, History, graphs of grammar, free from my own handwriting that coiled and cramped so badly that both I and my teacher were worn almost to yelling.

I sucked in my breath and picked at a knot. It loosened so the line looped out but only to draw in other loops that all pulled tight. This way, that way, every way was impossible.

I bit my lip, tasting the saltiness of blood, and remembered how I'd gotten myself slugged by the rusty-haired kid, the one named Riley. I'd tried to be his sidekick, to joke around, but Riley had gotten me wrong and called me "dope." So I swore at him and kids circled shouting, "Fight! Fight!" till I had to hit him, and Riley had to punch me back but he slugged me hard and in my face, and my lip began to bleed.

I stared up at the telephone line stretching across the river – a sagging horizon, draped with lures and sinkers twisting in the sun's first light.

"Next time I'll probably snag up there." I lowered the tangle, reel, all of it onto the railing and mourned into the mess: "Dad's going to know I took it. What'll he say when he sees the rod like this?"

An explosion answered me, a hollow eruption twenty yards up the river. Huge. Furious. The explosion ripped the river into an open wound. It raised a heavy pillar five yards high of churning mud and spray. It shook me and I dropped the rod.

Rod, reel, line, struck the water's surface.

I leaped forward, stretched over the railing, crying for my arms to reach but it was gone with only rings wavering where it sank. A sudden spray and the rings were swamped by the first angry wave.

Lost. It's lost, I told myself as the bridge shuddered under me. But how could the river explode? And how could I have dropped the rod? The waves still rolled, proof that the river did explode, but the waves wouldn't last and even proof wouldn't matter. The rod mattered and the rod was lost.

I twisted around to search but the rod did not miraculously reappear on land and no hand rose with it from the water.

"I can't go back." I imagined hiding in the woods, hitching to the city, or living on the road itself travelling on forever. Yet I knew I would go back. Just as I knew how my father and Uncle Steve would stare from the enamelled kitchen table, and how I'd look or rather how I'd look away, hesitating at the doorway as they laid down their cribbage hands. I'd begin some defence before I explained anything, while my aunt entered to make coffee but really to note my signs of guilt, and my cousins, delighted by the show, would conspire on the couch. I'd describe this impossible thing that struck the river as if it were something out of my comic books but with no white word-bubble reading BOOM!, no cartooned border to keep it separate from the world. All the while I'd be slouching and mumbling, knowing that Uncle Steve always said a mumble means a lie. Dad would tighten around his coffee cup, my mother would drift to the sink for a dishrag to rub against the worn Mactac counter, both of them wincing as my words tangled in confusion, while everyone decided what really must have happened.

"Ha! That gave it to her good!" The voice broke from a thicket on the river bank. Bushes shook and the silhouettes of two men dragged a long shadow into the water – a rowboat. The lean one sprang into it saying, "Get your ass in gear, jerk!"

The other one standing in the mud grunted the boat into deeper water, then stumbled in. "Oh, yeah, I'm the jerk. You think I don't know nothing about boats?" he whined as he pulled off his cap to run his hand through matted hair. "You're the one who's standing!"

"Okay, sailor, get it moving."

"You got to sit down, Jack."

"Damn it! They're rising."

Who were 'they'? I wondered. Was he talking about others like himself? Was the explosion some kind of signal?

The two men, the water, the river banks on either side focussed into vivid colour. I hid and watched.

"Over to the right!" Jack shouted. "Some sailor, you can't even row."

"How about you doing something, eh?"

"Dig the oar in the water, the left oar. Row with your left one."

I kept low, scrambling into the weeds at the end of the bridge while the men manoeuvred into midstream. I slid down the embankment into the bushes, thrilled to be a witness, a reporter like Jimmy Olsen, Superman's young pal.

"Nothing's happening, Jack. You said they'd come up. I got to be in Riverton by nine to open the garage. Hinkley's coming for a valve job."

Jack snapped back, "Stuff it, will ya?"

"Says who? Eh? Says who?" Even his anger sounded like a sulk.

Jack ignored him as he scanned the water. Eventually, he answered, "Hinkley's going to leave the truck on the lot and your boss never gets in till ten – so what's he going to know?"

"But, Jack . . ."

"Just shut up. You're bugging me."

Closer to the bridge, the sun touched their upper bodies. Light haloed Jack's bleached hair, the faintness of a moustache. He looked sixteen but could have been older, even twenty with features that were almost feminine, except they were set into a sneer as if he meant to ruin anything delicate about himself. I knew enough to fear this kind of angry mannish boy.

I wasn't worried about the other one, who kept whining. He was pimply and clumsy as an overgrown kid. He seemed to be more like me, helpless, thus somehow innocent. I was already planning to tell the police that "Whiner" was bullied into whatever they were doing.

"Here they come. They're rising!" Jack shouted.

"Look, Jack, they're everywhere!"

Jack slapped the water with his hands, "Come on! You're floating up to heaven. Come to Daddy."

I saw only clouds beneath the surface, slow dreaming ghost clouds seeking the real clouds reflected on the water. At first I thought it was one large fish, like some great whale rising. Then I saw there were many fish, mostly pickerel surfacing everywhere, white stomachs and gleaming scales bobbing under a skin of water. Some were dead. Others twitched in surrender. Stunned, drowned, they'd been dynamited.

My heart was firing in short wild bursts. I crouched lower in the weeds, the sides of my corduroys rubbing at thistles, my chin sliding along the cool stem of a bullrush. I was trying to recall what my Uncle Steve had said about dynamite and rivers.

"Those poachers, they don't care," he'd said. "They dynamite a whole bloody river and kill ten fish for every one they get."

Jack scooped fish with a long-handled net. Whiner held the plastic bags. The boat and the fish were being carried by the current, drifting so close to where I hid that I could see the sweat on Whiner's lip as he wiped his forehead with his sleeve. He spit into the water and I watched the spittle float towards me to finally ease against the pebbles on the shore. So very close. The boat scraped an outlying rock. A dozen pickerel bobbed along the shore. They would come for them.

I tried to think, should I run or stay? Or pretend I didn't know anything? Say I'm here by accident? Act blind. Unconscious.

"Who the hell are you?" Jack stood balanced in the boat with his feet spread against the inner ribbing. "What, are you deaf?"

I rose from the weeds, caught by Jack's stare, slipping in the mud towards him. I made myself look away, focus on a pickerel's wide dead eye.

"Maybe you're some kind of retard."

I stayed mute, choking on the wrongness of his words and staring down, fixed on the fish's eye, then on an eye-shaped pebble wet with the water's tongue, green pebbles, blue ones, many pebbles white and brown. Jack jumped to shore, his work boot grinding pebbles underfoot. "Hey, you look at me when I'm talking."

"Jack, he saw!" Whiner rocked in the boat as if cradling himself. "That's all we need! They're going to find out how we got the dynamite and . . ."

"Just shut up!"

Whiner clamoured from the boat desperate with an idea. "Hey, kid, how about some fish? Lots of fish!" Stumbling out, he grabbed Jack's jacket for support and pulled him backwards into water.

"Let me go!"

My chance. I skittered up the bank, breaking through the bushes to the road. I raced over wooden planks, the bridge a roller-coaster blur with Jack behind, pounding, panting, "Damn! Damn!" Words lost and stretching out. Whiner crying far behind, "Hey! Wait!" as Jack was getting closer.

I was caught, yanked back; shirt ripped, legs twisted, scraped on gravel. Jack towered overhead.

"You . . . you little . . ." Jack was breathless, his face was swollen and dark. "Want to get away, huh? . . . I'll fry your butt!" I was lifted and dropped, dangling by my collar. Sky, river, clouds, fields crashed about my ears.

"Thought you'd be smart, eh? . . . play around?" His words broke over me.

"No, Jack . . . don't hurt him!" Whiner yelled from somewhere.

My knees were scraped; one felt warm and wet through the corduroy. My head throbbed. Suddenly my back struck something hard. Jack had slammed me against the railing and I collapsed against him, the two of us, one in fear, the other furious, panting into each other.

I heard Whiner saying, "Jack, listen . . . he don't know us from . . . don't know a thing."

Yet I spit out, "You're Jack and you're . . . you're from Riverton . . . the garage . . . and you made me lose my rod . . . it's your fault, not mine!"

Too late. The words were out, all the worst ones, and already Jack was fiercer.

"You're really looking for it. Aren't you?" As he closed in, I saw his lips stretching back from small white teeth. "If you think you're telling anybody anything . . ." He bounced me against the railing in a slow, even motion, again and again. I wanted to fall onto him, cling to the softness of his denim jacket, to touch his boyish face, to sob, "No! No, please! Don't hurt me," into the heart of that mannish boy. But he propped me against a post and clenched both his fists.

"Don't, Jack," Whiner was pleading and I felt oddly sorry for him. "You'll just make it worse, Jack. You always make it worse."

Jack kicked the post, barely missing me. "Damn! It won't

just be the warden, it'll be Sargeant Vanier." He smirked as if to taunt himself. "He's been after me ever since that game in Ericksdale when I got him against the boards. He's going to love this. He'll come cruising into my folks' farmyard with his mountie lights flashing and he'll take me like a goddamn trophy!"

Whiner hovered at the edge of my vision, blocking out the sun. "Kid, how about some fish? For the old man, maybe?" I couldn't focus on the face, only his smells of sweat, gum, gasoline as I felt my knees dissolving.

A shadow hoisted me up and leaned me against the railing. Something flickered in the sun – a fishing knife with its row of teeth grinning into my eyes, and Jack's own bitter voice. "Want this? . . . sharp . . . if you know what's good . . . worth ten bucks."

I leaped over the railing. Something in me as powerful as Jack pulled me up, thrust out my hands and feet, manoeuvred me off the dark barrier of bridge, to toss me, with my shirt flapping like broken wings, head first into the reflecting blaze of sun.

And crashing through.

To be hugged by water. Dragged down by water until my eyes could open and see again – green shafts of light and mossy pilings. Dead fish, the ones that did not rise but stayed below, each one a marker on some wide path. No words. No sound. My lungs ached but I stayed. The fish seemed to want me. They were waving, nodding with the current. *Come with us. With shadows. It's quiet here and you can stay.* It seemed so easy to be carried by the cool dark flow.

Until my lungs screamed out and my arms grabbed towards the air. The upper light broke against my face. Sky blue. Field green. The wooden bridge all light and shadow. I swallowed air and water, choking as my hands reached for a cable wrapped around some pilings.

Dust and voices sifted down.

"You see him?"

"Jeez, Jack, he's been down too long."

"You looking or talking?"

"There must be lots of junk down there. He could be stuck on something."

"I was letting him keep the goddamn knife. He was crazy or a retard or something."

"Jack, what if he doesn't come up?"

Down again. Slowing my heart, my mind. Rowing downward like a water beetle along a shaft of light, I reached the grey riverbed speckled in greens and whites. My clothing swelled into fins. My cheeks filled, my throat blocked water as I floated with dead fish, so many more than had risen to the surface, suspended in a murky light curtained by darkness.

I stroked forward and back, a bowing stroke with my eyes open, my lips mouthing water, shaping some sort of song for the dead. Without words or sound I was nodding, chanting to them.

Arms and legs forced me up a second time, gasping and crying, until I could let the waves rock and calm me. And the sighing of wind.

I was jarred by a scraping far away, the metal hull of the rowboat pulled over rock. A break of voices. I submerged, stroking through the weeds, then turned in a dead man's float, letting my face bob among the lily pads near to shore. Eventually, after the bridge rumbled with the weight of heavy tires and the distant hill ground with gears, I understood that the men were gone. Yet I remained, gazing at the clouds as they shaped and reshaped themselves, dissolving even as they formed.

I broke the spell myself, with a deliberate plunge. This time I stroked to the river's bottom to search for what I'd lost. First I retrieved my runners, kicked off in the dive, where they were dangling like two more fish along the base of the pilings. I moved along the pilings to find my father's rod stuck upright in the silt. Its golden label, SPIN MASTER, gleamed in some trick of light. I gripped it as I rose and swam to the closer bank.

I crawled out across a bed of mud. My body was weak, trembling with its own weight, so I steadied myself on a flat large rock. Two legs, I thought, still streaming water, I'm some kind of creature with two legs.

My steps became firmer on the bridge, solid once I saw that my bike and tackle box were safe. I dropped the runners, leaned the fishing rod against the railing and whipped water from my sleeves. My back, especially my neck, felt stretched and a tingling at the base of my skull seemed to brighten everything before my eyes.

Something gleamed beside the box, like a long thin mirror, a shard of sky and cloud – it was the blade of Jack's fishing knife. Forgotten or left as a threat, a bribe, a prize.

I held it in my right hand, felt the sun's heat on it and its own hard weight. It had belonged to Jack, now it belonged to me. I didn't feel proud or excited or even tired. I only felt removed, as if I'd become a part of some great and distant order.

I tested the blade with the flat of my thumb, then looked to the tangle hanging from the rod.

A stroke of the knife.

Another.

The tangle sailed off the rod. It floated down, collapsing on the water. I watched it sag into the current and my chest released something that sounded like a laugh, as the tangle drifted with the dead fish into the shining river.

THE EARLY DAYS OF SHADOWMAN

I TOOK RILEY'S DARE, THAT SPRING DAY OF 1961 WHEN I WAS ONLY
ten years old. I climbed the main mast of the high back fence to
do my stunt. I shimmied up, past the grim hook of the laundry
line, to the nest-high top with the earth reeling way below me
and the sirens of the wind calling me higher, blowing my hair
cumulus, stratus, cirrus, but I stopped my ears from hearing
and clenched my legs around the wooden post so tightly that
my muscles knotted into wood.

I drew my yoyo from my pocket and wound the string to
tautness. Breathing in that wildness that was blowing over me,
I stretched out a hand and leaned into the sky. To perform my
trick, my offering to whatever had always kept me such a small
and timid boy.

With a flick of the wrist, I cast the yoyo at the sun.
Almost there, I pulled it back by its string and played it in
the air. It performed Around the World; the bright orb
circling around me, rising, falling, rising, falling, above me
and below me, as I became the world itself. Till the string
slipped from my finger and the yoyo broke its orbit,

plunging down and through the window of the old back door.

All my courage broke with that pane of glass. Riley, the kid who had dared me up the pole, took off. But I couldn't. This was my own back yard.

"Eh?" came an old voice from somewhere deep behind the door. "Eh? Who's there? You wait." It didn't come from the back door of my parents' store or from the door leading up the back stairs to the apartments. The voice came from behind the third door, the one with the window panes painted over that I'd cast my yoyo through, the one I'd thought nobody ever used. A dry, whistling voice called out, "Wait. I'm coming right away."

I slid down the post, heavy with dread. I tried to think of someone I could blame. It's my dad's fault, that's what I'd say. He stuck me out here.

One night while I had dreamed of flying over the moonlit towers of Gotham City and Metropolis, my father took my treasure of comic books and stowed it in the basement. When I found out, he ordered me outside where there was nothing, especially in early spring with everything dead and buried in the muck.

"It's all Dad's fault," I whispered to the broken glass, to the door and to the sound of slow, dry steps, coming closer, rising out of the ground.

"I'm coming. Coming." The door scraped open and an old man blinked into the sun. "Arthur? . . . ah . . . I thought you were Arthur knocking." He was bent, shrunken almost to my height and hung with faded work clothes. He nodded to me through milky eyes. "But, you . . . you."

"I didn't mean it, honest," I said.

"Sometimes Arthur comes to take me to Oscar's Delicatessen. I have some borscht, maybe a corned beef sandwich. But what's the difference?" he shrugged. "I can make my own borscht." He turned back toward the stairs.

Old Man Werner. This was the first time I had met him, the owner and caretaker whom my father called 'the mole'. "That old mole," he'd said. "Ever since his wife died he's gotten funny. He left his house and moved into his basement workshop. I don't see how he'll keep himself together, let alone the building."

"I'm sorry about the broken window, Mr. Werner," I said. "It was an accident."

"Window?" He looked at the broken pane. He fingered the long teeth of glass. "Yah, I got to fix it but I don't know when. There's so much to do."

"What are you going to tell my parents?"

"So who are your parents?" he asked.

"We rent the store from you and apartment number one upstairs. My dad is Murray and my mom's Deborah. . . . You know, we're the Steins."

"Oh, yah. So you're . . . uh."

"I'm Danny."

"Daniel, you grow so fast. Just like Arthur did."

"What about the glass?"

Mr. Werner studied the window. He drew a measuring tape from his pocket. "You tell your dad, you tell him . . . I been busy but now I'll fix it right away. Twelve by six." He stepped back and shrunk six inches. Another step, he shrunk again and faded as he descended into the half light below. His whisper sifted up. "I got some old glass somewhere. Twelve by six."

I shifted forward and back, vacillating between this tender ghost and the stony emptiness of the back lot. As he disappeared beyond my view, I spotted my yoyo on the bottom step, glowing candy red. Its string led into the basement. It lured me down, my hand trailing against the mortared wall. I stopped two steps from the bottom, crouched and grabbed it. I was about to rush back up when I heard the old man rummaging and I peered inside.

His workshop was a wizard's den with a cone of light above the clutter of a long wooden table. Twists of wrought iron and curls of cardboard were propped in a corner while odd cuts of plywood, pegboard, sheet metal leaned like strange letters spelled across a wall. At the end of that mysterious word was the figure of the old man himself, bending over a dusty store sign.

"Twelve by six," he told himself. "Yah, I got some old glass around here somewhere."

I wandered in, found a steel ball-bearing in a jar of screws and rolled it hand to hand, watching it mark an oily track across my palms. It slipped and with a flash of silver it disappeared beneath the table. I wiped the stain against my pants and poked through a Rey del Mundo cigar box, discovering brass numbers, odd keys, a broken lighter, the shiny gears from some intricate machine. Above the table were shelves of boxes, tins and mason jars. To the right was a panel of pegboard displaying ancient tools and instruments.

"What's this for, Mr. Werner?" I held up something that looked like a corkscrew.

"What?" he looked up from the corner. "Oh, so you came down. What's what? . . . that? That's, how do you say it? Aach, in the Old Country, there I knew how they called it . . . but here, what do they say?" He puzzled as his hand struggled to shape the word. "Yah, they say . . . a . . . a auger."

"Ogre?"

"It starts a hole in wood. Then I can stick in a nail or a screw." He retrieved the pane of glass, stripped off its yellowed paper, and cleared a place at the worktable. "That auger thing, it's like a drill except I do the twisting with my hand."

"How come they call it an ogre?" I asked.

"Do I know?" he asked me back. "It's a name. That thing beside you, they call that a ball peen hammer. That other thing in the jar they call it a . . . I don't know . . . they call it some different name. Who knows why? Do you know why they call you . . . what do they call you?"

"Danny. Or Dan or Daniel. Rita, from the cafe, she sometimes calls me Danny Boy."

"Yah, so you see. There's all kinds of names even for just one person. My name is Joseph or Joe or Old Man Werner. And before that, it was Yossel."

"Maybe the thing's called an ogre because ogres live in holes," I said.

"Hmmm."

"Or maybe because it's used to fight ogres."

"Look there," he said, "beside that ladder. That's a big auger for digging in the ground. That's how I built the fence outside. I dug holes with it three feet deep – for posts that stand six feet above the ground. And even higher. The post that holds the laundry line, it's fourteen feet high."

"That's high," I said.

"It sure is," he said.

"But it's a pretty old fence."

"Yah . . . that's right," he admitted. "It's old. And I'm old, too. I used to be a young man. It used to be a young fence."

I dragged out the tool by its crossbar, wider than my shoulders. I propped the bar against my chest and managed a single turn; it flaked a circle of rust onto the concrete floor.

Mr. Werner smiled. "You want to make holes? Use the small one. It's more your size. Here's a block of wood – go make some holes."

I gripped the hand-sized auger and dug fiercely. The pine was soft and soon I sank a line of holes to form a pattern. I was shaping an S for Superman. I turned around to show it off and saw the old man nodding to shadows on the wall, the pane tilting loosely in his hand.

"Sometimes I forget names," Mr. Werner said. "I even forget what you call a thing. I can still use it. My hand doesn't forget. And the auger? What does it need to know? The hand turns it and it digs. In the village, so many boys were called Yossel. Yossel Nossen, Yossel Lansky, Yossel Bendel, plenty of Yossels. We play in the field after studying Talmud. We hear, 'Yossel . . . come eat!' I run and Yossel Bendel runs. My stomach wants supper. Yossel is all it needs to hear. It don't need no details. So my legs run. Only, who is calling? It's Mrs. Bendel who's got more kids than she's got plates. Then just having the name, Yossel, isn't good enough. She says, 'Go to your own house. I got enough mouths to feed.' Oh, I could smell her fresh braided bread even in her doorway."

"Are you going to cut the glass?" I asked him.

"What? Oh, yah." His fingers tightened and my breath was

released. He set it flat, aligning it to the table's edge. "My son, Arthur, he says I forget to eat. He says I should live somewhere where I'll get meals served regular and right on time. Aach! So what if I eat at two or three instead of noon? Should a clock tell my stomach when it's hungry?" He lifted a glazier's wand from a narrow shelf. "You watch me cut with this. Maybe you'll learn something." He reached for a steel ruler. "What was it? Twelve by what?"

"By six."

"That's good. Between the two of us, we remembered the whole thing."

The wand rasped the pane and rasped my nerves so I had to clutch the bench to keep on watching. The old man tapped the wand once, twice along the groove; the glass pane snapped in two.

"In our shtetl, our small village, no one had a clock," he said. "But everybody still knew when to eat. No, wait, that's not true. Horowitz had a clock. He was a rich man, that Horowitz. He had a fur coat made from foxes and a cane with a silver head. And his clock was gold! – or for sure, it was brass – with three balls at the bottom that kept turning in a circle. First they turned one way and then they turned the other. Me and my sister, Rochel, we loved to peek through his window to watch them move. The clock faced into the room so even then we couldn't see the time; all that the clock told us was that Horowitz was a rich man. But what did it tell Horowitz? When he was going to choke on a bone? No.

"It's winter, late in the day, with the snow blowing so much that we can't even see across the road. Masha Pinsky, who takes in Horowitz's laundry, beats on our door. She says to my papa, 'Horowitz is dead. He choked on a bone.' Just like that. Papa goes with the others to sit all night with the body and make prayers. Me, I'm too young but I sneak out and look through Horowitz's window. The clock is still going. The balls are still turning."

The old man was gesturing with the glazier's wand and I could almost see that long-lost clock. Mr. Werner seemed to be drawn with broad cartoon lines; deep set eyes, slight curve of nose, a mat of silver hair tufting around his ears, he wasn't stooped but inclined, as if to greet the world with a self-effacing bow.

"My Arthur has that kind of clock," he said. "It's not exactly the same, but close. He's a lawyer now with a big house in Tuxedo. Sometimes, he takes me there for supper. We have pieces of chicken in cardboard cartons with these . . . these fried potatoes and a bun. He buys them at a pick-up restaurant. The whole family sits in the living-room on furniture that could be in a palace and we all eat out of cardboard cartons. This, Arthur calls 'a treat.' He says, 'Pa, it's like having a picnic right in your own home.' What am I going to say? Everybody is watching the television. But me, I'm watching the clock on top — the way the balls are turning. I don't say nothing to nobody. I just think things to myself."

A third stroke of the cutter. Then a fourth. Mr. Werner measured the glass again and nodded. He gathered his hammer, chisel, a pack of putty, then stooped to search deep in a battered coffee tin. He paused as if his hand met something strange that his fingers were deciphering.

"They can't have a regular funeral for Horowitz. It's snowing way too much. The snow keeps drifting like moving hills. We have to open the window on the second floor just to get outside. No, wait . . . that wasn't in Poland, that was in Canada, already. Before Miriam came over. Yah, I was working then for the Scotsman. He said to me, 'Joe, get to the barn and feed the horses.' So I had to climb out the window. It wasn't so easy — I could only see the hay loft where the barn should be but I had to do what the Scotsman said. He had such a temper! Yah, Miriam was still in Warsaw, waiting to come over. She was sending me letters with flowers pressed inside."

I imagined Old Werner as a young man dressed in farmer's overalls caught inside the glass dome of a giant clock. Snow whirled around the bottom as he stretched up to grab the rotating balls, before a snow drift overwhelmed him.

"If Spider-man were there," I said, "he'd shoot out a web and then you could grab onto it."

"What? A web? What kind of web?" he asked.

"Like a rope to the barn," I said. "So then you wouldn't sink in the snow."

"I walked on top of the snow. I sank to my belt but still I could walk."

The old man studied me as I tumbled out more words. "But Spider-man doesn't need a rope. All he has to do is shoot his web, it's like when I do my Shoot the Moon trick with my yoyo, except with Spider-man, it's not a yoyo, it's a web and the web sticks onto anything. He can even swing on it."

"Who's that?" he asked. "A man who's a spider?"

"Well, kind of . . . he's a superhero in the comics . . . like Batman. If Spider-man was there, if he was real, I mean, he'd have saved you. If you needed him."

"Spider-man? Batman? You like spiders?"

I dug another hole into the wood, reaming it far too wide. "They aren't spiders or bats," I said. "They're like that but not that part . . . the part that's . . ." I searched the deeper shadows by the wall as if my heroes were waiting there. Then I remembered they were stuck in the storage room of our basement. "Mr. Werner, how come . . . I've been down in the basement with my dad but I never saw this workshop. And where's the furnace and the room where my father stores our stuff?"

"Through there – that's your parents' side," Mr. Werner motioned to a steel fire door. "You've never seen my side before. The building is divided; on the top floor there's the apartments. On the main floor, there's the barbershop on one side and your parents' store on the other side. In the basement there is also two parts. This part is under the barber shop. It's got my workshop and my place to eat and sleep. Your parents' part of the basement is underneath their clothing store. The only connection between the two parts is through that door."

I studied the door, a bank vault door, a dungeon portal. "I wouldn't go in there," I said. "Not unless I'm with my dad."

"You don't like basements?" he asked.

I shook my head, frowning at the door.

"Me, I like basements," he said.

"I don't mind this one," I told him. "It's different."

"You like bats and spiders – you don't like bats and spiders. You like basements – you don't like basements." Mr. Werner smiled as he stood beneath the the workshop lamp, light streaming through his fine white hair. "Me, I'm an old man so I like basements." I nodded and grinned at his wrinkles drawing shadows. I thought, shadows, he knows all about them. He's Shadowman.

"It's quiet here," he said. "So I can remember things. Arthur says I'm forgetting, but I'm remembering. Plenty."

"Did you ever see The Sleeper?"

"What's that?" Mr. Werner asked. "Somebody who's sleeping?"

I pulled out my yoyo. "It's my best trick. First, it goes to sleep at the end of the string. Watch." I jolted the yoyo, dropping it the length of the string so it lay spinning on its axle; it became a blur, a phantom hovering around its solid core. For a moment we watched together in a shared trance.

"Now let's wake it up!" I yelled out and slapped the back of my hand. It leapt up the string into my grip.

The old man stared, first at the yoyo bright as an apple in my hand, then at me. He gauged the intentness of my eye, the sureness of my grip. "That's what I'd call a real wake-up," he said.

I looked to the stairs. The outer light had dimmed. "What's the time?" I asked. "I better get home!"

"Yah, I got to fix that window," he said. "And I've got some sweeping up to do in here. I didn't notice what a mess it's getting."

I hesitated at the first step and looked back. The old man was retrieving a broom from a pile of lumber.

"Mr. Werner . . . about the window."

"Yah, you can help me another time," he said. "You come back. You dig with the auger."

I'D VISIT MR. WERNER often over the next year and a half, stirring about the worktable as he drifted through his memories.

Perhaps my coming changed him, woke him up, because his stories grew more clear and livelier, and he did, too, as if he'd brushed himself off and gotten back to the work of living once again.

He guided me through my family's Passover seder, he taught me how to work with my hands, and with my head. He started me dreaming of a whole other world, woven by his memories and folktales, a world far greater than those of my comic books. I'd tell him things, as well, chattering about my family and school; neither of us needed the other to listen very carefully.

One time I found that I'd planed the end of a two-by-four into a paper-thin wedge. I'd been day-dreaming, had lost the wood and lost the day-dream and it was too late in the day for anything. Another time, I shuffled down the stairs, aching from an insult. Werner was working at a padlock. I pulled an end of lumber from the pile of scraps and hammered it with larger and larger nails until they split the wood. I tossed the broken pieces at the pile, then hunched over a coffee tin of loose nuts and bolts to sort and match. All this time not a word was spoken, not a look exchanged. As I threaded pairs of nuts and bolts together, I barked out my story.

I'd been watching two pigeons on a branch outside my classroom window. Their throats glazed with purple, their heads bobbed in a mystery of need as they jostled one another toward the end of the branch which bowed to their weight and tapped against the glass. It looked so golden in the sun, it seemed like Elijah's magic branch. Mr. Werner had told me how the spirit of the Prophet Elijah gave the Ba'al Shem Tov a branch from a wonder tree on Mount Carmel. The Ba'al Shem Tov carved it into a walking stick to call down miracles. When the Ba'al Shem's great deeds were all completed and he had died, Elijah took it back, returning it to the wonder tree to become a living branch again. And so I watched in awe as a golden branch tapped against the window, offering itself to me.

The laughter of my classmates blew the scene apart. My name was being shouted. Thirty faces cooed, hooted, and above them all was Mrs. Maitland commanding me to copy out a lesson all through recess.

"It wasn't fair," I complained to Mr. Werner. "I understood what she was teaching just as much as anybody. She picked on me."

"Did you explain about the branch?" he asked.

"Huh! What does she care? She's got no time for stories."

"Yah," he said. "Grownups got no time. But you got time for branches. And for comic books. And even to build and break with nails."

I felt my throat tighten. I lowered my head to the loneliness rooting in my chest.

"And me, I'm just the same," Mr. Werner said. "I got time to free a lock that doesn't even have a key – a lock to shut a workshop that's got nothing in it anyone would want to steal." His hand, rough as bark, rubbed across my cheek and came to rest upon my shoulder. "It's not so bad," he assured me. "We can't be standing at attention all day long. A child has got to build some hopes and dreams. And old people have a lot of memories that need putting into order." For a long moment we said nothing, we thought nothing and felt no differences between us. Though we worked and told our stories each for different ends, this dreamy silence from which all our stories seemed to come made the two of us one and the same.

"But when I was a young man," Mr. Werner said. "Ha! I had to work so hard, I didn't even have a minute. A minute was like a crumb to a starving man, a drop of water to a thirsty man! I worked and studied, studied and worked. My father, may he rest in peace, he wanted me to become a great rabbi. Even not so great, it would still have been a blessing. He was a hard-working man, my father. He knew about time like he knew about money, it was always what somebody else had, never him. He drove a wagon that carried water from the river to the town. Just water. But every night the two of us read together in the village study house, saving for candles so we could study longer. I learned about the Prophets, and the Holy Writings, the Mishnah, the Gemorah, the Commentaries, even the Kabbala that no student was supposed to even look at until the age of forty. My father's dream was that I should go to Ger and be accepted by the great Hassidic rabbi who lived in the way of the Ba'al Shem Tov, the one known as Sfas Emes, the Lips of Truth. But how? We had a big family and the youngest didn't even have a pair of shoes. Also there'd been troubles, a pogrom in our village – with people hurt and our house burned down by peasants. My father had to cut down trees to build another house and I had to do his work, drawing water from the river and driving it to Otvotsk. Already my mother was getting her sickness in the chest. . . ."

I pictured the young Werner, just my age but tall and strong, driving the water wagon to his village. A great storm was breaking over the countryside as he struggled with his panicked horse. The scene was drawn in one of those large panels that filled the whole first page of a Classics Illustrated comic book. In the following panel, lost and weary, he was entering Ger. In the next, he stopped at the study house, asking for directions home. The students made jokes about his ragged clothes, his sunburned face. Another one showed young Werner raising his reins, about to leave, when he overheard two rabbis arguing a complex problem and he offered a brilliant answer. A crowd scene showed scholars in fur hats, rich men in silken gabardines; everybody had a question.

I imagined more panels – young Werner welcomed by the great rabbi to his palace, then Werner in courtly clothes waving from a high tower to the rabbi who was leaving on a mission. The next panel showed the Black Duke leading a surprise attack upon the palace and then a half-page with Werner in the rabbi's study summoning spirits out of an ancient leather book to help him as the duke and all his men break in. The early scenes were green, the next were washed in crimson. The final ones glowed golden, promising more panels, all bright and thrilling.

THE DAY I RETURNED from vacation, at the end of the summer of 1962, the moment my parents released me from unpacking, I rushed back to the workshop. I'd been stuck in a crowded cottage with my parents and my uncle's family, escaping whenever I could to an old wooden bridge where I would fish and remember Mr. Werner's stories, telling them to myself in my own way, for only gleaming fish and gleaming words were able to ward off the dreariness of that cottage and my growing apprehension that I was somehow to blame for everybody being miserable.

I found Mr. Werner bent over the worktable as if he'd never left. His tools were in confusion and there were plates of food here and there, some looking very old. At first I merely thought he was in the middle of some big job.

"You should have been there, Mr. Werner," I said. "We went for hikes and bike rides and motor boating on the lake. Once we drove into the woods looking for a berry patch and the car conked out. Uncle Steve couldn't get it going, he couldn't even find the instruction manual. He was swearing at the car like it was a donkey and Aunt Judith was yelling that we'd be stuck there overnight. Finally we started walking back to the main road but my cousin Searle said he was going to stay and live off rainwater. Uncle Steve turned all purple. He shouted, 'Searle, you're so spoiled you won't even drink Pepsi, it has to be Coca-Cola!' That's when Aunt Judith said, 'Where's Lonny?' So everybody started looking for Lonny!" I lost my breath, felt giddy and amazed. This story was a wonder that I'd discovered. Suddenly, the weight of that time, the anxiety and boredom fell away, not by a lie – for none of it was made up – but something else had emerged in the telling, magically transforming everything. And I was the magician.

My mind reeled; there was so much to turn into stories – a motorboat ride so close to shore I thought we'd crash into the trees; a bear at the cottage window and my aunt's hysterics when we tossed it potato chips; the night we tented in the backyard and Lonny, needing to pee, wandered through the dark into Mrs. Hiebert's cottage and how she screamed for the police. Story after story took on a glamour under the work lamp's cone of light, so that even my awful cousins, my overbearing aunt and uncle became hilarious characters, their foulest traits turning into whimsical eccentricities in a world I shaped with words.

I decided to tell about the fishing rod. "I was fishing with the Spin Master. And there was this explosion, I mean, I'm talking about a real kaboom! Like one big shout!"

It was all welling up: the two men in the boat, the floating weeds and ghostly fish, the singing edge of the fishing knife, even the calm I'd found afterwards that would shelter me from the misery of that cottage; all this was rising, glowing between me, the teller, and Mr. Werner, my listener. As I rushed into the story I knew there was something more moving through it, something that could make it even greater and Mr. Werner was the one who could help me find it.

The old man seemed to be concentrating on something in the shadows. I stumbled on in my excitement. "I hid in the bullrushes so I could see and two guys showed up in a boat – teenagers, but tough ones and I was scared but I had to stay to be a witness . . ."

"By the beard they dragged him."

"Pardon me?" I asked.

"By the beard. They were hitting him with sticks." Mr. Werner's hands were locked together as if he were struggling with himself, trying to break the grip. "I wanted to run out of the bushes," he said. "To do anything but we don't dare be seen. Mama, she holds Rochel to her breast. She don't want her seeing – even seeing such a thing is like being hit."

"What's wrong, Mr. Werner?" I asked him. "Who was getting hit?"

"We hear Reb Sender. I think he's crying or else begging. It's no shame if begging saves your life. But no, he is singing the prayer for dying, 'Shma Yisrael – Hear, O Israel, the Lord Our God, The Lord is One!' Over and over. And the peasants are laughing; hitting and laughing. Then, Janusz, the woodcutter, the one who stutters, the one who in the spring crawled out of the forest with a cut foot. It was Reb Sender who bandaged him and Janusz kissed his hand. Like a dog licks, that's how he kissed. 'Y-y-you save my foot, G-g-god love you!' But now Janusz is lifting his axe high over Sender's head and he brings it down with all his might!"

I listened, stunned, as Werner wheezed, his words tearing into coughs, straining to speak as the scene changed to another and then another: a search for a child among gypsy wagons; an argument with his father who said some girl he liked was not properly religious; a party in the back of a tailor's shop for a young soldier, Werner's best friend, who would never return, and others from his past who kept coming back as ghosts. I finally backed away and up the stairs, trying to excuse myself, but he could not hear or see me.

"He's a fool, not a doctor, talking words just to frighten. A 'condition'. What's that supposed to mean? And why should I waste money on pills that make me sicker? Twenty dollars. My sister, Rochel, is starving . . . sixteen years old . . . teeth, hair falling out. For twenty zlotys she can eat and live."

FROM THEN ON, every visit was a risk. Sometimes Mr. Werner seemed himself. An hour might pass in jokes or silent work before the shadows deepened along his eyes and his memories took him further than I could go. A story would unravel into shifting scenes. Characters would merge. A Polish soldier, a Winnipeg policeman on a dike of sandbags, a foreman hollering atop a pile of lumber, they all became a single man emerging in different places, at different times. A sobbing woman had me constantly alarmed. She was dressed in black, clutching a kerchief to her mouth. But was she the woman who mourned over a child dead of diptheria? Or was she crying beside a burning house? Werner's mother, sister, wife? I asked him but at first he didn't hear. I asked again as clearly as I could. Finally I shouted and he startled to his feet. He hushed me and gripped my hand, whispering, "Get away while you can. Don't tell anyone about us or they'll come looking."

I wanted to stay away but his memories held us both. I was caught in arguments with people I'd never known. I worried with Werner about his wife forming a union for garment workers, agonized as if we were really waiting for her to come safely home. I wanted the crying woman, whoever she was, to stop crying, to rebuild the barn, to have another child, to do anything that would free me from her.

Mr. Werner's memories must have stayed with me even in my sleep for I'd wake up with the same tightness in my jaw and shoulders as I'd felt in the basement workshop. Yet, when I tried to recall my dreams I sensed only dark and furtive movements in my mind.

The first week in September, I announced to Mr. Werner that school had begun, hoping this would free us both to be the way we were before. He was sitting on the stool, bent over the worktable. There was no light except from the stairs leading outside which only served to raise a dimness along his back. He mumbled something about a bike that had broken just when he needed it to ride to a union demonstration. After gathering a pair of pliers, screwdrivers and a jar of bolts, he lifted a loose ball of rope and strings out of a drawer and tried to pull some wire from it. I noticed something red; it was my lost yoyo with its string tangled in the mess. I wanted to free it but Mr. Werner kept pulling at the wire and soon the yoyo was swallowed up. Muttering, he shoved it all back into the drawer and carried his tools to the other end of the room to look for a bike that was not there. When he stopped, he seemed to soften. Returning, he laid down the tools and looked at me like the person I used to know.

"I'm sorry, Danny," he said. "I'm remembering so many things that I feel bad about and I keep thinking how they could have turned out different. But what can I do? It's too much work for me." He buried his face in his hands.

I climbed up the stairs, looking backwards, then hesitated at the outer door, afraid to let it close and leave him in that darkness. For a moment, I thought of hunting out the mess of string and wire, cutting my yoyo loose and using it to delight him once again but I knew even then that no child's trick of light and colour whirling on a string would bring the old man back.

I called down to him, "See you in the workshop, Mr. Werner. I'll come visit you tomorrow," and knowing that I wouldn't, I let the basement door close shut behind me.

TWO SPIRITS HAD COME DANCING

NO ONE ON THE BUS SEEMED TO SEE OLD YOSSEL WERNER AS HE entered; not the driver whose thoughts were tied to traffic nor the workers and the evening shoppers heading home. All their faces were turned away, too weary for the weight of another's eyes.

Old Werner did not look up either, so deeply was he brooding about the spirits who had appeared to him again last night. He took a seat and gripped the crossbar in front of him. Two spirits had come dancing, showing themselves as swirls of phosphorescent white in a dark corner of his basement workshop. The first one was his wife; he could tell her by her shawl and by her flowing waist-length hair. But the other one, so much fainter and obscure, the one who circled her as she gently rose and sank in a spiralling waltz. Who was that man?

Werner stared through the rattling window at the trees, their autumn leaves ablaze in the lowering sun. Burning, he thought, but not burned up.

"Lo, the bush was burning yet it was not consumed." This came to him as words written upon parchment in the ancient Hebrew and scented by the wooden spicebox that his father used to place nearby for revival in case either he or Werner might drowse during their long nights in the study house.

There was a bush whose flaming leaves
Each spoke a holy word.

He remembered his father singing this old song, never drawn with ink or held by paper but living in the coiling laugh and sigh of Yiddish, the Jewish common tongue, the language of the street, kitchen and bedroom, of folklore and family tales.

His father's words were composed of earth and air, Werner decided, like the man himself whose body smelled of pipe tobacco, sweat and the damp hay of the stable, whose breath was ripe with pickled herring and the homemade peppermint schnapps that he would decant at the end of every Sabbath with a rousing tune and a calloused hand rhythmically beating the supper table into life.

But either way, Werner mused, I never saw that fire. And no bush either.

Werner watched the last of the sun sink behind the Main Street shops. The canopy of elms darkened into smouldering clouds as the bus rolled on. It rocked him forward and back in the manner of his father when he prayed, who would lean towards and away, eyes fluttering in the ancient trance of their people, his father who worked by day and studied by night, carting water for the village, yet signing his name with the letters Samech-Tet, signifying a direct descendant of the high priestly Jews of mediaeval Spain. When those ancestors had suffered their Dispersion, being expelled in 1492, they returned to the Hòly Land to become scholars and mystics of the Kabbala. There they clung for generations to rocky perches in the mountain city of Safad, even after an earthquake levelled it. Safad, City of Earth and Fire.

"A ruined city in a ruined universe," his father had intoned, hands grasping the worn edges of his prayer book. "What better place to search for God's lost sparks?" Werner's father held to a Kabbalistic vision of Creation which described the Divine Substance contracting Itself into vessels. The vessels burst apart, creating the universe in an expulsion of fire and earthen shards. Humanity's great task was to retrieve those scattered sparks and return with them to the Source.

Something crowded beside Werner on the seat, a grey bulk with bulging shopping bags between its legs. It drew in a wheezing breath, then exhaled with a listless groan. Again and again, it added its shallow rhythm to the rock and rumble of the bus: wheeze, groan; wheeze, groan.

Old Werner found his own breath keeping pace. He shifted inside his padded canvas coat. His feet rubbed inside their crusty work boots. He adjusted his wool cap but it kept itching at his scalp. His body felt frail and shrunken, an old seed rustling in its husk.

How did I get so small? he wondered. How did my clothes all get so loose?

He imagined his last few teeth dropping out, his hair shedding in the next strong gust of wind. "Nothing fits anything anymore," he said aloud.

This interrupted the wheeze and groan beside him. Werner looked to the profile of chin, lips, nose; the rest was covered by a dark wine scarf. He spoke to the lips. "Everything's gotten hard and loose."

The lips tightened. Without moving they grunted in agreement, a muffled note that broke into a cough. Soon it began again. Wheeze and groan.

You must be earth and earth, Werner decided, identifying the composition of his companion. There's no part of you that's fire or air or water.

Werner studied the other travellers on the bus. He imagined embryos inside dusty bottles; dimly formed beings, transparent in their foetal sacs. Each body held its spirit like a trapped light, a faint luminosity; one was hovering underneath a heart, others wavered behind a mouth or eye, and another struggled down toward the genitals.

They're stuck inside their bodies, Werner told himself. Each one's like a ghost in a haunted house. It can't leave but it can't rest. And there's nothing it can find in there that does it any good.

"They call it a temple but what happens if it's a ruin?"

Werner asked the bulk beside him. "What happens when it's a wreck that you can't keep fixing?"

The bulk straightened. "Huh? . . . you talking to me?"

"They say your body is a temple for the soul."

"My body? Who says?"

"It doesn't matter who," Werner replied. "It only matters if it's true or if it's not."

It fell silent, not even a wheeze. Grey lips parted slightly. A watery eye swivelled into view and then away. The bulk spoke again. "Excuse me." It rose to sway up the aisle of the bus, exposing a surprise of flesh above its black boots; a woman's heavy calves.

Too late for desire? Werner wondered. He closed his eyes to summon a memory of women. He imagined dim figures far below him, as if in the bottom of a canyon. One of them gestured to him, her voice lost in the depths.

Werner tried to remember himself with the firm body of his youth, scented with shaving soap and talcum powder. He recalled the clatter of his shoes as they'd climbed a stone staircase, his laughter in a marbled concert hall, the sparkle of a woman's hatpin and the nape of her neck veiled by auburn hair. When she had turned to greet him with deep chestnut eyes, he had felt his skin electrify, as if belt and buttons, layers of clothes all vanished so that he and she were two naked bodies about to meet.

This still is not desire, Old Werner told himself. This is just a memory of desire. It's the remembering that's strong, not the wanting.

Werner gazed at a row of apartment blocks as the bus passed by. He was attracted to the occasional lit window suspended in the darkness, each an illuminated panel of an interior life. In one, a woman was gazing out, the lace curtains draped behind her like long white wings. Further on, another window revealed an older woman pointing across a table at a man, who was shaking with laughter, or anger, or fear. Another window held a boy with a toy airplane. He was crashing it against the window frame. Once. Twice. The bus rolled past.

"It all started with the boy, you know." Werner heard his wife Miriam's voice, alive again and as warm and musical as when they had been young. He turned to see her just beyond the window of the bus, in their bedroom as it used to be in Warsaw almost sixty years before.

"What boy?" Werner asked, without speaking his words aloud. "Are you talking about the boy who visits me, my friend, Danny?"

"All his questions. The boy got you thinking about things you'd never understood. He even got you praying on Passover like some Old Country rabbi." She lay in their wide feathered bed, the brass bedposts gleaming at her back like a golden gate. "Then when he left you . . ."

"Danny went with his parents. On a vacation."

"He's back but now you're telling stories that frighten him."

"I can't help what I'm remembering. I love the boy. I wouldn't hurt him."

"He was good for you at first. You came alive and got a chance to tell some stories, have some fun. But now you've gone too far, Yossel. You've taken on old troubles that are best forgotten."

"I can't be everything for the boy. He needs to be with friends his own age."

"And who do you need to be with, Yossel?" she asked, sliding off her shawl to reveal her ivory shoulders, firm young breasts.

"You're a ghost now, Miriam," Old Werner warned her. "It's a sin to make love with a ghost."

She laughed with moistened lips. "You never worried about sin when you wanted me before. Or when you wanted your other women."

"I had no other women."

"Liar. It's a sin to lie to a ghost. And not as pleasant as making love. Come to me, Yossel. I can't come to you."

Werner leaned towards her, his forehead pressed against the quivering glass of the bus window as he watched her ease beneath her sheets. "Miriam," he whispered.

"Come, Yossel." She called but it was the fragrance of rosewater that drew him into her bed.

"My only love," he whispered as he used to when his young body used to press against hers, his lips brushing her ear, her neck. "I was always faithful."

"In your way, you were faithful," she yawned, "but not in my way."

"Those others, they meant nothing to me."

"And now," she answered, her eyes closing, "they mean nothing to me."

"That's because you have someone else yourself. Admit it, Miriam."

"Make love to me, Yossel. While you can."

"I saw you with him last night, and twice before that. Three times altogether in the shadows of my workshop. You were dancing with him. Was he your lover in this world, too?"

"I forgave you for your women long ago, Yossel." Her words were drifting off. "No one has ever come between us."

"Then what has come between us?"

Miriam, the bedroom, the scent of rosewater were gone. Werner gripped the restbar of the seat. He felt cold and stiff. Two seats ahead, a window was jammed open and the draught carried a damp chill. Yet his stomach and chest were burning.

Who is her lover? He bent into his pain. Who's that man dancing with her in the Other World while I'm left here with ashes in my mouth?

"Something wrong, old fellah?" The ruddy face of the bus driver startled Werner. The eyes were stern, the hat military with a shining badge and a hard black brim.

"Tzo? Tzo ty chcesc?" Werner flinched. What? What is it? He wanted to cower in the corner of the seat.

"Look, let's not have no problems. Understand?"

"Problems?"

"That lady with the shopping bags, she says she sat next to you and you had some kind of problems."

"I am sorry."

"You got to watch what you're saying to people."

"I am sorry."

"Where do you live, huh?"

"Ulica Pañska. No . . . I mean . . . Stella Avenue. I live at 119 Stella Avenue in Winnipeg."

"That's back in the North End. We passed it twenty minutes ago. Now listen, I'm writing you a note. You wait at that bus stop across the street and you show the note to the driver, understand?"

"Yah . . . I . . . I understand."

OLD WERNER KNEW as he approached the house that it was not 21 Pañska Street, Warsaw. And he knew that he was no longer a young man dashing from a trolley car after work in 1903, a man who'd left the cramped quarters and boundless visions of the study house in his muddy Polish village so he could walk the spacious boulevards of Warsaw and save for passage to Canada. He had no gift of day-old poppyseed torte or back-row tickets to the symphony or a rose plucked from the Krachinsky Public Garden as perfect as any ruby. Werner's hands were empty because there was no Miriam waiting for him on the other side of the door at 119 Stella Avenue, Winnipeg, in 1962.

As he entered, he placed his coat, work boots and cap in the closet by the door. He gathered up the month's worth of letters and flyers that had been slipped through the mail chute. He carried them unread into the kitchen where he dropped them into a brown paper grocery bag. The kitchen was lined with paper bags, each full of mail that Werner would neither read nor throw away. He glanced at the calendar unchanged since November 1960.

It was a year and eleven months ago, today, he thought.

The eleventh day was circled with a heavy lead pencil, the day of Miriam's death. A week after her funeral Werner had sealed up the house and moved into the basement workshop of their commercial building on Main Street. He returned to the house on the eleventh of every month to pull off the dust covers from the living-room furniture and sit in one of their two matched reclining chairs. He'd listen to Dvorak's *New World Symphony* on the gramophone, recalling how they'd first heard it together played by the Warsaw Philharmonic, how it burst from the orchestra, rising above the marble pillars and the gilded gods to resound against the great hall's painted heaven.

This time Werner didn't enter the living-room at all. He headed for their bedroom, the one room he'd not entered since his wife had died.

Werner drew the sheet off the long cedar box at the end of their bed, Miriam's "big hope chest," as she'd called it. Before she'd died she told him to clear it out, saying there was nothing in it worth saving anymore.

How could she treasure all those things for so many years and then let it all be trashed? he wondered. Was there something in there that she was ashamed to leave behind? Something that might reveal her lover?

Werner lifted out the top wooden tray, filled with old purses and cloth bags of costume jewellery. Underneath it were layers of momentoes, the residue of Miriam's seventy-five years.

He knelt beside the box, riffling through the top strata: obituaries of their friends, old greeting cards and invitations, her union badges and certificates of service, a bag of feathers and shells from Gimli beach, a hat box of family photos. But nothing, not even a cryptic note, to give him any clue of a hidden life.

Below this, he reached their middle years, almost all given up to their three children: report cards, class photos, programs from school plays, swimming certificates. A stack of party hats, some waxy cake decorations; Cindy's hospital release when she broke her leg at camp; two braids of Marsha's hair that the girl herself cut off with sewing scissors after some tearful argument with her sister; a chocolate box of dried-out pens, coloured string and ribbons.

A cardboard tube with a tight roll of children's drawings caught his attention. Werner pulled at the drawing closest to the core. It slid out dry and curled up like a scroll, reminding him of the old handwritten parchments he and his father used to study late into the night, mystical works forbidden to the young.

"I SHOULD NEVER HAVE let you read those writings," his father, Avram Werner, had told him as they sat together for the last time in the synagogue. "It made you want to learn too much, too soon. Now you're frustrated and you want to give up everything."

He'd just told his father he was leaving for Warsaw and from there emigrating to Canada. But he'd said nothing about leaving with Miriam, who was known for her own forbidden reading in socialism and secular philosophy.

"Already by eighteen you've mastered all the rabbi understands," his father whispered, not wanting to be heard by those who prayed nearby. "Remember that night when the rabbi spoke about how the Shekhinah, God's Holy Spirit, was separated during the struggles of Creation? You interrupted. You described the Shekhinah as God's womanly being. You said that God and the Shekhinah would join together again at the End of Time with all the joy of a wedding night. What a look the rabbi gave you! He began accusing you of reckless thoughts not fitting for an unmarried man when suddenly the door blew open. I'll tell you now what I should have told you then – that was a wind on a windless day. I heard it rustle like a long stiff robe. As it blew in, I saw the nails of the floor boards sparkle with a soft blue light – that wind was the Prophet Elijah offering you a blessing." His father's breath was sour from fasting, for it was Yom Kippur, Day of Atonement.

Before Yossel Werner could respond, his father was called to the front to open the Ark of the Covenant. Werner watched him approach the dark oak cabinet carved with guardian lions. He opened the doors to reveal the Torah, three feet tall. It had a purple velvet coverlet embroidered with sacred words, and adorned by a silver breastplate etched with the symbols of the twelve tribes. The two poles that held each end of the scroll were wrapped in silver and topped with ivory crowns. Avram Werner lifted the Torah out of the Ark and held it with both arms, resting it against his left side. For a moment he swayed as if he wanted to dance with it the way he did each year on Simchat Torah when he would carry it out of doors into the ecstatic centre of a swirl of singing men.

Instead, he looked across the dark rows of men hunched into their books to his son and gestured with his hand. *Take the Torah, receive this honour meant for me and carry Her around the congregation.*

Yossel Werner could only stare stone-faced past his father's eyes. If there is any blessing coming through that door, he thought, it's meant for you, Papa, not me. You've known miracles. You've seen angels and now Elijah on the wind. But all my books and prayers are still just words. Even if I spoke the thousand sacred names of God at once, I wouldn't see a candle burn the least bit brighter. As if his father understood, he lowered his eyes and leaned his cheek against the velvet cover of the Torah.

Young Werner's chest had felt heavy since morning despite the ritual of knocking at it with his fist, a gesture repeated all through the day-long service in order to arouse the spirit for atonement. It became heavier as he'd prepared to tell his father that he was leaving, for he knew how badly that would hurt him. But now that Young Werner had told him, the weight became something else: hard and unyielding, a barrier that nothing could penetrate or escape. So he watched impassively as his father carried the Torah through the room, and he remained impassive even when his father returned it to the Ark, and did not rejoin him but stayed at the front to pray, nodding to the Torah as if it were his sole companion.

Young Werner mouthed the syllables of each prayer but only for appearance's sake. At sunset, after the Prayer for the Dead, the service reached its climax; the cantor called out, "Tekeah Gadola!" summoning the rabbi to raise the ram's horn for the Great Shout, the final trumpeting call for heaven's gate to open. His father, still at the front, called out as well, gazing east as if his shout and the horn's long blast could carry him past the Torah, through the Ark of the Covenant's wooden wall, the synagogue's whitewashed wall, and even beyond the reaped and darkening fields.

Werner looked back instead, trying to see through the ornate screen that divided the men from where the women prayed. Though he could not see Miriam, he knew that she was in there, waiting, for he could sense her close and thinking of him. Just a few more days, Miriam, he thought, and we'll be married in Warsaw. Then we'll always be together.

THAT'S HOW IT WAS, Old Werner mused as he rested against Miriam's cedar box. We left for Warsaw, then for Canada. We built a life and a family; a whole world, just the two of us.

Old Werner unravelled the child's drawing. He pressed it flat upon the floor beside the box. It was one his son, Arthur, had drawn when he was only eight years old. Werner remembered how Miriam had set the boy on a pile of new pine boards and had given him crayons and this very piece of paper. It kept the boy occupied while she and Werner constructed the high fence in the back lot of their building on Main Street.

The right half of the picture was dark blue with silver stars and moon and a golden sun streaming over the horizon. The left half showed a brown fence with Miriam and Werner inside. She had long black crayoned hair and a flowing yellow dress, her body slightly tilted off the ground. Werner was drawn as a smaller stickman but with massive hands and a huge hammer. He was building the fence around them which rose to the top of the picture like a dam or a fortress wall. He was nailing boards against the highest post that would also hold the laundry line while Miriam was handing him the last two boards that would close them off completely.

But now she's gone, Old Werner thought. And I'm alone, stuck here by myself.

His heart was roaring in bursts of pain. Arthur's crayoned picture slid from his hand and he leaned against the wooden box. He managed to fumble a small tin out of his shirt pocket but as he opened it, a dozen nitroglycerin pills scattered at his feet. There was one left in the tin and he pressed it to his tongue.

Papa, Miriam, even little Arthur, I've failed them and I've lost them, he told himself, his vision blurring as if he were inside a cloud. There's nothing left, he thought. Just memories.

"Then let them go, Yossel, and come to me." Miriam's spirit spoke to him from a light that was streaming upward in a pillar. He resisted and gradually he felt himself steady, the room take focus. Miriam's spirit stood in the outside hall framed by the bedroom's doorway.

"Don't show yourself like this, Miriam," Werner said aloud. "You're too much like a dream."

"The Talmud says a dream left uninterpreted is like a letter left unread."

"And don't quote Talmud. You, who were so proud to be an atheist."

"You don't need to believe in souls to have one, Yossel. Just like you can follow what I'm saying, even if your mind's locked shut. Listen with your heart or with your belly. Even with that old thing in your pants. There's lots of ways to listen."

"Then you tell me what I want to hear, Miriam. Who's your lover?"

"Jealous now after all these years?" she teased. "Jealousy's not love, it's private ownership."

"It's easy for you to talk about love. You've got what you want."

The spirit spiralled gently in a way that made Werner think of clay spinning on a potter's wheel. "Would you sooner I was dancing with the Torah?" she asked. "Or maybe that would make your papa jealous."

"Don't mock me, Miriam."

"You're too serious, Yossel. Even death isn't so serious."

"Was it Svenson, that tall shop steward, the one who'd bring you home after union meetings? You wrote his phone number on the wall."

She shimmered. A vaporous arm wrapped itself around her waist. "You want one more memory? Another stone for your Wailing Wall? Then remember when I taught you how to waltz in Warsaw behind the bandstand at Krachinsky Gardens. Remember how you held me in your arms."

"What are you telling to me?" he asked her.

"You're my lover, Yossel." Her light shifted into an aura of blue and purple hues.

"The man I used to be, all those years ago? That man's more dead than you are."

"No, Yossel. My lover is the part of you that loves me perfectly. The part that has no memory for anything but love."

Werner turned his face towards the wall. "Leave me alone. I'm just a crazy old man."

Werner kept staring past the wallpaper curling from its plaster long after the spirit had gone.

Finally, though his chest was still a tight band of pain, Werner began to search again, digging deeper in the box toward the layers of their earliest years. A stack of mail, piled at one end, collapsed across his hands, letters they'd written to each other before Miriam joined him in Canada in 1906, along with letters from their families, all ending abruptly in the fall of '39. A final one was stamped the International Committee of the Red Cross, dated in Geneva a year after the war. No members from either of their families had survived Europe's storm of souls.

He pushed the letters to one side but they kept sliding back until he lifted them out in handfuls and dropped them to the floor. Beneath them he found a trove of odd keepsakes: a bar of perfumed English soap, cracked and powdery. A ring of skeleton keys. A jar of buttons. Three pairs of long white gloves. A box filled with old reading glasses. Two Polish passports, health certificates. Then a spread of old newspapers in Polish, Yiddish, English, each wrapped in dry-cleaner's cellophane.

As he lifted the pile of papers he saw a lacy cuff reaching up from the bottom of the box – it was the sleeve of Miriam's wedding dress. Werner dug towards it, clearing everything else away. He found her dress carefully folded, the pleats still sharply pressed. Beside it was a crystal water jug — their wedding gift to one another – and inside the jug, a piece of bridal cake, dry as dust. Werner held the dress in his arms. "Miriam," he whispered. "Come back to life."

THE MORNING SUN STREAKED the window, waking Werner on the bed. He was surprised to find Miriam's wedding dress beside him and so many things scattered across the floor. "Miriam!" he called out as he headed to the kitchen, thinking he would find her making breakfast. He was surprised at all the bags of mail, and at the furniture covered in sheets.

The living-room looks so funny, he thought, all covered up like that. And he laughed out loud. He'd talk to Miriam and she'd explain it. But Miriam wasn't anywhere in the house. She must have taken little Arthur out to play, maybe to walk the girls to their music lessons or to buy groceries at the corner store. He was getting impatient. There were so many things he needed to tell Miriam and also he wanted to be with Arthur. He decided he needed to spend more time with the boy.

He found his coat, work boots and cap in the front closet. There was important work to do behind their building but he'd find a way for Arthur to join in. He would get the boy a small hammer so he could help rip off the boards. He could imagine little Arthur already, leaning forward in concentration though his face seemed to be merging with others', even with his own at that young age. But he was certain that the boy would be happy with the hammer, eager to get something done. And he knew that Miriam would be pleased that he was getting rid of the fence. Werner had decided the fence was just no good. He was going to take down that fence today.

THE LAST DAYS OF SHADOWMAN

I HAD TO SHUT THE DOOR ON HIM, HAD TO STOP VISITING altogether. The old caretaker's stories had been so wonderful when I had first heard them in his workshop a year and a half before, but they changed as he began reliving times too painful for a boy to hear. He had lost all sense of himself, became morose and impossible to speak to.

Though I had stopped seeing Mr. Werner, had tried in my mind to resist, deny, forget all about him, some part of me must have kept travelling with his thoughts, and leaving me exhausted. I was tired all the time. My body ached. Meals, chores, school lessons were oppressive, forcing themselves into my crowded brain. I still remember how my teacher eyed me coldly as I mumbled any answer to keep her at a distance, how my mother plagued me with vitamins and healthy foods. She checked my temperature and theorized about a growth spurt, a change of seasons, and how the first month of grade six was bound to be hard. Later, I heard her on the phone asking for the guidance counsellor.

Then everything broke through, one morning in October

as I crossed the wasteland of Mr. Werner's back lot on my way to school. There was the old man pushing against the high post of the fence. I hadn't imagined him, didn't want to imagine him outside his basement workshop. Especially not in that cold morning light, struggling to wrench loose a heavy post with the old fence boards piled at his feet.

"Arthur," he called to me. "Come and help."

I stifled a nervous giggle. I knew it wasn't funny but the laugh was shaking out, as if to greet what I'd been fearing for so long.

"Mr. Werner. I . . . I'm not Arthur. I'm Daniel."

He squinted. The post was more than twice his height and rough, really just a tree trunk with its branches cut and bark stripped off. When I saw how its blistered paint had scraped the flannel of his shirt, the last of my laughter broke against my heart.

"Arthur," he called me again. "The post has got to come out. It's rotten . . . it's no good no more."

"You can't do it, Mr. Werner . . . you're too old." I pressed my thumb against the handle of my lunch box. I couldn't look at him, only stare at the cracks in his boots, at his heels worn to the nails. They were slipping on the boards, a fine dust rising like smoke around them.

"Son, we got to get rid of this," he said. "We don't need no fence. It's gotten in the way of everything."

"Your son Arthur's all grown up. He's a lawyer. You visit him on Sundays and there's a clock . . . remember the clock with the balls that turn?"

"Horowitz is dead. Dead a long time."

"Please, Mr. Werner, this isn't fair!"

The old man strained again, rocking the high post back and forth. "You just wait," he groaned. "Between the two of us, we'll change everything."

The desperation in his eyes drew me to him at the post. We gripped it from opposite sides; he pushed and I pushed it back, again and again, trying to keep his pace as we worked to rock it loose.

"Now push . . . and again . . . push," he grunted but I lost the rhythm and the post struck me on my cheek. I slipped on the boards, falling to my knees.

"Wait," I yelled.

"No! I can't wait." He was gasping. "No more. No longer." He clung to the post, rocking with it back and forth.

All I could think to do was run, to stumble out the gate, rush to my parents in their store and wail. So my father would take over, so my mother would hold me and press her soft hands to my face.

Instead I stayed.

"Mr. Werner," I cried to him. "I jumped into a river."

"What? What river? There's no river."

"Not here," I said. "It's far away. I was fishing and I dropped my rod, then I had to jump in after it."

"A river is dangerous," he said. He stopped, leaned against the post, trying to catch his breath. "I was never allowed in the river. My parents said it had a monster. A cruel man confessed his sins to the river so the sins would wash away. But they all sank to the bottom. They grew into a creature of earth and water – all mixed up wrong – it waited in the deepest part to drown young children."

"It was dark in the river," I answered. "I swam to the bottom. I saw everything."

"But what about the monster?" he asked.

"There was no monster down there, nothing that wanted to hurt me. And I got back what I lost, my fishing rod. Remember the Spin Master fishing rod? You helped me put it together."

"Yah. We played Moses with the rod and you made the Red Sea open up."

"That's right, Mr. Werner. Remember how I got in trouble later when I took it into Borkow's Funeral Chapel?"

"Yah, that's right," he said. He eased himself down, his hand on my shoulder for support so he could sit beside me on the shaky boards.

"This time I took the rod to a real river," I went on. "It was early. The sun was coming up all big and yellow and there was

199

no one else around. When I got to the bridge I saw a big fish jump right into the air. . . ."

I told my story to Mr. Werner, the one I'd tried to tell him before but couldn't. It became my first, best story as he sat next to me, trying not to wheeze, trying with all his failing strength to listen, to imagine the boy who was me and who was also him and others, too, the boy who would give himself to a river just like he would be giving himself to another and much deeper river, and who would struggle out again, whole and well and with a precious gift. While the sky turned above us, ragged with clouds and fluttering wings.

THREE DAYS LATER, I stood outside the padlocked door of Mr. Werner's basement workshop, kicking at the dust. I hadn't been allowed near it. My mother had kept me in bed all the first day with *Reader's Digests* and Roman Nugget Bars, tall glasses of Seven Up with coloured straws. The next day, my father had taken me to fish at Lockport. He'd showed me how to lift and toss heavy rocks without hurting myself and he helped me carve a whistle with my fishing knife. He even told me jokes that he'd remembered from when he was a boy.

The third day was Saturday and both my parents were busy in their store. They'd left me with a jigsaw puzzle of swans on an Irish lake with some decaying mansion in the background but I could only brood, staring out at traffic, clicking the television on and off. I even scanned the newspaper left at the kitchen table – *US Sinks Cuban Patrol Boat – Brant Sees War Over Berlin – India Warns China She'll Fight.* Like everything else, the headlines made me cramped and nervous, as if something had to burst. Finally, I couldn't stand it any longer.

I stared across the lot at the mound of rotten boards around the high fence post. It was there I'd last seen Mr. Werner before my father hurried me away. He was propped in my mother's arms, his eyes closed, his head slumped to one side as a policeman and two ambulance attendants crowded around. Dean, the young butcher's apprentice, was there, too, and Mr. Nojuk from the cafe. They were hanging over him on either side and staring down, both of them as pale as he was.

I didn't hear any siren taking him away but when my mother returned she said, "They took Mr. Werner to the hospital. No, Danny, he won't be coming back. An old man like him, well, he shouldn't have been living down in that basement. His things will be cleared out, his son's making the arrangements. There's so much down there to get . . . get taken care of." She'd hesitated as she shut my bedroom door. "Danny . . . it's really the best thing for everyone." But later that night, I heard her weeping and when I came out of my room, I saw she'd lit a memorial candle in a glass.

The padlock to the workshop door wasn't really locked. It couldn't be; it could only hold the door shut. Mr. Werner had lost the key, so he "fixed" it by making it appear to lock. I twisted it the way he'd shown me and the tumblers all released. Opening the door, I looked down at dust floating over sunlit stairs.

"Mr. Werner?" I called out.

Empty. Silent.

I whispered the door shut, replaced the lock, and turned to go.

CRACK! the door rapped. I jumped away.

"Mr. Werner, is that you?" The door was silent. I touched it, reading the stillness of weathered grain, the vacancy of its window panes. Not even a vibration.

Another CRACK! above my head. My arms flew up. "I'm sorry! I'm sorry!"

A boy's green-eyed laughter. "What a sucker! What a gutless chicken!" It was Riley, the rusty-haired kid, sitting on a remaining section of the fence, grinning down at me. He lit a firecracker and tossed it.

CRACK! It exploded in the air.

"Boy, did you ever jump!" His feet drummed a rumble on the fence boards. "Ooh, stampede. You better run!"

"You're the gutless chicken," I yelled. "You ran that time I broke a window with my yoyo, this window right here in the door." I flung a fist of gravel, pocking the boards beneath him.

"Ah, go on!" Riley swung behind the fence, hanging on so that only his head showed above it, with his chin resting on the ledge. "You want target practise, huh? Try just me."

"You look like a pumpkin," I teased. "Hey, pumpkin head!"

"That's right, I'm all ready for Hallowe'en. Boo hoo, bugga boo!" His head seemed to dance along the fence with his mouth gaping hollow and toothy.

"You're nuts!" I laughed.

"Who, me?" He rose as if his head were drawing up his body until he stood balancing on the fence. "Who's Mr. Wormer," he asked. "Some kind of wormy boogie man?"

"It's Mr. Werner, stupid. He's my friend."

Riley landed with a spring in front of me. "Then why are you so scared to go down there?"

"Not me. I'm not scared."

"You're scared to death!"

"I'd go anywhere except . . ."

"Except what?"

"You might lock me in."

"I won't, I swear it." He crossed his heart with two fingers and he kissed them.

"Okay," I said. "But you come down with me."

We entered cautiously, watching each other for any false move, until we reached the bottom.

Riley narrowed his eyes. "What's all that junk in there?"

"They're Mr. Werner's tools and stuff he's working on, important stuff. Just leave them alone."

"What about that door?" He pointed to the steel fire door.

"Bet you won't touch it," I said.

He sprinted through the dark, slapped the door and rushed back. "Ha! It's just a door," he laughed, his eyes shining with fear. "Where's it go?"

"It goes to the other side . . . to the basement of my parents' store. My dad keeps things down there like my box of comic books."

"So let's get them."

"Why should we?"

His eyes quivered green. "You see? I knew you were gutless."

I thought of Batman, Spider-man, Superman, all prisoners in the dark. "I'll go." My heart throbbed in my ears so I hardly heard myself. "But you have to stay . . . and watch."

The door opened easily – hardly a creak. Beyond it, the shifting darkness had the hollow moan of an empty bottle.

"You scared?" Riley's voice was impossibly far away.

"I don't know," I answered.

"You've got to hum something, like a song."

"I can't."

"Go like this." He hummed some silliness without a tune.

"I can't."

"Okay, I'll hum it. You just listen."

I entered with a slight bow, Riley's humming as my lifeline. I whispered to the darkness, "Mr. Werner is my friend. Mr. Werner is my friend," softly so as not to disturb, only to soothe whatever might be watching. Stiff-backed, I shuffled forward, my hands probing till they touched the furnace. Cold and empty, a relief of darkness, nothing more.

"I'm just here to get my comics," I said, seeing something out there like an after-image; a glow like Mr. Werner smiling at me through hazy eyes, parting shadows, stroking them away, directing me to the white clapboard storeroom that held my comic books.

I fumbled open the storeroom latch and moved into the blackness. My foot met something lying on the floor. It was soft and heavy. I cried out, "Oh!"

"What's there?" Riley's voice was cracking.

"I don't know."

"Well, find out, Danny."

It was the fleshy weight of damp and rotten cardboard. "It's okay," I called back. "It's my box of comics. Just keep on humming." I cradled the box and hurried toward the dimness of the doorway, then scrambled through and rushed past Riley.

"Wait up," he yelled as I pounded up the stairs.

I burst into the air and sun just as he caught me by my shirt. I dropped the box on the ground. "I got them. Look!" I tried to say but began giggling, giddy with the residues of fear; and Riley giggled, too, all loose limbed, with his red hair shaking wildly. I collapsed, tumbling over the cardboard box even as I was tearing it apart, "My comics! I got them back! All of them!"

I shook off the basement mortar from a Batman comic. It showed the superhero and his young friend, Robin, writhing in a pit under a giant magnifying glass. Their gloved hands hid their eyes as the Joker cackled high above them in his stainless steel control booth. Bits of mortar still stuck to the illustration, giving it a third dimension. As I crouched to brush away the last bits of rubble, I felt myself entering the scene like a giant clearing off a landslide to save two tiny victims. I was surprised to see the cover so discoloured, the paper so stained and veiny, and to hear it crackle in my hand, exhaling peppery mould.

"I guess it got wet down in the cellar," Riley said. "Then it got dried out."

"Look," I mumbled. "All my comics are the same – they're all wrecked."

"Aw, that's too bad." His freckled hand drifted unexpectedly onto my shoulder. "Hey, we can air them out. My mom puts stuff outside all the time and then they're fine."

We spread the comics on the ground in three long lines, pages opened to the sun. I inspected, walking up and down the rows, trying to focus on the pictures, to follow the adventures from square to square. Impossible. They didn't seem like anything anymore, these glories of my childhood, just a senseless blur. Certainly nothing like the stories I'd begun to tell.

"What a useless mess!" I said.

"They look weird, huh?" Riley added.

I poked a comic book with my foot. "It's like some animal that's all squashed on the road."

"Yuck! You're sick!" Riley was laughing again, in his deep chortling way. "They're like some kind of . . . turtles."

"Butterflies," I said. "See, they're all spread open like pairs of wings."

"What, you a sissy?" he scowled.

"Then how about tongues? See, the wind's got the pages turning. They're all like tongues. Yackety yack." We jeered at their senseless flappings but soon I fell silent. And then I asked him for his matches.

"You want to shoot more firecrackers?" he asked.

"You get that bunch of comics. I'll carry the rest," I said. We collected them in a pile beside the high fence post. I tore out pages and stuffed them under the boards. I struck a match.

"You're crazy!" Riley warned me. "You'd better not blame this on me."

"They're my comics," I told him. "And this is Mr. Werner's fence. He wanted to get rid of it because it was no good anymore. And me and Mr. Werner, we were friends."

A gust of wind swept the pages into flames. A rotten piece tore loose and fluttered upward. Then another. Suddenly, unquestionably, the wild-haired boy and I were the closest of friends. We circled Mr. Werner's post, its base already bright with tongues of flame. A sudden blaze and pages tore in leafy shreds. We leaped the boards that soon were hissing at our feet. And we laughed, ripping and tossing more pages to the singing pyre. The smoke surprised our eyes with tears, but we kept laughing. For we were delighted by the fire and by the sudden animation of those old paper heroes, and delighted by the restless wind that swirled them high and sparking into the open sky.

The Cover Artist

Elaine Halpert was born in Toronto in 1957 and received her B.A.A. in Photographic Arts from Ryerson Polytechnical Institute in 1984. She has travelled extensively to discover new subjects and develop her techniques. Her work has been seen in many parts of Canada and has appeared in advertising and other commercial venues. She is currently represented by Zone Gallery in Winnipeg, where she lives with her husband and twin daughters.

SUICIDE EWIN PROGRAM
181 Higgins Avenue
Winnipeg, Manitoba
R3B 3G1